Prairie Wife

Prairie Wife

The chronicle of a Kansas family in the early
1900s

Adult Fiction

Cover photograph:
Eliza Glenn Vaughan Griffith, age 31
November 1897

Published 2019
Printed in the United States.

ISBN: 978-0-578-22009-3

Kansas

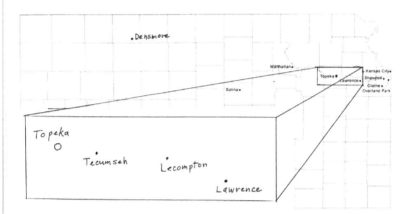

Topeka

Tecumseh

Lecompton

Lawrence

Densmore

Manhattan

Salina

Topeka

Kansas City
Shawnee
Lawrence
Olathe
Overland Park

Major Characters

Eliza Glenn

her parents Elizabeth and Alexander Glenn
siblings include Jane, Jake, and Mate
   first husband Joe Vaughan
   second husband Pierce Griffith

Pierce Griffith

his parents John and Binnie Griffith
siblings are Laura, Charlie, Mollie, and Frank
   first wife Nannie Thompson
   second wife Eliza Glenn

Children of Pierce and Nannie Griffith
   Ralph, Ross, John, and Ruth

Children of Eliza and Joe Vaughan
   Harry, Sadie, Nellie, Irene

Children of Eliza and Pierce Griffith
   Enid
   Glenn

TABLE OF CONTENTS

This is a work of fiction, based on the life of my great-grandmother.

Chapter 1

1897

Her hands shook as she stoked the fire in the cook stove to make coffee. The cabin smelled of soot and mildew. A mouse skittered along the floor and squeezed behind the cupboard. Fishing a coin purse out of the coffee can, Eliza counted the pennies and nickels and then slipped the purse into her pocket.

She picked up an empty whiskey bottle from the floor and set it quietly on the sideboard. The ache in her chest sharpened as she bent over. *How can you tell if you have a cracked rib?* she wondered.

Through the small window came the faint glow of approaching dawn. This hour of the morning was usually a calm, unblemished time when she could be alone with her thoughts. Today, her muscles ached. Her head pounded. The dark shapes of the furniture loomed menacingly in the shadows.

Eliza Vaughan, her husband Joe, and their three daughters lived on an island in the middle of the Kaw River, which flowed through the northeastern corner of Kansas. On the western half of the island were several fields and his family's cabin, and on the eastern half of the island, forest and marsh. In addition to their small farm, the family made money by providing early morning breakfast to fishermen and duck hunters who came to the island.

This morning, Eliza was preparing a meal for Mack and Bud, a couple of their regulars. She poured coffee into a crockery jar, fastened the wire bail over the lid, and wrapped it in a cloth. Then she fitted the jar inside a tall, narrow leather pouch, added biscuits and ham, and fastened the top flap.

She tiptoed to the bedroom door. Joe was still asleep. *Good*, she said to herself. Moving back to the cabin's main room, she set the rocking chair upright and bent low over the two sleeping children.

"Wake up, girls," she said in a soft voice. "It's early, but you need to get dressed now." She folded down their blanket and rubbed the girls' shoulders.

Sadie, six years old, sat up and yawned. "What is it, Mama?"

Nellie, three, grimaced and rubbed her eyes.

"This morning you're going to help me take breakfast to the fishermen." Next to each of the girls she lay out a flannel chemise and drawers, petticoat, long brown stockings, and a dress with a ruffle at the bottom. She herself had slept in the dress she wore the day before.

"Shh! Now put on your clothes, but don't make any noise. If Papa wakes up, he'll be grouchy as a bear." Their faces took on a pinched and worried look as they put on their clothes.

In the kitchen Eliza opened the lower cupboard and retrieved the travel bag she had packed the night before. Hearing a sudden thump, she clasped her hands to her breast, then relaxed. One of the girls had dropped a shoe.

She slipped into the bedroom. Joe was sleeping on his back now and snoring lustily. She picked up baby Irene and the little one started to cry. Eliza quickly returned to the main room, changed Irene's diaper, and let her nurse from one breast.

"You'll get more later, sweetie."

Eliza buckled the straps of Nellie's shoes, then gazed around at the battered wooden table, the four splintery wooden chairs, the cook stove, the sideboard, the children's bed, and the two narrow windows. After living for years in drafty, dilapidated wood-frame houses, she had loved this old stone cabin. It didn't keep mice or insects out, but in wind and storm it felt snug as a rabbit's nest.

Time to go. Have I forgotten anything? She picked up a framed picture, weighed it in her hand, then placed it gently back on the sideboard. She settled the baby on her hip, handed Sadie the travel bag, and picked up the pouch of food for the fishermen.

Eliza and the girls stepped outside into the early morning chill of late September, into the familiar smell of damp earth and moldering leaves. The air was still. A silver sheen on the trees and bushes muted their usual colors. Cicadas chirred.

Sadie, her eyes dull and sleepy, clasped the travel bag against her chest with both arms. A lock of hair escaped her bonnet. "Mama, why are we. . .?"

"Hush," her mother whispered. "Don't talk yet." Sadie and Nellie exchanged a puzzled glance and followed their mother to the edge of the river. A frog croaked from a clump of muddy weeds. Gravel crunched under their shoes as if they were stepping on cockroaches. Crows cawed from a tree. The girls shrank from the sound and squinted up at the dark branches.

The family rowboat, its white paint peeling, lay on the broken shale bottom side up, with the two oars beside it. Eliza was quite capable of dragging the boat down to the water by herself, but she discovered that Joe had chained it to a tree. Her shoulders slumped, and she tried not to panic.

She stared across the expanse of tranquil gray-brown water toward the town of Tecumseh, two miles away to the south and west, obscured by morning fog. Sluggish waves lapped at her feet. She breathed in the rich mineral smell of algae and mud. A fish jumped out of the water and fell back in with a splash. *There's no help for it. We will have to rely on the fishermen. But I mustn't frighten the children.*

"Come, girls." Eliza turned back from the shore and set off briskly toward the interior of the island. Sadie and Nellie hurried to keep up.

Some distance from the cabin, their mother slowed her pace. "All right, let me explain. First, we are going to have a picnic, then take breakfast to the fishermen, and then we'll visit Grandma and

Grandpa." Eliza's parents lived on a farm near Lecompton, fifteen miles east of Tecumseh on the railroad line.

"Goody, goody!" said Sadie.

"Not so loud, sweetheart."

Nellie bounced up and down, making the ties of her bonnet dance. "Goody, goody, Grandma, Grandpa," she chanted in a quiet voice.

They made their way past a watermelon field, where large, green-striped fruits gleamed against the sandy soil. It was their second crop of the summer and the only field under cultivation on their seven-acre farm. The melons were doing well, and if they didn't have an early freeze, Joe might be able to pay off their debts.

After the field, Eliza and the girls walked along a trail that wound its way into a dark wood of birch and cottonwood trees. This early in the morning, the path was almost indiscernible. Twigs clawed at their clothes, and dew-drenched leaves splattered their faces. They walked silently in single file. Sweet, tangy, and earthy scents enveloped them as they made their way past different kinds of bushes and trees.

Cicadas buzzed in rhythmic waves, warblers twittered, and every once in a while a meadowlark burst forth with its melodic phrase. Eliza walked ahead of the girls to clear away any spider webs. Baby Irene started to fuss, but Eliza jiggled her up and down and kept walking.

"How much farther is it, Mama?" asked Sadie, trudging behind her mother. "This bag is heavy."

"Just a little farther, honey. Here, let me take that." Eliza stopped to knot her shawl into a carry-sling for the baby. That way she could carry the pouch for the fishermen in one hand and the travel bag in the other.

After a while, the trail opened out into a small clearing. Next to a rock shelf, water seeped from a bed of deep green moss and trickled away in a tiny stream. Raccoon tracks crisscrossed the damp ground. The rocks shone under the water, and iridescent blue damselflies hovered around the spring.

"Look, Mama, fairies!" said Sadie.

"Well, isn't that something!" Eliza smiled, and her eyes sparkled. "This is perfect place for a picnic!" She unpacked the travel bag. The air smelled fresh and clean. Sadie and Nellie sat on a fallen log and spread their dresses over their knees to warm them. Egrets flew overhead on their way to the marsh. Sparrows quarreled over a seed pod that had fallen to the ground.

Eliza doled out pancakes and ham, then filled their tin cup several times at the spring.

"Why are we eating breakfast in the woods?" asked Sadie, fully awake now.

"See how beautiful the world is in the early morning?" replied her mother. "The trees are waking up. The birds are waking up. The sky is waking up."

Nellie pointed to the sky, where streaks of pink had materialized on the belly of a large pale gray cloud. "The sky is waking up." She spread her arms wide, beaming.

Eliza sat on her folded shawl and gazed at the lofty, overarching trees, the blackberry bushes, and the moss underfoot. She listened to the spring as it burbled over the rocks. It almost seemed like an ordinary morning.

This was her favorite spot on the island. She unbuttoned her blouse and took her time feeding baby Irene, whose hair was beginning to curl in wisps.

"Sweet, sweet baby," Eliza murmured. Irene, nursing eagerly, reached out and grasped her mother's thumb.

"If I was a bird," announced Sadie, "I could fly anywhere I wanted. I would visit Grandma and Grandpa every day. I would sit way up high in the trees and watch people."

"You is not a bird," said Nellie.

"I was saying if I was."

"You a girl."

After feeding and diapering the baby, Eliza repositioned the combs holding her long hair in place and stood up. The sky was brighter now, and a slight breeze had sprung up. Leaves rustled. A twig snapped.

Instantly, she was alert. No, nothing. *Must have been a raccoon or a deer, coming to drink at the spring.*

"Okay girls, let's go!" Her leather shoes made a squishing sound, and the hem of her brown skirt was muddy. *Wish I could change out of these wet clothes. Oh, well.* She guided the children out of the woods and toward the marsh. Sadie and Nellie had never walked this far before.

They emerged from the woods at the highest point of the island as the sun rose, and Eliza stopped for a moment to appreciate the view. Below them lay the river, the marsh and, on the far bank, a patchwork of green and yellow fields as far as the eye could see. The Kaw River, which meandered through Kansas to join the Missouri River en route to the Gulf of Mexico, was dotted with tiny islands, most of which were inhabited only by ducks, geese, deer, rabbits, and squirrels.

Vaughan's Island, where the family lived, was one of the larger islands on the river, and it had belonged to her husband's family for decades. Before that, it was a hideout for outlaws.

"I'm tired, Mama," said Nellie. "It's too far."

"We're almost there, sweetheart. Can you see the fishermen? Let's let them know their breakfast is here." She spied a rowboat among the reeds. "Halloo! Wave, girls, then they will be sure to see us."

A boat with two men eased out of the shallows. Bud and Mack waved. The men were around sixty years old and wore yellow-brown canvas jackets, wool caps, and oilcloth pants.

"They're nice fellows," Eliza told the girls as they scrambled along behind her. Down by the dock, a pungent smell of rotting vegetation rose from the water, and the air was alive with insects.

Bud hopped ashore and tied the boat to the weather-beaten dock. "Mornin', ma'am." Mack shoved fishing tackle aside, reached back for a bucket, and stepped out of the boat.

"What you got in there?" Sadie asked.

"Channel cats," said Mack, tipping the bucket for her to see.

Bud added, "One of 'em was really big, must be ten pounds!"

"Looks like you caught quite a few today," said Eliza, impressed. She unpacked the pouch, handed the men biscuits and ham, and put the jar of coffee on the ground between them. They squatted on their heels and ate their breakfast.

"Mighty fine grub, ma'am. Hits the spot!"

"Thank you." She smiled and quietly watched them eat. A mosquito whined nearby, and Eliza shooed it away from the baby's face.

The girls gathered around the bucket to stare at the glittering fish, which had brownish-green skin and droopy, string-like mustaches.

"Can I touch 'em?" asked Sadie.

"Go ahead," replied Mack. "Touch 'em if you want." He chuckled. "I got a grandson just about your age."

"You'll get your hands sticky," warned Eliza.

"That don't hurt nothing, Mother," said Mack. He grinned at the girls. "Catfish are ugly, but they're sure good eating."

After Nellie peered into the bucket, she put her hands behind her back. "They gots teeth," she said.

He laughed. "Those fish can't bite you. They're dead."

Sadie leaned over the bucket and picked up a fish with both hands, then flopped it back in. "Eww!" she said, wiping her hands on her dress.

"Think we'll head back, soon's we clean the fish," remarked Bud.

"In that case, I wonder if you could help me out of a bind," said Eliza, swallowing hard. "I mean, could you please give the children and me a ride into town?"

Bud looked dubiously at their boat. "Hoo boy! I don't know, ma'am. Our boat isn't big enough for the two of us plus all of you. Can't Joe take you across?"

Her throat tightened. Eliza studied the two men in front of her. She hated to tell lies, but events of the past few months had given her no other choice. She tilted her head to one side. "I'm supposed to go over to my mother's this morning, and Joe is still asleep."

Mack snorted. "Getting his beauty rest, is he?"

His companion guffawed. "I hear he's been hitting the hard stuff lately. Probably can't lie down without holding on."

She gritted her teeth and forced a smile. *They'll tell Joe that we went to visit my folks, but I don't care. Where else would we go?*

Mack paused, watching Eliza closely. He gave her the briefest of nods, then turned to the other fisherman. "How's about you gut the fish, Bud, and I take the lady and her kids across? Be right back."

"You giving me the dirty work?"

He cackled. "It's because you do such a good job."

Bud gave his friend a shove. "You lazy son of a gun! All right, I'll clean your fish today, for her sake."

"Thank you!" said Eliza. "This will really help me a lot."

"I might as well give you the money now too," answered Bud. "Here's a dollar, ma'am, payment for our week of breakfast meals."

"Thank you very much."

"Get those youngins of yours some candy to eat on the train." He winked at Sadie. "You like candy, don't you, girlies?" Sadie and Nellie nodded.

"Well, that's more than enough to buy candy for the both of you."

The men unloaded the boat and put the fishing supplies onto the dock. Then Mack, Eliza, and the children climbed into the boat, which wallowed back and forth in the cloudy, brown-green water. Waves sloshed against its side and spread outward in shining ripples.

Mack adjusted the oars and began to row from the stagnant edge of the marsh into the main channel of the river, against the current. The paddles dipped and swirled through the choppy water, making a ka-slup, ka-slup sound. Sadie sat calmly on the seat, while Nellie held tightly to the side of the boat. Irene sat upright on her mother's lap, looking at everything and not making a peep. Eliza felt tense and jumpy. *If we can just catch the next train. . .*

The Kaw River was two miles wide, full of clay and silt, and had unpredictable currents—not a river for swimming. Trees grew right down to the bank in some places, and in other sections, rocks and sand sloped down to the river's edge. Mack rowed slowly.

"I got to keep an eye out," he explained. "The sandbars shift day to day, and also there's strainers—tree trunks and rocks under the water that collect weeds and brush. It don't take much for a boat to get stuck or capsize, 'specially when it's this heavily loaded."

Water gurgled against the prow of the boat. A dozen mallard ducks swam noisily near the shore: quark, quark, chitter, chitter. A flock of red-winged blackbirds rose from a tree, scattered into the sky, and wheeled toward the huge cottonwood and sycamore trees on the opposite shore.

"I seen a turtle!" called Sadie, pointing.

"Yup," replied Mack. "Painted turtle over there on that log. If we're lucky, we might see a bald eagle or a heron. They hang around these wetlands. Lots of fish and frogs for them to eat."

"Baby fishies," squeaked Nellie, watching the quick-moving silvery bits swarming in the water.

"Shiners. That's what catfish eat, and they grow big and fat. Then we catch 'em and eat 'em!"

At last the boat drew near the town on the south bank of the river. Despite consisting of only a few streets, Tecumseh had a fine concrete boat landing because it had been a steamboat stop before the railroads came.

As the boat approached the dock, a loud train whistle split the air. An engine with two carriages roared past, gaining speed. Eliza froze.

"There'll be another train before long," Mack assured her.

They thanked him for the ride and walked to the station.

"A family ticket to Lecompton, please."

"Twenty-five cents, ma'am. Next one in an hour, at 8:10."

"Thank you."

Nellie tugged at her mother's skirt. "Mama, candy."

Eliza sighed. "You just ate breakfast."

Sadie jumped up and down. "Candy, Mama, please! The man gave you lots of money so we could buy some candy."

Eliza frowned and whispered, "The candy here is probably stale." She patted Sadie's shoulder and continued in a normal voice. "Let's buy some candy in Lecompton. By then, the regular shops will be open, and you'll have more kinds to choose from." They stopped at the depot toilet, then waited at a bench near the train platform. Sadie and Nellie tried to teach baby Irene to play Pat-a-Cake, then the two older girls sat facing each other and played more clapping games.

Eliza stared for a long time in the direction from which the next train would come. *Please God, let Joe sleep late today.* How could she leave him after eleven years of marriage? Eliza put her hand over her mouth to stifle a sob. *I have loved him all these years, at least it seemed like love, but the most important thing is that the girls are safe.*

Chapter 2

As she waited on the bench, Eliza thought about a former schoolmate of hers who had married a drunkard. After the woman divorced her husband, she took a job as cook for a banker and his family. They let her bring along her two children, and she cared for them while she worked. Then the children got sick, and when the woman stayed home to take care of them, she was fired. Eventually, she had had to put them into an orphanage. Eliza promised herself, *That will never happen to my children.*

A whistle sounded in the distance.

"Lookit, here comes the train!" Sadie shouted. Hastily Eliza got to her feet, with the baby in one arm and the bags in the other.

Sadie and Nellie jumped up and down as the train chuffed into the station. The engineer leaned out of the train window and gave a hand signal to the depot agent. Then, grinning at the children, he pulled the whistle cord an extra time: too-whoo!

The girls yelled, "Hurray!" and danced around. The wrinkles on Eliza's forehead smoothed somewhat as she helped the children climb onto the train and find a seat. The carriage, which held few passengers this time of day, had wooden benches arranged in facing pairs.

The engineer was chatting with the depot agent. *Let's go, let's go,* Eliza urged them silently. In a short while, the train glided out of the station in a cloud of noise and smoke.

They disembarked in Lecompton fifteen minutes later. Sadie and Nellie waved goodbye to the engineer and watched the train vanish down the track. Then they looked around the train platform, which was empty except for some men stacking wooden crates.

"Where's Grandpa?" asked Sadie.

"He didn't know we were coming," Eliza answered calmly. "This is a surprise visit, so we'll get a ride to the farm with Uncle Jake. He always comes to town on Thursdays because of the auction at the sale barn." *The fat's in the fire now,* she thought, twisting the fringe of her shawl. *But as soon as we get to Mother and Father's, we will be safe.*

Lecompton was a town of around 400 people, with broad streets, brick sidewalks, and several large stone buildings dating back to the time it was the territorial capital of Kansas. The capital city was changed to Topeka when Kansas became a state in 1861.

Eliza and the girls waited outside the candy store until it opened at 9. Inside the store, Sadie and Nellie spent a long time contemplating the rows of glass jars filled with lemon drops, burnt sugar peanuts, chocolate drops, licorice laces, and jewel-like jellybeans.

"No chocolate, girls," said their mother. "That's too messy to eat when there's no place for you to wash up. Why don't you get butterscotch drops or an all-day sucker?"

"I want chewy candy, Mama," said Sadie.

"How about candy corn?" suggested the saleswoman, who stood behind the counter in a blue and white striped apron, "or Tootsie Rolls? They won't melt in your fingers." The girls selected several kinds of candy and then the family went to a bench in front of the feed store to wait for Jake.

The street teemed with people who had come to shop at the feed store, the general store, the dry goods store, and the livery barn. Wagons rattled along the street, raising small clouds of dust. A group of horsemen, whooping and whistling, drove several dozen bawling cattle toward the train station to be shipped to Chicago.

As the sun broke through the clouds, the day grew warm. The older girls piled their jackets in a heap. After Irene was fed and changed, she went to sleep. Eliza held a bonnet above the baby's head as a sunshade.

Sadie practiced jumping off the armrest of the bench while Nellie crouched underneath, poking Sadie's shoes through the slats. Eliza jerked to attention whenever she heard boots thumping along on the sidewalk. *I sure hope Jake comes to town today.*

By the time the girls finished their candy, they were thirsty, but Eliza was afraid that if they dashed into a store or cafe to get something to drink, they might miss Jake. The girls complained for a while, then chased each other around the bench.

A long whistle sounded. A train was arriving from the west, the direction in which Tecumseh lay. Eliza's heart beat fast, but Joe did not appear. He must not yet realize that they were gone.

After a couple of hours waiting in front of the feed store, they all were exhausted. Sadie sat limply at one end of the bench and pouted. Nellie leaned her face against her mother's arm and whimpered. The baby woke up and began to cry. Eliza put Irene onto her shoulder and patted her, but the baby wailed at an ever-increasing volume.

"Hush, Reenie! Don't cry, precious. Where's my happy girl?"

"Hey, has the circus come to town?" boomed a man's voice. "I see two monkeys here. And the loudest baby in the world."

Sadie and Nellie ran to him. "Uncle Jake!"

"Hi, Sis. Looks like you could use a hand." He lifted Sadie and Nellie, one in each arm, and whirled them around as they cheered.

"Am I glad to see you, Jake!" said Eliza, "With the baby crying, I didn't hear you come." Her younger brother was a lanky fellow in black pants, a white collarless shirt, and a tan vest in a flowered pattern. *The mustache is new,* she thought.

He smiled and raised his eyebrows. "Do you ladies, by any chance, want a ride out to the farm?"

"Yes, please."

"Yay!" yelled the girls.

"Let's go then!"

"I must say, Jake, you look pretty spiffy for going to a livestock auction."

"Ta-da!" He sauntered around in a circle, showing off his clothes. "There's a dance in town tonight and, after the auction, I thought I'd stay for that. But I don't mind a detour. You and the monkeys go climb into in the wagon. I need to pick up some salt. Back in a few minutes."

Eliza and the girls waited in the wagon as the proprietor of the feed store loaded a couple of salt blocks. The horses stamped their feet, blew air out of their nostrils, and swatted flies with their tails. Then Jake untied the lead rope from the hitching post and climbed into the wagon. He snapped the reins and clucked to the horses. The wagon rumbled down the street toward the Glenn family farm, half an hour's drive away.

The homestead owned by Eliza and Jake's father was fertile bottomland, and he grew wheat, oilseed rape, and barley as cash crops. He also raised pigs, chickens, cattle, and turkeys, and he kept a couple of milk cows for the family's use. In the field next to the house, swaths of freshly mown hay were drying on the ground.

The frame house and the stone barn had been built ten years ago when his older sons were teenagers. Alexander had hired a man with a portable sawmill to cut the lumber, and he and the boys had put up the buildings themselves. Downstairs, the farmhouse had a parlor, kitchen, laundry room, the parents' bedroom, and the guest bedroom. It had six rooms upstairs. There were ten children in the Glenn family, but now most of them were grown.

The scent of freshly cut alfalfa wafted over them as the wagon rolled to a stop beside the farmhouse. Jake engaged the brake, and Eliza watched through a haze of tears as he helped Sadie and Nellie climb down.

The screen door slammed as Sadie and Nellie darted inside the house to see their grandparents. Jake took the baby and, with his free hand, helped Eliza alight from the wagon.

"Here you go, Sis." He returned the baby to her. "Troubles with Joe?"

She nodded and spoke in a choked voice. "Thanks for being such an angel and bringing us to the farm. I know you wanted to stay in town today."

He shrugged amiably. "I can go back later." He held the halter of the near horse until she moved out of the way, then he guided the team toward the barn.

Eliza trudged toward the house. *The most important thing is that the children are safe.*

Elizabeth Glenn, a short, sturdy woman in a dark blue shirtwaist dress, high-topped shoes, and full-length apron, held the screen door open. Her gray hair was parted in the middle, combed flat and smooth against her head, gathered into a tight bun in the back.

"Hello, Mother."

"Come on in, honey." Elizabeth gave her a quick hug, then looked askance at her daughter's rumpled white blouse, faded brown shawl, and none-too-clean skirt. "How nice you came to call."

Eliza laughed despite the tears in her eyes. "I must look like something the cat dragged in."

"Always glad to see you." Her mother looked at her searchingly. "Is everything all right?"

Eliza hesitated and gave a wry smile.

"I was in the midst of darning socks," Elizabeth went on hastily. "Want some coffee? I'll make a fresh pot." She went to the cook stove. "The girls are sure full of energy today. They got a quick drink and ran out to the barn."

Eliza inhaled deeply and looked around the bright and airy kitchen. The polished oak floor gleamed. She put her bags on the floor, pulled out a chair at the table, and sat down heavily.

"Mmm, I smell apples. Oh, Mother, it's so good to be home!"

Elizabeth looked up sharply. "Let me get you an apple turnover. Baked this morning," she said. She cleared away the sewing supplies and placed a pastry and a glass of water in front of her daughter. Then she made coffee and poured cups for both of them.

Sitting down, she held out her arms for baby Irene. "Come to Grandma, punkin! Oh, if you aren't a sweet bundle! Hi, Reenie! Got a smile for Grandma?" She bounced the baby up and down in her arms.

"Mercy, this child needs a dry diaper something fierce. Let me get her changed."

Eliza opened the travel bag and handed her mother a fresh baby dress and the last clean diaper. Elizabeth carried Irene to a side table and got her cleaned up.

"There! That feels much better, doesn't it? Look at you! Growing like a weed! Yes, you are. Yes, you are. Three months old already. What a big girl you are!" The baby gave her a broad toothless grin.

"Babies grow up so fast." Elizabeth caressed the baby's head and chucked her under the chin. "Your other girls have brown hair, but I have a notion Irene is going to be fair. A little blondie."

After a short while, she passed the baby back. "Grandma's got to start cornbread for dinner," she said.

Elizabeth took a bowl from the shelf and spoons from a drawer. She got cornmeal and lard from the pantry and arranged the cooking items at the other end of the table. Eliza held the baby facing outward so she could watch.

"It's been hot and humid this week," the older woman remarked. "Indian summer, it is. Cold at night and hot in the day. Whoo-ee! Some nights Father and I have to leave the door and shutters wide open."

Half listening, Eliza examined a shelf of decorative plates on the wall. Then she turned to look directly at her mother. "What would you say if, er, well, if the girls and I came to live with you and Father?" She swallowed. "For a few months at least?"

Elizabeth stirred milk into the dry ingredients. "So that's why you look so bedraggled today," she said finally. "Well. I would never interfere in anyone else's marriage, Eliza, and I do not want to hear the specifics of what is going on between you and Joe. You're a grown woman, thirty-one years old. Capable of handling your own problems." Her mouth took on a harsh twist.

"You might not approve, Mother, but I have decided to leave Joe. He's taken to drink, and the long and short of it is, I'm afraid that one day he would hurt us." She leaned her head against the back of the chair. Tears nevertheless came. They ran down the side of her face and into her hair.

"Even if he doesn't mean the cruel things he says, I have to leave him. For the children's sake, if not for mine."

Elizabeth tipped the cornbread batter into the baking pan with stiff and clumsy motions. "I swan, what *is* it you do that provokes your husband? I had hoped you'd settle down. Not be so strong-minded. Resign yourself to a wife's proper role."

"I don't do anything to him!"

"You have to let Joe wear the pants in the family, you know." Elizabeth opened the oven door and flicked a few drops of water inside to make sure it was up to temperature.

"Men want to conquer something. It's in their blood. Women are the ones who protect, who help things grow. You were our first girl, right after the three older boys. You watched them climb trees, ride horses, and ice skate, and from the time you were knee-high to a grasshopper you wanted to do anything they did. You grew up half boy, wandering the pastures and fields and riding horseback. In those formative years your father, for some reason, hmmf, didn't see fit to curb you."

Elizabeth shoved the pan into the oven, bent down to position it, then closed the oven door with a bang. Her own father had been stern, and sometimes her voice took on his unforgiving tone. She frowned at her oldest daughter and bit her lower lip. "You need to realize, my dear, that acting bold and confident makes some men feel threatened."

She stepped to the window and looked into the distance. "I love these nice big windows, though they cost Father a pretty penny. We have lived in this house for twenty-five years." She sighed, then glanced back at Eliza.

"I have borne eleven children and lost only one. Your father and I worked hard to give our children a good upbringing, and in return we expect them to be respectable people of fine character."

Then her posture softened. "Eliza Ann, your hair looks a fright! When's the last time you had a shampoo? Though I know life gets topsy-turvy when you have a new baby. Let me get Alpha in here."

Before long, Eliza's younger sister Alpharetta slipped into the kitchen and awkwardly emptied an armload of cucumbers from her apron into a bucket. She pushed aside her long side braid and cleaned her hands noisily at the washstand.

"Hi, Eliza," she said. "Getting warm out there."

"You seen the girls?" asked Elizabeth.

20

"They are helping Father and Jake brush down the horses."

"Fine," Elizabeth replied. "Alpha, honey, could you keep an eye on the cornbread and get the rest of the dinner going?"

"Anything the matter?"

"Never you mind about that."

Elizabeth pumped a bucket of water and put it to heat on the stove, then carried a washtub inside and set it on the side table.

Irene began to cough and fuss. "Baby girl, baby girl," crooned Eliza. "I've carried you hither and yon today, haven't I? You poor thing! Are you hungry again?" She unbuttoned the bodice of her blouse and put the baby to one breast, then the other.

Elizabeth's eyes crinkled fondly. "I never tire of watching babies' little expressions." As soon as the baby was sleeping soundly, she shifted her attention to Eliza. "Now, young lady, your hair is in desperate need of a wash. Let me get things situated, and then I'll see to your hair."

Her mother's voice sounded loud beside her. "Ready?"

Eliza jerked to attention and burst into tears. She had almost fallen asleep.

"Sakes alive! You must really be overwrought. Come, my dear, stand here and lean over the washtub. The water is nice and warm."

Eliza removed her combs and hairpins. Her mother poured a stream of water through her hair, then worked Castile soap into a lather and massaged it into her scalp.

"Oh, Mother! That feels wonderful."

"Well, I want to get your hair thoroughly clean." Elizabeth hummed a little song. Her fingers were gentle and thorough.

"This reminds me of old times," she said. "When you were a girl and too scatterbrained to care for your hair properly, I washed your hair every Saturday. Remember that? I knew that when time came for courting, you'd be glad it had been kept in good condition." She lifted Eliza's dark, heavy tresses and rinsed out the soap.

"Pretty soon, you'll feel like a new woman." She carried the washtub to the yard and emptied it, then filled another pitcher and added a spoonful of apple cider vinegar. As Elizabeth poured the vinegar water through her daughter's hair, Eliza wrinkled her nose at the smell.

"What in the world?" said her mother abruptly. "Eliza Ann, do you. . . There's something sticky in your hair. I have to wash it out." She added more soap and rinsed again. She stared at the water, which had a slight pink tinge.

"Is that blood? Sweetheart, what happened? Are you hurt?"

Eliza sniffled. "It's hardly bleeding anymore."

"Hold still," said her mother in a practical tone. "I want to have a look-see." She parted her daughter's hair, searching the scalp with deft movements.

"I see the cut. Doesn't look too bad. I think it's just the one. For some reason even small scalp wounds bleed a lot. Okay, let me make sure your hair is squeaky clean." She got more dilute vinegar water and rinsed a final time with plain water, and then she rubbed Eliza's hair partially dry with a piece of flannel. Leaving a comb on the table, she went to the stove to check on how Alpha was coming with the dinner.

Returning to discard the dirty water, Elizabeth glanced sharply at her daughter. "You might as well take a complete sponge bath, honey. Just pull down your blouse and chemise. I'll wash your back."

She replenished the warm water in the pitcher and brought a washcloth. "Here you go. Remember, it's good to keep your breasts very clean when you're nursing."

Eliza unbuttoned her blouse and slipped out of her chemise, letting them hang from the waistband of her skirt.

Elizabeth gasped as she caught sight of the green and purple bruises on her daughter's arms and side. "Oh, sweetie. . ." She gently washed her daughter's back.

Eliza closed her eyes and let it happen. "My left shoulder about gave out, carrying Reenie all day," she murmured.

"Alpha, could you please fetch one of my everyday dresses?" called Elizabeth. "And some clean underthings? We need to scare up a change of clothes here. . . And don't let anyone in the kitchen for a few minutes."

Elizabeth's dresses were too big for Eliza, but Alpha was sixteen years old and slender; a dress of hers would have been too small. A high-necked style was unhandy for breastfeeding, but Eliza could wear her mother's shirtwaist dress until the skirt and blouse she had been wearing got washed.

"Finish up your bath now," said Elizabeth, handing Eliza a towel. "Tonight, we will speak to your father."

Chapter 3

After the noon meal Eliza washed the clothes she had worn when she arrived, in addition to Irene's diapers. She hung them on the clothesline to dry, then went upstairs to find a secluded place to take off her mother's dress and feed the baby. There were six rooms on the second floor of the farmhouse—one for Jake, one for Alpha, another for the hired man, plus the sewing room, a storeroom, and a spare bedroom.

Opening the door of the spare bedroom, she was taken back to her childhood by the pleasant scent of lavender. Her mother always sprinkled lavender water on sheets when she ironed them.

As Irene nursed, Eliza caressed the baby's back and snuggled her close. *Each of my children has been so different. What sort of person would Irene grow up to be?* This baby liked to be where the action was, and she made a lot of noise until someone picked her up.

There was a light tap at the door, and Elizabeth leaned into the room. "When the baby falls asleep, sweetheart, bring her down to the kitchen. Alpha and I can watch her and keep the older girls occupied for a couple of hours. You, my dear, need a long, uninterrupted nap."

"Thank you, Mother," she murmured. "I'm about ready to drop."

Eliza woke several hours later, feeling more rested than she had in weeks. Her gaze wandered over the familiar oak furniture and flocked wallpaper. On the wall was a portrait of her grandmother and a painting of a moonlit landscape. Basking in the scent of lavender, she could almost imagine that she was still a teenager, sharing this bedroom with her younger sister Jane.

Then she noticed her skirt, blouse, and underclothes were draped over a chair beside the door, freshly ironed and ready to put on. Her eyes misted. *How thoughtful!* Her mother paid attention to details.

Eliza got up and dressed slowly, taking care not to touch certain places or bend in some directions. Then she combed her hair and twisted it off her neck. *Everything is going to be all right now.*

She paused to examine her image in the shelf mirror: tawny complexion, well-defined nose, round chin, wide brow, and long neck. *I'm not bad looking, am I?* People often remarked about her unusually expressive eyes.

Out of curiosity she opened the jewelry box sitting on the bureau and lifted out an amethyst pendant on a silver chain. Standing before the mirror, Eliza held the necklace to her throat for a moment. She sighed. It was lovely, but too delicate for her strong features.

Time to get busy. She went downstairs, diapered and fed the baby, then donned an apron and helped her mother by putting a measure of wheat through the grain mill, ready for bread-baking tomorrow. Next she sliced cucumbers thinly and put them in salt water. Later she would rinse them and add sour cream, vinegar, and sugar.

Elizabeth had lain down earlier with a headache and so, to keep the house quiet, the others were working in the garden. It had a big area for vegetables and a smaller area for flowers. Nellie picked bugs off the tomatoes, Eliza hoed, with Irene in a carry-sling, Alpha dug carrots and onions, and Sadie gathered flowers to put in vases.

"Look at all this food!" exclaimed Nellie. "Grandma and Grandpa *always* have enough food."

Supper consisted of sausage, sauerkraut, fried vegetables, and apple turnovers. Elizabeth asked, "When will your next crop of watermelons be ready to sell, Eliza Ann? I'm looking forward to eating some and making pickles with the rinds." Jake wasn't there for supper, as he had gone to the dance.

"Not long now."

"A couple more sunny weeks," said Eliza's father, Alexander, "and that'll do it. Here, we're 'bout finished with haying. If the weather stays dry, we can drill wheat next week."

Alexander was a balding man in a work shirt and overalls, still strong and fit at sixty-seven. He had recently hired a man to do the heavier farm work. Jake was the only one of his seven sons still living at home, and in a couple of years he, too, would be out on his own.

The hired man, Alva Daley, mostly talked with the children during the meal. He blushed whenever he looked at the women. He told Sadie and Nellie, "If you clean your plates I'll give you a piece of peppermint candy from my pocket."

Alexander had some news. "Jake heard uptown that there was a train wreck five miles east of here yesterday morning. Fault of the flagman. Both engines were damaged, but nobody was hurt."

"Merciful heavens!" said Elizabeth.

"I wager it was at that big curve," said Alva.

"They need an extra signal lamp out there," Alexander remarked.

Elizabeth turned to the girls. "Did you help Grandpa and Alpha milk the cows this evening?"

Sadie and Nellie brightened. "He sits on a one-legged stool," said Sadie.

"That's so I can jump back quick if the cow's about to step on me."

"The kitty drank the milk," said Nellie, giggling.

"Yes," Sadie chimed in. "Grandpa squirted milk right into the kitty's mouth. It was so funny." She bounced on her chair and glanced at her mother. "This is a happy house, Mama."

"Yes, it is," answered Eliza. A shadow passed over her face. *Children need a stable, organized household with kind people around them.*

Later Elizabeth and Eliza discussed what they might serve at their corn shuck they were hosting in a few weeks' time. In addition to roasting ears, they decided on fried chicken, baked potatoes, and raisin crumble.

After Alva had retired to his room and the girls were asleep on the floor of the spare bedroom, the family switched its attention to the current crisis.

"Now then, what's this I hear about you having marriage troubles?" began Alexander.

"Joe has been in a bad temper recently," said Eliza, shifting uneasily in her chair, "and it seems to be going from bad to worse. He yells at the girls. Flies into a rage over the smallest things." She hunched her shoulders and drew into herself. "I am afraid of him, Father."

"That sounds serious. I take it this has been going on for a while?"

"Unfortunately, yes. I think Joe never got over Harry's death. He wanted so much to have another son. Then we had Sadie and Nellie, and this time when I was expecting, he was sure it would be a boy. But it turned out to be a girl."

"Can't you and Joe patch things up?" asked Elizabeth. "Invite him out here to the farm for a nice hot meal. Or perhaps the preacher could have a word."

Eliza pressed her lips firmly together. "Well, Mother, it's not that simple. Ever since I got pregnant with Irene, he hasn't been the man I married." Her voice took on a grim tone. "Last night he got drunk and said he would kill us all."

"You can't be serious!" her mother gasped.

Alexander went pale and stared at his hands. "I can hardly feature. . ."

Looking from one parent to the other, Eliza gripped the edge of the table until her knuckles were white. "So I have decided to leave him. No matter what. Our marriage is over." She slumped in her chair and blew air slowly out of her mouth.

Her father was silent for a few moments. "You can't stay married to a man like that, of course not." He nodded to himself. "Eleven years of marriage is more than enough time to reveal a man's character. I thought Joe never had a lick of sense, and he complained constantly. But he was your choice for a husband, and I hoped for the best. The question now is, how are you going to support yourself and the children?"

Eliza leaned her forehead on her hand. "I'll think of something," she said quietly.

Alexander paused, then steepled his fingers and cleared his throat. "Well, for the time being, you will live here, and that's final. Just care for your little ones and help Mother. Don't count on her for unlimited babysitting, of course, but take it easy for a while. You just gave birth, my dear, and you need to rebuild your strength. In due time, we will consider the next step."

"Thank you, Father." She gave him a grateful smile.

"As for you, Alpha," he continued, "with Eliza Ann helping at home, go ahead and go to high school if you want. She can handle the milking by herself, and the two of you can manage the garden. I don't want Mother overdoing things at her age.

However, I for one wouldn't mind having a baby around again. It's been years since we had a houseful of little shavers, hasn't it, Mother?" He smiled and patted his wife's hand. "There are times when the house almost seems lonely without a baby crawling around."

Eliza gave a big sigh. In a few months she would have to turn her mind to earning money, but for the foreseeable future, they were safe. Her father and brother would protect them.

The next morning, Alexander and Jake traveled out to Vaughan's Island. "No reason to wait until Joe knocks on our front door and makes a scene. I'll make sure there's no ambiguity about your intentions, and Jake and I can fetch the rest of your clothes."

"Thank you, Father. That would be wonderful." She touched his arm lightly. "And if you could also bring the picture of Harry Benjamin. . .?" Her father nodded.

Several hours later, Alexander handed Eliza a pile of clothing and several framed photographs wrapped in a towel.

"I told Joe I was sorry that things had taken this turn, but he was no longer welcome on my farm. If he showed up, he would not be allowed to see you or the girls, at least for the time being."

Eliza's hand flew to her mouth. "What did he say? Did he get upset?"

"His state of mind is nothing for you to concern yourself with. I told him to contact you through my lawyer." Elizabeth looked relieved, and Eliza began to relax.

Eliza spent the rest of the day doing laundry, trying to get the cabin's musty smell out of their clothes. It was hard for her to believe that the ordeal of dealing with Joe's anger was now over.

The following week, her younger sister Mary, known in the family by her nickname Mate, visited for several days. A short, energetic woman, Mate was twenty years old and had recently gotten married. She had a fair complexion, well-shaped brows, short nose, and a sweet smile. Sadie and Nellie showed their aunt everything that was new on the farm, and then Mate played leapfrog with them.

That evening, after the other members of the family had gone to bed, Elizabeth, Mate, and Eliza stayed up late, chatting and sipping small glasses of port. The parlor windows were propped open to catch the evening breeze. The chirp, chirp of crickets drifted in from the window.

Eliza sat on one end of the couch and Mate on the other, curling her own hair. She folded sections of her damp hair into strips of rag, rolled them tight, and fastened them with pins. The two sisters, although thirteen years apart in age, had been close ever since Mate stayed with Eliza to help her when each of her babies was born.

"I don't bother to curl my hair," remarked Eliza. "No matter what I do, it's coarse and frizzy. I wish I had soft, shiny hair like you."

"It's true, I'm lucky. It has a natural wave. Well, I got good hair, and you got an hourglass figure." Seeing the blush on Eliza's face, she laughed. "Well, Sis, you have to admit you're well-endowed. But tell me, how long are you and the girls here for?"

Eliza looked somber. "Mother and Father have said we can live here for the time being. I'm getting a divorce."

"A divorce! Good heavens! How did that come about? Give me the inside scoop!" Mate moved closer and clasped her knees to her chest.

"Well, see, Joe had this idea that we could make extra money by taking a hot breakfast to hunters and fishermen who came out to the island. They had complained that the cafe in town didn't open till 7 a.m. So for several months now, I've been taking breakfast down to various customers around 5:30 in the morning. Joe makes the arrangements, and I make the food and carry it down to the customers. I don't mind the extra work, and that way we can afford to buy coffee.

"The other night Joe and I had an argument because I told him I wanted to keep this week's money for myself. The watermelons are almost ready for market anyway, and I didn't think he would mind too much, but he got mad and accused me of stealing his money. He grabbed my neck and choked me, then at the last minute he got hold of himself and stopped."

Elizabeth and Mate looked alarmed but said nothing.

"Later, I was sitting in the rocking chair nursing Irene, and he came up and gave me a big wallop on the shoulder with his fist, and that knocked over the rocking chair. I was hard-pressed not to fall on top of the baby. He threatened to kill the children and me, and then kill himself."

Mate gaped and clasped her hands to her heart. "You poor thing! And you and the girls out there on the island with no neighbors nearby! My God, it's hard to believe. Just a few months ago when Reenie was born, I stayed with you and he seemed like a perfectly nice fellow."

"Well, with you there he was on his best behavior."

"Oh, Eliza! I'm so sorry."

"So I'm leaving him. The girls and I are safe here, and that's the important thing. I have a feeling we made it out by the skin of our teeth."

"You must've been scared to death out there. Thank heavens you managed to escape. But if that's the sort of man Joe really is, good riddance!"

"I don't hate him, Mate. But when he got physically violent, I had to put my foot down. No second chances. Why couldn't he have talked over his problems like an adult, I'd like to know, rather than flying into a rage?"

Mate grimaced. "Seems to me that if your marriage had been true love, he would never have acted like that."

"Fiddle-faddle!" broke in Elizabeth, twitching her skirt into even folds, "It has nothing to do with the ins and outs of his personality." She frowned at her two grown daughters. "You girls assume you can pick a husband by finding a man you enjoy keeping company with."

She sniffed. "Men don't change. You have to find yourself a good family man and provider, then grow to love him, if you can."

"That sounds awfully old-fashioned, Mother," replied Eliza in a mild tone of voice.

Mate added, "It's not always easy to tell whether a fellow is a good family man, you know. In any case, I prefer the modern way of making sure you and the man get along as friends before you get married."

Elizabeth jerked her chin upward. "Mark my words, girls. I know whereof I speak."

Eliza thought back to when she had first met Joe. They had gotten acquainted at a dance, when he said he had been struck by her "smoldering" eyes. The two of them had started up a conversation and found that they were the same age. He was funny and entertaining. He told her his name was Joseph but he went by Joe, and he had been born on an island in the Kaw River. Eliza had seen islands from the window of the train but was surprised to learn that people actually lived there.

The next week, Joe borrowed a rowboat and took her out to explore his family's island. Deer flitted through the woods. Mallard and teal ducks paddled in the marsh. She imagined how romantic it would be to live out in the pristine wilderness.

By the time she and Joe got married, however, someone else was renting the island. For the first couple of years of their marriage, they lived with his parents and helped on his father's farm.

Mate leaned back and clasped her hands behind her head. "Joe was fun to visit with. He told lots of stories. I remember going out to his folks' farm when the whole gang came for that sleigh ride. What year was that, do you remember?"

"Must've been back in '88. Because it was before Harry Benjamin was born. I wasn't even expecting yet."

"We had a lot of good times."

"Joe and I didn't have two cents to rub together, but we were happy. His father supported us, to tell the truth."

Elizabeth spoke up. "It was such a shame about baby Harry."

Eliza's face clouded. "Yes. Only eleven months old when he died. My darling little angel. . ."

Her mother said, "That place you and Joe rented later was a poor excuse for a farm, if you ask me."

"It was all we could afford, Mother. We borrowed money to buy horses and machinery, but farming just didn't pan out. Some years we broke even. Then Sadie and Nellie came along, and it seemed like we always needed things. Once we were in the hole financially, it was almost impossible to get out. Sometimes we didn't have enough food, and I had to give the children my portion."

"Oh, babe!" said Elizabeth, wringing her hands. "I'm so sorry. Who would have thought? I did notice you looked peaked there for a while."

"Well, I didn't want you and Father to know. I took care of the house and the children the best I could and tried not to complain. There was no way I could run outside and help Joe with the farm work and leave the babies alone in the house. Besides, some of the time we had a hired man."

Her mother gazed into the distance. "Joe's father wasn't that successful at farming either, so maybe Joe never learned how to farm properly."

"I expect it was partly my fault," said Eliza. "As a girl, I paid no attention to saving money. Growing up, we always had enough of everything, and I didn't give much thought about how to scrimp and save."

"There's no need for a housewife to be a skinflint," her mother retorted. "If you are frugal when you can be, then your savings will tide you over any setback."

"Right, but you do need to have a *certain* amount of money." Eliza rubbed the back of her neck. "Where was I? Oh, yes. When I was expecting Irene, Joe gave up the farm and took that job in town. Although we had more money, then he started spending evenings at the saloon."

She looked down and shook her head. "I keep running through these things in my mind, trying to understand where our marriage went wrong. Joe became more difficult to get along with, and sometimes he would slap me around. I don't believe he meant to hurt me. He wasn't getting ahead in life, and he was so frustrated he just didn't know what to do.

"Also, Joe is impulsive. He doesn't think things through like Father does. And whenever I said we needed more money, he accused me of criticizing him. Which I was, honestly. Anyway, last spring Joe quit his job and we moved to the island.

"I told myself that it would be a peaceful place to live, and the children could play in the woods. At least we would have plenty to eat, what with having fish, nuts, watermelon, and berries close at hand. Joe and I planted a big patch of watermelons to sell, something he had dreamed about doing for a long time.

"It was whiskey that made things go bad. It's like it made his mind unravel. I tried to be a good wife, but the other night, when he said he would kill the children and me, there was no more need to brood about how to deal with him. Our marriage was over."

Mate covered her face with her hands. "Horrible! I can't imagine it." She crossed her legs, then asked in a hesitant voice, "What're you going to do now, Sissy? Teach?"

"Heavens no, I'm not a teacher type. But I'll come up with something, by hook or by crook. Life goes on, and I have to rise above the situation. One fortunate thing is that the girls and I have our health."

Mate said, "I'd be scared to go out in the world all by myself."

Eliza shivered and wrapped her arms around her shoulders. "I'm not a coward, but I'm not exactly brave either. Just because you go through something and are still alive, doesn't mean you are brave. Nevertheless, I'll find a way to support my girls. I don't want them to suffer because of me." She threw her hands wide. "Look, I have no choice."

Elizabeth clucked her tongue. "Enough of that kind of talk! I can hardly feature that any child of mine would get a divorce."

Mate said, "Mother, this is obviously not Eliza's fault."

"A divorce, for whatever reason, brings shame upon the family. Now Eliza will never have a regular place in society. She will be alone in the world. My grandchildren will grow up the products of a broken home, and my daughter will be dependent on charity. . ."

"Charity!" murmured Eliza. Her cheeks sagged.

"What I mean is that in future years—after we're gone, for instance—people may give you a job as a cook or housecleaner because they pity you, since you have children to support. And you will probably have to get clothes from the poor box at church."

"Mother! Although I'm getting a divorce, my life isn't over. I'm a strong woman, and I'm not going to spend my years boo-hooing about a broken marriage. You never know—maybe I'll open a bakery on Main Street. Wouldn't you say that was respectable?"

Chapter 4

For their appointment with the lawyer, Eliza and her father dressed in their Sunday best. They drove into town without speaking, each of them tired and preoccupied. Ahead of their wagon, the rough surface of the road shone with early morning dew. Nellie had had a bad dream the night before and roused the household with her screams. It had taken an hour to get her calmed down.

The dusty anteroom of Jeb Hudson's law office was as dark as a closet, its single window partially obscured by a green velvet curtain. Eliza and Alexander had sat in the leather-covered armchairs and waited until the previous client had left and Mr. Hudson motioned for them to enter.

"Please, have a seat. We have a lot to discuss this morning." On the lawyer's roll-top desk was an inkwell, a pen tray, a loose sheaf of papers, a spike for paid invoices, and a cloth-bound ledger lined up parallel to the edge of the desk. Along the wall was a set of glass-fronted barrister bookcases filled with legal reference books.

Mr. Hudson shuffled the papers on his desk into a neat pile, slipped them into a buff-colored folder, and deposited it in a drawer. He then selected another, thinner folder and opened it on his desk.

"I have learned quite a few things about your estranged husband," Mr. Hudson said, cocking an eyebrow at Eliza. He riffled through several sheets of paper and selected one document.

"Yes. Well. First of all, Joseph Vaughan is not his real name."

"What?" exclaimed Eliza. She grabbed the armrests of the chair and leaned forward. She and Alexander stared at the lawyer.

"As a matter of fact," continued the lawyer, "his correct legal name is Joel, Joel V. Vaughan. Joseph Vaughan was his older brother. Joseph was part of a group of men who hunted wild horses and sold them. At the age of nineteen, Joseph unfortunately disappeared and was never seen again. He must have been planning to get married, though, as his father had signed this affidavit giving him permission to marry under the age of twenty-one."

The lawyer gestured toward the document. "What seems to have happened is that your husband used his brother's affidavit in order to get married. Joel was only 16 years old when he married you—not 19, as he claimed."

"I'll be damned!" Alexander raised his eyebrows and shook his head.

"Dear Lord, what else wasn't true?" said Eliza, fumbling with her handkerchief. "When we got our marriage license, I remember Joe signed his name J. Vaughan. 'Course I thought nothing of it at the time."

"Wait!" interrupted Alexander. "Does this mean that their marriage wasn't valid?"

Mr. Hudson twisted his mouth to one side. "No, you have only four years to contest a marriage, except in cases of bigamy. Here, the question is moot since she and Joel were married more than ten years and they have minor children."

Alexander asked, "So it has no bearing then on Eliza's divorce petition?"

"Since Joe did not sign a business contract or mortgage using the false name, it is significant only in that it throws light on his relationship with the truth. For instance, begging your pardon, ma'am, if he were to testify in court that you had committed adultery, in order to swing the custody ruling his way."

"I was *never* unfaithful to Joe," said Eliza, her eyes flashing.

"What I'm saying is that he *might* try to besmirch your virtue, and we have to be prepared for that possibility." Eliza glanced at her father, who sat stony-faced.

Mr. Hudson looked apologetic. "If he did that, we could sue him for slander, but apparently Joel has no money so a judgment in our favor would be of little benefit. Eliza, do you know of any other assets owned by Joe?"

She was still adjusting her mind to Joe's lie about his name. "Er, no, we do not. The island where we lived belongs to his father, including the cabin and the furniture."

"Very well," said the lawyer, paging through the file. "By the way, I did receive a letter from your husband. Joel has asked to be reimbursed for the items you took from the house."

"Always a hustler, that guy," said Alexander, suppressing a laugh.

"As I understand, Eliza, you only took clothing for you and the girls and a few photographs, right? So we won't need to get into a scrap with him over that."

The lawyer spread his hands wide. "Judging by your deposition last week, I believe there will be no difficulty for you to obtain a divorce from Joel on the grounds of extreme cruelty. You are a virtuous woman and did nothing cruel to him in return. Alexander, you should make yourself available as a witness, though, in case you are needed to vouch for the extent of her injuries.

"Judges don't like to grant divorces, and in particular they try to weed out cases where a husband and wife make false claims of abuse or adultery in order to obtain a desired divorce. Thus, when we present our evidence, we want to leave no doubt that you have been mistreated.

"Assuming your divorce is granted, Eliza, the judge will probably award you custody of the children, since all three are girls and 'of tender years,' which is to say, under the age of seven. We are lucky on that score. However, judges have a lot of discretion in custody matters. We are scheduled to appear before Judge Hazen, who is one who believes that a father has a natural right over his children unless he is clearly unfit.

"Therefore, Eliza, I would recommend that you make a strong statement when you go to Topeka and testify. Don't be shy when you get on the witness stand. Speak loud enough for everyone in the room to hear. Tell the truth, certainly, but in order to ensure that you are awarded custody of your daughters, I'm afraid you will have to describe your husband's cruel acts in detail."

Mr. Hudson drummed the fingers of one hand on his desk. After a few minutes of silence, he put the papers in order, closed the file folder, and stood up. Eliza and Alexander stumbled to their feet.

"See you in court," the lawyer said, shaking hands with both of them, "and don't worry. I think the case will go our way." Grinning, he rubbed his hands together.

As they left the lawyer's office, Eliza took her father's arm. "Well, that's got the ball rolling. It feels like I'm being disloyal to my best friend, but I have no other choice. The children must be protected."

Alexander reached over and patted her hand. "It can't be helped, my dear. And Hudson will make sure the paperwork is up to snuff."

The divorce hearing was November 1, 1897. Eliza and Alexander left the farm early to catch a train to Topeka. Alpha came along to help take care of Irene, as there was no way to know what time of day their case would be called.

The weather was cold and windy. Eliza dressed simply in a full skirt of dark red satin, a high-necked white blouse, her mother's white shawl, a coat, and a conservative gray bonnet. Alexander wore a black suit, hat, and cloak. Although the baby fussed in the open wagon when they were buffeted by the wind, she was quiet and well-behaved on the train.

They took a taxicab from Topeka's train station to the corner of Fifth and Van Buren. The Shawnee County Courthouse, a four-story brick building sitting by itself in the center of a grassy square, had multiple arches in front and a tall clock tower on top.

The Glenns dusted off their clothes, climbed the stairs to the entrance, and passed through the double doors into a high-ceilinged central hall, their footsteps echoing on the marble floor. After inquiring at the cloakroom where they were supposed to go, they climbed another staircase to the second floor and sat on a long wooden bench outside the courtroom.

Eliza and Alpha chatted in a distracted way while Alexander paced. Occasionally, a clerk would emerge and summon other individuals for their court hearings. Eliza kept an eye out for Joe but didn't see him. Would their case be able to proceed if Joe did not appear?

After the noon recess, their lawyer paused briefly on his way back into the courtroom. "Not long now," he said. "Ours is the last case of the day."

Finally, at 3 p.m., the bailiff opened the enormous wooden door and the clerk called, "Vaughan versus Vaughan, petition for divorce." Eliza, Alexander, and Alpha, carrying Irene, rose and were ushered into the courtroom. Some people filed out of the room, while others shifted their chairs, chatted, and coughed.

The Glenn family looked around the large courtroom, which smelled of furniture polish, tobacco smoke, and beer. Eliza finally spied Joe, who was sitting in the visitors' gallery and must have come in earlier. He wore a poorly fitting suit, and his face was bloated and puffy. Seeing him for the first time in two months, she shuddered.

Eliza perched on the edge of her chair, clasped her hands tightly in her lap, and watched as Mr. Hudson submitted their paperwork to the judge and presented the basic facts of the case.

Elizabeth and Alpha had helped Eliza fix her hair that morning. Although a few strands had come loose, her hair was braided and wound around her head in an old-fashioned style.

Eliza wrung her hands. Her pulse raced. *It will be over soon,* she tried to reassure herself. She picked up the baby and patted her back.

Would the lawyer deflect any hostile questions? Would her father be asked to testify?

Suddenly, it was time. She stood up and walked to the witness stand, carrying Irene on her shoulder. *That way she probably won't cry, and besides, it might make me look virtuous and maternal.* Mr. Hudson's eyes beamed his approval.

Eliza was sworn in and seated. She rubbed her fingers back and forth on a rough spot on the chair to stop them from trembling. Mr. Hudson looked through his notes and began to speak.

"Mrs. Vaughan, please tell the court how you would characterize your marriage."

She looked directly at Judge Hazen, a chubby, bald man with side whiskers and a stern demeanor. *He is probably a father himself and would want the best for his own children.*

"Until this year, I suppose our marriage was not that different from many others. Joe and I quarreled at times, and occasionally he came home intoxicated. After we moved to the island seven months ago, however, things got much worse."

Eliza held her head high and spoke in a clear voice that commanded attention. Her cheeks were flushed, and she appeared as forthright and determined as an Old Testament prophet.

There was a sudden commotion in the gallery. Joe Vaughan sprang to his feet and, with strain visible on his face, he barreled toward the door. Sidestepping the bailiff who sought to block his way, Joe opened the door and left the courtroom. Slam!

The audience murmured and pointed. Bam! "Order in the court!"

The judge paused. "Go ahead, counsel. Let the witness continue." Mr. Hudson gestured for Eliza to go on.

"We moved to the island this spring. Joe thought I would not be able to get away, so he treated me worse than he ever had." A few spectators nudged each other.

"Did Joel Vaughan ever strike you?" asked the lawyer. The courtroom grew absolutely quiet.

"Yes, many times, I would say." Eliza winced as she thought back over the difficulties of the past several years.

"Before we moved to the island, we used to have troubles, but they never amounted to much. He would apologize after and say he was sorry for losing his temper. The last several months, though, he would swear at me, strike me, and say all manner of things." She took a deep breath. "Then one night he took down his razor and ran his finger over the edge. . ."

She stifled a sob and forced her voice to be steady, "I could hardly believe my eyes. He claimed he was going to kill the children and me, and then kill himself." She took out a handkerchief and wiped her eyes. "When he said that, as far as I was concerned, it was the end of our marriage. Later he fell asleep. The next morning, very early, I took the children and fled to my father's home."

At last, the ordeal of giving her testimony was over. Irene had not made any noise. As Eliza sat down again in the gallery, Alexander gave her an almost imperceptible nod. Her breathing gradually reverted to normal, and Alpha put an arm around her shoulders.

Then Joel Vaughan was called to the witness stand. When the baliff informed the judge that the individual was no longer present, the judge pronounced his verdict. "Complaint against the accused sustained, divorce granted, with the customary equal division of personal property. Sole and exclusive custody of the three children is granted to Eliza Vaughan, without conditions." He banged the gavel.

"All rise!" called the bailiff. Everyone stood respectfully as the judge got up and departed to his chambers.

Eliza, Alexander, and Alpha found themselves pushed out of the courtroom by the crowd. The corridor teemed with clerks, lawyers, policemen, journalists, and spectators, all talking at once. Cigar smoke clogged the air. With trembling hands, Eliza handed the baby to Alpha.

Mr. Hudson appeared beside them and clapped Alexander genially on the back. He opened his briefcase and produced a leather-bound bottle of whiskey and several small silver cups. "Congratulations!" he said. "May I offer you both a drink?" Eliza shook her head.

"As a matter of fact, sir, I believe I *could* use one," said Alexander. The two men drank a small whiskey.

"A convincing performance," the lawyer said to Eliza, bowing slightly.

"What are you talking about?" she muttered with a wan smile. "Those tears were real. Come on, Alpha, let's get the baby away from this cigar smoke."

Sitting on the courthouse steps, Alpha tittered. "I don't know how you did it, Eliza," she whispered, looking at her feet. "You are so brave. Gosh, if I had been up there, with everyone staring at me, and me starting to cry, I would've been too embarrassed to go on." She covered her mouth with her hand.

"It *was* hard. I had to steel my mind to keep talking, but I had to do it. Children are the most precious things in life. That really hit home to me when we lost Harry."

Two days later, at the farm, Elizabeth was going through the day's mail when she suddenly stopped and sought out Eliza.

"What in the name of heaven is this?" she demanded, thrusting a newspaper in front of her daughter's face.

"Oh, no!" exclaimed Eliza as she caught sight of the headline: TRAGEDY OF THE ISLE. FORTUNATELY MRS. VAUGHAN

ESCAPED IN TIME. An article in *The Topeka State Journal* described Eliza and Joe's divorce proceedings, blow by blow, as if in a penny dreadful.

"Who would have thought my divorce would be written up in the newspaper?" Eliza grumbled, her cheeks pink. *At least it wasn't on the front page.*

"Sounds to me like you made an unseemly public display in that courtroom."

"For goodness' sake, Mother! I had to speak plainly in order to get custody of the children."

"Our family's dirty laundry, printed in the newspaper for everyone to see! There's no chance now that the circumstances of your divorce can be kept secret."

"I'm afraid you're right. That horse has left the barn. Also Joe has probably talked about me to his no-account friends at the saloon. But Mother, we 've lived in the Lecompton area for years, and people know we are a family of good character. I expect that the talk about my divorce will die down after a few weeks. After all, I'm an ordinary woman. Why would people be interested in my private life?"

Elizabeth turned abruptly and pressed a hand to her bosom. "Eliza Ann, you just see this from your own selfish point of view. Think of how I feel! In a few weeks, Father and I are going to celebrate our fortieth wedding anniversary, and it will take away a lot of my happiness in that occasion if gossip about your divorce spoils our special day."

Eliza patted her mother's arm. "Don't worry, Mother. I think things will go all right. If people ask, I will tell them in a matter-of-fact way that Joe and I have separated, and then change the subject."

A few days later Elizabeth asked Eliza, "Have you explained to the girls why you're living here with us? I'm worried about whether they can adjust to not having a father."

Elizabeth was knitting, as Eliza kneaded bread dough on the kitchen table nearby. Push, push, turn. Push, push, turn. "Yes, Mother. I've talked with them, and they've asked questions, as is to be expected. Far as I can tell, they have accepted the situation."

"Well, least said, quickest mended. And there's nothing gained by you running Joe down when you talk to them. You're easy in your own mind about what your actions?"

Eliza wiped her brow with her sleeve, keeping her face expressionless. "I do not regret getting a divorce, if that's what you mean. Honestly, I thought so many times about leaving Joe that when I left I had no misgivings. It's all behind me now. And as the children get older, I expect their memories of him will dim, and the hard times will almost be forgotten."

"You are mistaken, my dear. Some things you don't get over—like not having a father."

Eliza swallowed. "I know, but we all have to accept what life brings us, right? The important thing is that the children are safe." Her eyes brimmed with tears and she spoke in a subdued voice. "I am very grateful to you and Father for taking us in."

"Parents never stop loving their children," Elizabeth replied crisply, bending over to count her stitches.

Some days later, Sadie and Nellie moved into their new bedroom, which had formerly been the sewing room.

"Grandma made you these butterfly curtains especially," said Eliza. "What a pretty room!"

"Whee! Whee!" said Nellie, leaning against the bed, arms outstretched. "A big bed." She climbed onto the bed and curled up like a cat.

"Are we ever going back to the island?" asked Sadie, biting her lip.

46

"No, we live with Grandma and Grandpa now," her mother replied.

"Well, what about Papa?"

"He still lives on the island. He was feeling very angry, and we had to leave before someone got hurt."

"When he stops feeling angry, will he come and live with us?"

"No, sweetheart, we won't be living with Papa again. I'm afraid this is a grownup thing that you're not old enough to understand."

"Papa doesn't like us anymore?" asked Sadie.

Eliza straightened her daughter's braids. "He's going through a difficult time."

Nellie traced one of the quilt's butterfly designs with her finger. "Papa hurted you."

Eliza nodded. "Yes, Papa was yelling and hitting. That's why we couldn't stay."

Sadie said, "It's not nice to yell or hit."

"No. I asked him to please stop, and he wouldn't stop."

Sadie twisted the end of her braid. "I used to yell and hit, but I'm a big girl now."

Eliza swept both children into her arms. "You and Nellie are very, very good girls. And if you yell or hit once in a while, I know that you are just children who are learning how to behave. It's a completely different thing if a grownup does it." She kissed them. "Now, don't worry! I will always love you and take care of you and keep you safe."

After Sadie and Nellie scampered downstairs to play, Eliza remained sitting on the bed, deep in thought. *My three girls are probably all the children I will ever have, and that is rather sad. Well, unless I remarry, which is not likely at my age. At least the girls are close enough in age that they can play together. But it would have been fun to raise at least one little boy.*

Chapter 5

Soon Eliza took on many household tasks at her parents' farm. During the winter Sadie and Nellie, wearing their little-girl pinafores, helped her in the kitchen, and in summer they worked together in the garden in the early morning, when it was cool. She explained to the girls everything she was doing.

The garden was a mature plot with rich compost, easy to weed, with tomatoes and vines on trellises, cabbages on dirt mounds, and a sturdy fence to keep out chickens and rabbits. Sadie and Nellie also sometimes rode the gentler horses, under their grandfather's supervision.

At supper Eliza would ask Sadie and Nellie, "What new things did you see today?" She was always interested to hear what the girls had to say. Elizabeth, although somewhat indulgent with grandchildren, felt that the girls should 'get all their wiggles out' when playing outside, and sit calmly and quietly at the table.

"Don't fidget, Sadie!" she would say. "Act like a lady."

One evening Elizabeth frowned at the bowl of dessert. "Something's wrong with the custard. Not enough nutmeg."

Alexander replied, "It does seem a bit out of the ordinary. I like it though."

Eliza smiled. "Well, Nellie was helping me, and we got a little too much vanilla poured in, but anyway I thought it might be a nice change to have something different."

Jake spooned out a second helping. "It's good both ways."

Elizabeth sniffed. "Next time, please make the recipe like we do it in this family."

"All right, Mother." Eliza tried not to smile. *She is so predictable.*

One day Alexander, Elizabeth, Alpha, Eliza, and the children were shopping in Lecompton when they saw a wagon down the street with a big sign saying "Watermelons, 25 cents each." Next to it stood Joe, wearing a threadbare suit and a jaunty bow tie. Customers gathered around the wagon to listen to his amusing patter and buy watermelons.

All at once Joe stood in front of Eliza, blocking her way. He gave Irene a fleeting caress, then leaned into Eliza's face, glaring.

"You vicious, shameless woman! Just *had* to get revenge, didn't you?"

Her throat tightened, and she could hardly get her breath. "Hello, Joe. I wish you well."

"Ha!" he hissed. "Because of that grand performance of yours at the courthouse, I can't even rent a room in this town." He gripped her shoulder, squeezing harder and harder. Eliza's face began to crumble. Beads of sweat formed on her brow. She raised her palms ineffectually against his chest.

Alexander was immediately beside them. "How're you doing these days, Joe?" he exclaimed heartily, holding out his hand for a handshake. "How's the watermelon business?" As the two men shook hands, Alexander rested his free hand lightly on Joe's shoulder, turning him smoothly so that Joe's back was to Eliza.

Eliza's cheeks burned. She staggered a bit and tried to recover her composure.

"Papa!" exclaimed Sadie and Nellie, running toward Joe. Just before reaching him, the girls stopped and wrapped their arms around Alexander's legs. Joe squatted down and grinned at them.

"I've missed you little rascals, that's for sure."

He glanced up at Alexander and shrugged. "Sorry, can't stop to visit. Better get back to my customers." He sprinted back to the wagon, where people were looking around for the vendor.

"I want to buy a couple of those nice big watermelons," announced Elizabeth, and the family began drifting toward Joe's wagon.

Alexander fell into step beside Eliza and tucked her hand into his arm.

Elizabeth made her way to the display. "Hello, Joe," she said. "How's business?"

"Going great guns," he said, gesturing to the crowd. "How many would you folks like?"

"Two, please," said Elizabeth. "How are you doing, Joe?"

"First-class," he replied with gusto. "And I'll give you an extra melon at no charge." He picked up a watermelon. "Where's your wagon?"

"Let me give you a hand with that, Joe," said Alexander. "We're just down the street here." Alexander, Joe, and Jake carried three large watermelons to the Glenns' wagon.

"Well, thanks a lot! Best of luck to ya," said Alexander. "We have to go now." He took Sadie and Nellie gently by the hand, and the family moved away from Joe's wagon.

"Bye, Papa," the girls called. He gave them an offhand wave.

The last Sunday in November, Elizabeth and Alexander celebrated their fortieth wedding anniversary. Eliza and Alpha prepared a sumptuous buffet, and many friends and relatives came to the farm for the event. Mate had curled Sadie and Nellie's hair in ringlets. When people asked Eliza about Joe, she simply said that she and Joe had permanently separated.

A photographer took a formal portrait of the anniversary couple, as well as other family pictures. As quickly as she could, Eliza escaped to the kitchen. *It's good to have pictures, but I always feel like an ugly duckling next to Mate. She almost always takes a cute picture.*

1899

Alexander Glenn's farm was just a few miles down the road from the farm of his sister Jane, a widow with two daughters. When Eliza was young, she and those two girls, plus Nannie, another cousin, spent a lot of time every summer at Aunt Jane's house. The four of them were around the same age and they loved playing together. Since Eliza's sisters were much younger than she, those three cousins felt almost like sisters. Nannie, who had a sweet and gentle disposition, was a special favorite.

As an adult, Eliza kept up a regular correspondence with Nannie, who lived in western Kansas and was married and had a family. In her most recent letter, she had said that she was pregnant again and not feeling well.

"If things should go wrong during childbirth," she wrote, "I have made my peace with God, but what would happen to my children if I die? Pierce is not the sort of man to raise them by himself. I lie awake at night worrying about that sometimes."

Eliza had replied promptly. "Please, take good care of yourself. Chances are, your upcoming confinement will go well, like it did with your other four children. But if something should happen to you or, heaven forbid, you pass away, I promise I will make sure your children are faring well."

Just after the first of the year, they learned that Nannie had had a miscarriage and died. Alexander, Elizabeth, Mate, Eliza, and Irene traveled by train to western Kansas to attend the funeral. Alpharetta stayed home to take care of Sadie and Nellie.

At the funeral, Nanny's husband Pierce assured the relatives that he had hired a motherly sort of woman to keep house for him and the three boys. Nannie's parents, the Thompsons, who lived nearby, were going to raise one-and-a-half-year-old Ruth.

1900 (the next year)

Sadie was in third grade now, Nellie would start school in one more year, and Irene was an active and talkative toddler. Alpha, who didn't want to go to high school, had taken a day job as housekeeper for an elderly neighbor.

"With my arthritis," said their mother one afternoon, "I'd really have to scale back the size of the garden if I were doing it all myself. How is it, Eliza, that you manage to accomplish so much day after day? And I must say, without fuss," she said admiringly.

"Well, I don't know exactly. I just do a stand-up job, then a sit-down one."

Elizabeth pressed a hand to her bosom. "I do hate to think of what life would be like if I didn't have you girls here to help out."

"Well, Mother, you could hire a day woman to come in."

"You're right, of course, but I wouldn't feel comfortable with a stranger in the house." Eliza was glad to be appreciated, and she was grateful to her parents for taking them in. Yet she often gazed out of the window and wished she were in charge of her own household again. It was not easy for her to take a back seat to her mother after being used to making her own decisions.

Elizabeth insisted that Eliza wear a corset every day and have her hair put up nicely before starting housework, even on laundry day. Eliza sometimes wondered if her mother, who had such strong opinions about how things should be done, had been that persnickety when she had done all the daily tasks by herself.

Every month or so, Alexander, Elizabeth, Eliza, and sometimes the girls, took the train into Topeka to buy supplies not available in Lecompton. For example, Eliza bought shoes and books. The women looked at dresses and hats, and Alexander attended the livestock auction. Before returning home, the family often stopped at Harvey House, a big restaurant next to the train station.

Joe Vaughan had disappeared, and the Glenns heard that he was working in a hardware store 130 miles away. He had remarried and was still going by the name Joseph. Hearing about Joe's change of scene made Eliza realize with a start that, although housework kept her busy, she was still doing many of the same tasks and seeing the same people as when she was a girl.

One evening after the girls were in bed and Alpha was out dancing with her beau, Alexander said, "I stopped by Jane's on the way home today. She just got a letter from the Thompsons. Apparently, Nannie's husband, Pierce Griffith, hasn't been able to find a housekeeper. It's been over a year now since Nannie passed away. Although the Thompsons are raising the baby girl, Pierce needs a reliable person to look after the three boys so he can do his farm work, but right now he doesn't have anybody."

"But I thought he had hired a housekeeper," said Eliza. "Oh dear, those poor little boys, with no mother!"

"I don't know what the difficulty is. Jane says Pierce has hired a whole series of housekeepers, and they all quit after a few weeks or months. Finally he got a husband and wife couple, but the man wanted more say with the farm and the cattle, and of course Pierce wouldn't stand for that. So, for a while now, he and the boys have been on their own.

"Maybe you ought to go out there and keep house for him, Eliza. When we were there for Nannie's funeral, he said the job was yours if you wanted it. Over the long term, him and the boys batching is not good."

"It does sound like the situation is not the best." She rested her chin on her hand. "It's such a shame that Nannie died."

Elizabeth stood up to clear the table. "Pierce should've gotten the doctor right away when her bleeding wouldn't stop. Although I'll grant that it might not 've changed the outcome."

"It might be fun to go look after the boys," said Eliza. "I can cook and keep house as well as anybody, even if Pierce *is* particular. Besides, it would be nice to have money of my own."

Alexander nodded and leaned forward. "Griffith has a good head on his shoulders, I know that. He deals in high-grade cattle and seems to have astonishing luck at knowing when to buy and sell. A few more years and he will probably be well-to-do."

"An opportunity like that doesn't turn up every day," observed Elizabeth.

"Well," said Eliza, "If you're sure that you two would be all right here without me, I have half a mind to do it. After all, Pierce is not a complete stranger. He and I have chatted at family dinners, and cousin Nannie was a dear friend of mine. I'd love to do something to help her children."

"Give it some thought, sweetheart," urged her father. "You're welcome to stay here as long as you like, but I can imagine that living with us old folks might feel tame to a young-blooded person. Mother and I will get along fine. Go see a different part of the country. If it doesn't work out, you can always come back home."

So Eliza wrote to Pierce saying that she would be willing to take the job.

A few days later, her sister Mate arrived at the Glenn farm for another visit. Mate's son Earl was nearly two and beginning to walk. Irene was two and a half. Sadie and Nellie had fun leading the toddlers around by the hand and playing with them. Eliza and Mate rolled up their sleeves and dove into spring cleaning their parents' house, giving the laundry room a good scrub and beating dust out of the carpets.

When Elizabeth went to town for a Women's Christian Temperance Union meeting one afternoon, Eliza and Mate put their feet up and had a private conversation.

"Being housekeeper for Pierce and his boys might be a good job for you," said Mate. "You'd be earning your way in the world. Though it's hard to think of you living way out in western Kansas. I would be sad to see you go, Sissy." She gave her a little smile.

"I'd miss you too," replied Eliza, "but all I know how to do is raise children and keep house. What other jobs could I get? I never liked school, and I'm no great shakes as a seamstress. I've thought of moving to town and selling cakes door to door, or working as a cook in the hotel, but then who would take care of my children?"

"This sounds like it would be a nice job." Mate clasped her hands together. "You'll make some money, and at the same time be able to take care of your girls."

Eliza nodded. "I hate the thought of living so far away from you and Mother and Father. It might be interesting though and, of course, I'd meet new people. You and I could write letters, and you could come visit me sometimes. It's not *that* remote, you know."

She stepped to the window to check on the children. They were crouched down in the dirt with some old spoons, pounding dry shards of mud into powder.

"I don't know," Eliza murmured, turning back. "I'd like to do it, and yet I wouldn't." She looked squarely at her sister. "In any case, it's time for me to take charge of my life. It's no fun just marking days off the calendar. It would be good to try something new, but this might turn out to be a mistake. I just don't know."

"I think it would do you good to get away from home, at least for a while. I know you're not totally happy here, Sissy. Mother's been a real grouch ever since she went through the change." The sisters tittered.

"Reenie is almost three," said Eliza, "and you know how kids are at that age. She's a saucy little thing and jabbers away all day long. Mother and Father are older and set in their ways and, as much as they adore the girls living here, they would probably prefer less hullabaloo. Sadie and Nellie are still young enough that they could adjust to a new place.

"Also, I feel like a fish out of water here in Lecompton. Without a husband at my side, I don't fit into the social scene. I'm always the fifth wheel. And people of the older generation think of me as a girl."

Mate stretched her arms and yawned. "Honestly, if it was me, I don't think I would take the job. Living out on the prairie with no family close by. . . Just be careful. You wouldn't want Pierce to get the impression you are a woman of easy virtue."

Eliza braced her shoulders. "I'll just do my work and not allow any unwanted intimacies. If he pushes things in that direction, I'll tell him no. My girlfriends here are either trying to get pregnant or wishing they weren't pregnant. Listening to their endless troubles doesn't make getting married again sound very appealing." They giggled, then looked sad again.

Mate wrapped her arms around Eliza. "Buck up, Sis. It'll be an adventure!"

"Right! I've set my sail. Only time will tell if it's the right choice. I'll figure things out as I go."

Five days later, in the middle of March, Elizabeth found a thick envelope in the mailbox. "Here's a letter for you," she said to Eliza, smiling. "Also, we got a Ladies' Home Journal if you would like to read it."

"Not right now, thanks." The letter was from Pierce, offering her the position as his housekeeper and asking where he should wire money for her travel expenses.

"Hey, I got the job!" she shouted. "That man's desperate, all right. He's asking me to come by April 1 or earlier."

"Bless my soul! That's wonderful news," said Elizabeth. "My women friends have felt so sorry for you, and now I can tell them that you have bright prospects at last. Not much time to get ready for the journey, though."

The week went by with dizzying speed. Alexander bought a couple of stout wardrobe trunks, Elizabeth knitted mittens and scarves, and Eliza shopped in Topeka for clothes, books, and other items. Living far from a city for the foreseeable future, she wanted for each of them to have three changes of clothes for summer and three for winter.

Pierce had written that she and her children would share a room at his farm. She assumed that his house would be equipped with the usual kitchen utensils such as skillets, irons, and churns, and so she planned to bring only a few items he might not have, such as an egg beater and a long-handled slotted spoon.

Eliza confessed to her mother, "I do have a few qualms about whether my children will get along with his boys. They are similar in age, but don't know each other at all."

"Just keep them organized and busy," said Elizabeth, patting her arm. "There is always plenty to see and do on a farm. Sadie will walk to school with Ralph and Ross, and you'll just have Nellie, Reenie, and John most of the day. Don't worry, honey. I expect everything will work out fine."

All too swiftly, the day of departure arrived. "It's a cool, clear morning," announced Alexander. "Perfect traveling weather." He and Jake fastened the buckles on the traveling trunks, loaded them into the wagon, and tied them down.

"Everybody ready?" asked Jake. "Hop in, and we'll be on our way."

"Goodbye, Alpha," Eliza said. "I'm going to miss you so much. It's been fun doing things together." Alpha hugged her sister and the children, then stepped back as Eliza reached out for Elizabeth.

"Goodbye, Mother. Thanks for everything! Don't work too hard. I'll write soon." Eliza gave a warm hug to her mother, whose face was streaming with tears.

Jake helped Eliza and the children climb into the wagon. The men sat in front, and Jake took the reins. Eliza wore a plum-colored traveling suit and held Irene on her lap. Sadie and Nellie wore identical green plaid dresses. As the wagon rumbled along toward town, Eliza and the girls waved their handkerchiefs to Elizabeth and Alpha as long as they could see them.

They arrived in Lecompton twenty minutes early. Alexander and Jake loaded Eliza's trunks onto the baggage cart and then stood around the platform, discussing hog prices with some other men.

"Mama, I'm hungry," said Nellie.

"My goodness, right after breakfast? How about an apple to tide you over?"

"I want an apple, too," said Sadie. Eliza sliced an apple and divided the pieces between the two girls.

After a short wait, a train whistle sounded in the distance. People edged nearer the tracks. Sadie was standing too close, and Jake eased her back.

Steam boiled into the cool air as the train moved slowly into the station. The whistle blew again, and the girls waved as the engineer came into view. The train braked to a stop, wheels squealing.

Rail workers loaded cream cans, wooden packing crates, and Eliza's two travel trunks into the baggage car. The depot agent rushed around and double-checked the paperwork. The doors of the baggage car were closed and locked. Bam! Bam! The conductor banged a step stool onto the ground in front of the passenger car and beckoned.

Eliza hugged her father and Jake goodbye. "Thanks for everything! I'll write soon." Gathering up her skirt, she stepped onto the stool and climbed three metal steps into the railroad car, then reached down for the baby. Jake boosted Sadie and Nellie directly up into the carriage, saying "whoop-de-doop," and handed Eliza her valise. Some people were already on board, going to the city.

Eliza found an empty seat and called the girls to the window. "Wave to Grandpa and Uncle Jake!" The train engine rumbled louder as it built up pressure, then there was a quick toot, and the bell began to ring, warning that departure was imminent. The chugging of the engine grew loud, and there was a puff of dark gray smoke. With a forward motion, the couplings between the cars clanked together, one after another, and the train began to roll down the track.

The train picked up speed, and the carriage swayed. Eliza and the girls settled into their seat. For better or worse, they were on their way to western Kansas.

Chapter 6

A bearded man wearing a suit and carrying a large leather case entered the train car. He greeted them pleasantly, sat on the seat opposite them, and took off a new-looking hat, putting it beside him. A traveling salesman? He smelled of beer. Irene eyed the stranger and whimpered, and Eliza distracted her with a toy.

A few minutes later, Nellie spoke up. "Mama, I feel sick. My stomach. . ."

Eliza immediately said in an undertone, "Sadie, please move to the middle so Nellie can sit at the window."

"I don't want to. Then I can't see as good." She wiped her nose on her sleeve.

"I know, sweetheart, but if Nellie's stomach is upset, she needs to have the window seat." Sadie sighed and the girls exchanged places.

The man across from them stretched out his legs and fell asleep. As he relaxed, his boots leaned against Eliza's skirt, pinning her leg to one spot. Irene fell asleep in her mother's arms.

The girls fell quiet. Nellie huddled in the corner and stared vacantly out of the window. Sadie swung her legs idly back and forth and observed the passing landscape. As the train rounded a bend, light gray smoke floated back from the engine.

Sadie turned from the view and gave her mother a radiant smile. "There's no telling what adventures we might have!"

Eliza patted her cheek. "That's my girl. And don't wipe your nose on your sleeve. Use your handkerchief, honey."

The train to Topeka followed roughly the path of the Kaw River, and in some sections it chugged along near the water's edge. As the train neared Tecumseh, Eliza pointed to Vaughan's Island. "Remember when we lived in the old cabin and went back and forth to town in a boat?"

"Oh, yes," said Sadie, perking up.

Nellie shook her head. "I just remember you telling about it." She squinted. "I don't see any cabin."

"It's hidden behind the trees," replied her mother.

"Does Papa still live on the island?" asked Sadie.

"No, he moved away some time ago."

"Maybe pirates live in the cabin now."

Eliza pursed her lips. "I suppose that's possible. Most likely, it's rented to hunters."

"I remember there were lots of ducks," said Sadie, "and inside the cabin it was kind of dark."

"That's right," said her mother. "It didn't have many windows. We lived on the island, and then we lived with Grandma and Grandpa. And now we're going to western Kansas, and we'll live in a different house. But wherever we live, we are together." She put her arm around Sadie, and the girls lapsed into silence again.

Would Pierce be satisfied with her work? Would she like him? At family dinners, she recalled, he liked to tease people. He could also be charming. Nannie had never complained that her husband drank to excess or hit her. So that was one thing Eliza wouldn't have to worry about.

What if we ended up falling in love, and he asked me to marry him? I've missed having a sex life since the divorce, and he IS an attractive man. No, better forget that fantasy. If it happens, it happens. I'm afraid though that he'd prefer a younger woman as a wife. I'm over thirty.

62

Although living with her parents for a few years had been a tremendous help, Eliza wanted to establish a stable family group of her own, with or without a husband. *I'm a mature woman, and my happiness does not depend on the moods of a man.*

She resolved to be businesslike and friendly with Pierce, but not take anything for granted. She would simply do a good job taking care of his house and children.

After an hour the train slowed and blew a long, moaning whistle. The part of the trip from Lecompton to Topeka was familiar to them. The train clanked noisily from one track to another as it bumped through the spider web of tracks leading into Topeka's enormous train station. The wooden frame of their carriage creaked and swayed. The engine's warning bell rang continuously.

The man sitting on the seat across from them pulled his feet back abruptly and sat up. "Beg pardon, ma'am." He put on his hat and gently slapped his face with both hands.

The brakes made a long, loud screech. The carriage shuddered, and the iron connectors clunked together. Then with one last jolt the momentum eased, and the couplings bumped against each other a final time. The train came to a complete stop, and the engineer released steam pressure in the engine with a loud hiss.

The bearded man leaped to his feet, grabbed his leather case, and clambered down the steps. Eliza retrieved her valise from under the seat and lifted Irene onto her shoulder.

"Let's go, girls." They made their way into the depot, which was swarming with passengers. Eliza got in line at the ticket office to buy Pullman tickets for the next leg of their journey. This afternoon they were going to ride on a first-class train with a dining car, and then the next day Eliza and the girls would take a local.

After she bought tickets for the afternoon train and arranged for her trunks to be transferred, she said, "Now let's go to Harvey House.

Where we ate the other time, remember? Since our train doesn't leave until 3 p.m. we might as well enjoy a leisurely dinner."

The restaurant was busy, but it had a serene atmosphere. Each table was set with floral-painted china, heavy silverware, and artfully folded linen napkins. They followed the maître d' to a table, and he handed them menus. Climbing onto a chair, Nellie giggled and immediately dropped her menu on the floor. Sadie sighed dramatically and retrieved it. A friendly-looking waitress in a black dress and long white apron approached their table.

"Tea, iced tea, coffee, or milk?"

"Coffee for me, and milk for the girls, thanks." The waitress placed the cup and glasses in such a way that the drinks maid would know what to pour into them.

"The two ready-to-eat specials available today are steak and hash browns, or tuna casserole and salad. Or would you prefer to order from the menu?"

"We have plenty of time," replied Eliza, "so I'll order from the menu. Let's see. You have English peas au gratin, filet of whitefish in Madeira sauce, roast sirloin of beef, lobster salad in mayonnaise. Entree and two side dishes, 75 cents." She studied the menu, then turned to the waitress, who stood politely at her elbow.

"I'll have stuffed turkey, boiled sweet potatoes and French slaw, and the girls will share a baked veal pie and English peas *au gratin*. And could you please bring a banana for the baby? Thank you." The waitress bowed and left. When Eliza and the girls visited the restaurant's restroom, they marveled at its marble walls and shiny brass fixtures.

Sadie and Nellie dawdled over their meal, looking around the room at the big ceiling fans, the hanging lamps, the forty or fifty customers sitting at tables, waitresses rushing to and fro, and businessmen standing at the bar. Eliza fed Irene a few bites of turkey and dressing and then mashed the banana into small bites for her.

Suddenly a waiter rang a big metal gong with a wooden hammer. The girls dropped their forks and stared.

"That's to let the waitresses know when a train is about to arrive," explained Eliza. "Some trains stop for just one hour so the passengers and crew can eat. The train conductor wires ahead with the number of people who will be eating, and then the restaurant makes a special effort to serve those customers quickly so they can get back on the train."

She smiled. "There's lots of interesting things to see here, aren't there? But don't forget to eat your dinner, girls, or you'll be hungry later."

"What will Pierce's farm be like?" asked Sadie, eating her food again.

"I expect it will be like Grandma and Grandpa's, only smaller. I'm sure there will be a barn and cows and horses."

"Will they have a dog?" asked Nellie.

"I don't know," said Eliza. "Would you like it if they had a dog?"

"If it was a nice dog."

"Nana!" prompted Irene. Eliza gave her another bite of banana.

"As I told you, he has three children for you to play with, boys about your age. Their mother was one of my best friends when I was growing up, and she was a very nice person. If you are polite and friendly to the boys, I'm sure you will soon be good friends."

After dinner, they made their way back to the station and were plunged into a chaos of color and noise. Passengers, baggage men, messengers, and candy sellers threaded their way in and out of the crowd. Carts with bags of mail were loaded and unloaded. Officials used megaphones to announce train arrivals and departures.

A young man in a brown uniform tapped her sleeve. "Porter, ma'am?" His straw hat had a ribbon that said Union Pacific.

"Yes, please," she said, grabbing their tickets from her valise. "Thanks for rescuing us! I must say, this crowd is overwhelming."

"Car 59," the porter read from the tickets. "I'll get you there safe and sound, ma'am. Follow me." He took her arm and propelled her along the platform, muscling past groups of other passengers. Eliza walked quickly to keep up. She held tightly to Sadie's hand and Sadie, in turn, reached back for Nellie.

"I'm not a baby," shrieked Nellie, and wriggled out of Sadie's grasp.

"Come on! Or you'll get lost," said Sadie through clenched teeth, grasping Nellie's sleeve.

"Coming through," the porter called loudly, opening a path for them through the milling crowd. Finally, he stopped beside a large brick-red car. "Here is your coach car, ma'am. Sit in any seat you like."

"Thank you very much!" Eliza gave the porter a generous tip, and he helped her and the girls climb into the carriage. They paused for a moment in the outer corridor to catch their breath. Then Eliza opened the inner door with a whoosh, and they stepped inside.

Suddenly, the noise of the crowd was muffled. The interior of the Pullman car had an aisle down the middle, with two rows of dark red plush seats facing forward and beautiful lamps built into the ceiling. The car smelled of pipe tobacco and furniture polish. Eliza chose an empty seat, put her valise in the upper storage compartment, and placed her bonnet in the netting above the window.

"This is like for princesses," said Sadie in a hushed voice, examining the carriage from one end to the other. Most of the passengers in the car were men in business suits. An elderly couple sat erect in their seat, with a large heap of parcels between them.

"Maybe this train has ice cream," said Nellie.

66

Outside, a train official shouted several times in a singsong voice, "Union Pacific Westbound: Junction City, Salina, Hays City, Denver, Salt Lake, San Francisco. All aboard!" Eliza leaned back in the soft seat and gazed around to admire the Pullman car, where every detail had been carefully thought out for the passengers' comfort.

A middle-aged woman in a flowered dress strode down the aisle in a cloud of perfume. She carried a parasol in one hand and a pink hat box in the other. Catching sight of Eliza and the girls, she raised her eyebrows and stopped.

"What a darling little sprite!" she said. "What's her name? How old is she?"

"This is Irene. She's two and a half."

"Gorgeous curls," said the woman. "Oo, the boys will have to watch out for her one of these days. Are you and the children traveling by yourselves?"

"Yes, we're going to western Kansas." Eliza introduced herself and the older girls.

"My son and I are on our way to Colorado Springs to visit my parents," the woman said. "We're on our own, too. Pleased to meet you! My name is Emma Fahrengold. Harold, my husband, couldn't come, too busy with work. You know how men are. If you don't mind, we'll sit right here behind you."

"Yes, of course, please. You're welcome to sit with us."

The woman gestured to a young man behind her. "I told Gareth—this is my son Gareth, he's fourteen—that we might as well go right to the dining car and get a cup of tea. But now that we've met you, I think we will sit here. A waiter will come through before long with the drinks and snacks trolley."

The train gave a series of short whistles and lurched forward. Emma made a desperate grab for the edge of a nearby seat. "Dear me! I'd better sit down before I fall down." She gave a full-throated laugh and plopped down in the seat behind them.

They could feel a low throbbing of the engine through their feet. The engine hissed, heavy doors slammed, the cars clanked together, the warning bell rang, and the train began to ease out of the station. Chuff, chuff. The engine pulled hard and belched black smoke. After a few minutes the train chugged along, gaining speed, and with a long whistle they were off.

After the engine noise had subsided and settled into a steady rhythm, Emma moved up to sit with Eliza and Irene. Sadie and Nellie sat with Gareth in the seat behind them, and he offered to show the girls his card tricks.

"I never know what clothes to pack this time of year," said Emma. "April weather is so changeable. We need things for the city, and also we want to spend a few days at the ranch. It might be unseasonably warm, and then again, it might snow like crazy. What kind of clothes did you bring?"

"I don't know about the weather, but we have all of our clothes with us. I'm raising the girls on my own, and we're moving to western Kansas. I've taken a job as a housekeeper on a farm owned by a widower with three boys. So it will be quite an adventure."

"How enterprising!" said Emma. "You have a lot of spunk, starting a new job in a new place. I'm impressed!"

"Nothing ventured, nothing gained," Eliza replied with a twinkle in her eye.

"I guess! Well, you do seem like the kind of person who is up to a challenge."

After a while, the children's chatter became loud. Eliza turned around and handed them some strings from her valise so they could play

Cat's Cradle. Gareth taught the girls a few new variations of the game. Irene toddled back and forth from the adults to the children, holding on to the seats. She peeked around the corner at Sadie and then at Emma, giving each of them a dazzling smile.

Later, a waiter came down the aisle with a jingling cart that held tea, coffee, and sweets. "Would you ladies care for some refreshment?" he asked. "And would the young people back here like cake, or perhaps ice cream?" They all chose something to eat and drink.

The train rattled and chugged through the afternoon. Eliza paid no attention to the towns they passed, as they weren't getting off until 6:30 p.m. The two women chatted, and Eliza got the children playing "I spy with my little eye."

At first call for supper, the two families stood up, eager to stretch their legs and go to the dining car. They chuckled as they were jostled to and fro by the swaying of the car. When they had to step from one carriage to another, however, the train noise was suddenly at full blast. The ground rushed dizzyingly underneath their feet, and particles of soot flew into their faces.

Nellie backed away from the door. "I am *not* going out there!"

"Come on, Nellie, I'll hold your hand," coaxed Sadie.

"No!"

Gareth suggested, "What if your sister holds one hand and I hold your other hand?" Nellie calmed down somewhat, and the group carefully stepped from one carriage to another until they reached the dining car, which had tables with tablecloths.

"Oh," mused Eliza, "Just like at a restaurant. I had pictured special tables with rims to keep the plates from sliding around."

Emma said, "I don't believe the train bumps enough to make things spill. Except for soup, perhaps." They had a pleasant meal, then made their way back to their seats. Emma and Gareth accompanied them as far as the lounge car.

"Gareth and I are going to stop here," said Emma. "I like to have a cocktail before settling for the night."

"We get off in Solomon City in twenty minutes," said Eliza, "so the girls and I had better get back to our seats. Have a good trip, Emma! I've really enjoyed talking with you." The women embraced.

"You have a good trip too." Emma handed her a women's magazine. "Here, take this. It's got some cute patterns for little girls' dresses. Lots of luck with your new job!"

Eliza and Sadie held Nellie's hands as they slowly made their way from one car to the next and back to their seats, their path lighted by beautiful frosted-glass lamps in each car.

Then it was time to disembark. They left the transcontinental train, and Eliza made arrangements for the next part of the journey, which would be on the Missouri Pacific line, Solomon Branch. They shivered in the cold as they waited at the ticket window.

Once Eliza had purchased tickets for the next day's journey, she checked the family into the town's only hotel. They discovered there was no hot water available, and the beds were saggy and uncomfortable. The whole family was exhausted, Nellie was whining, and Irene insisted on being carried.

"I know not what to call this place," joked Sadie.

Her mother laughed. "No rest for the wicked or the weary, I'm afraid. At least this hotel is cheap."

The next morning, Eliza and the children had to be satisfied with a meager breakfast of coffee and cookies, the only food available at the station that early. Eliza also had some apples and cheese in her valise. They caught the train at 6:15 and traveled all day, stopping at every town along the way—usually to pick up or unload freight, though

70

occasionally passengers got on or off. A few flakes of snow fell in the morning, but by noon the sun had warmed the frosty air. At noon the train stopped in Kirwin for an hour at a restaurant.

They arrived in Densmore, their destination, at 4 in the afternoon. Eliza and the girls stumbled down the steps almost in a daze, and the train continued on. The family was stiff and grumpy from sitting so many hours on a hard wooden seat. It had taken two long days to make their way from one side of Kansas to the other.

The Densmore station had a very small depot, hardly bigger than a hut. "Where do you want these, ma'am?" asked the depot agent, wrestling her trunks onto a cart.

"I'm not sure. I expected that someone would be here to meet us."

"Well, we don't have no public storage here, ma'am. You could try the livery barn. You're welcome to leave 'em on the cart until five o'clock, but then I have to lock up."

"Thank you. I'll see what I can do."

Eliza scanned up and down the street. *This is annoying.* Hadn't Pierce received her letter saying what day they would arrive? Densmore had only one train a day, so it was obvious what time he needed to pick them up. Or did he suppose that they would stay overnight at the hotel? Well, she refused to be buffaloed by the situation. She had enough money for whatever would be needed.

"Mama, I'm hungry," said Nellie.

"Let's get some candy," said Sadie.

"Candy!" echoed Reenie, pulling on her mother's skirt. Eliza surveyed the deserted train station and what she could see of the town. Where was Pierce? She crossed her arms and waited.

Eliza had never seen such a sleepy town. It consisted of a few dozen houses and a street with no stone curbs or boardwalks, just a dirt thoroughfare lined with hitching posts. On one side of Main Street were a hotel, a hardware store, a general store, and a post office. On the opposite side were a newspaper office, a creamery, a bank, and a livery barn. A bit farther along, she could see a red brick church and a lumber yard. Four wagons were parked in front of the saloon, and a dog slept in the middle of the manure-dotted street.

After half an hour, Reenie threw herself onto the ground and began to wail.

"Oh, honey, I'm sorry. We are all tired, aren't we? But right now, I better get our trunks seen to, and time is short. Girls, please watch Reenie. I'll be back in ten minutes."

At the livery barn, Eliza arranged for someone to pick up her luggage and store it temporarily, then she hurried back to the children. Even way down the street she could hear Reenie. Sadie and Nellie sat listlessly on the ground. Their hands were grimy and their hair ribbons askew. Reenie sprawled out on the ground, face-down, dirty from top to bottom.

"We need something to cheer us up," decided Eliza. "How about some food?"

"Oh boy, food!" said Sadie and Nellie. The family walked to the hotel, which fortunately had a cafe. They freshened up the best they could in the hotel bathroom, then traipsed into the cafe for an early supper. Eliza ordered simple and hearty fare for everyone, and then made the meal last longer by ordering desserts and a second cup of coffee.

"It's been a long day, girls, and I bet you wish you were back at Grandma and Grandpa's and in your own beds. I feel that way myself. But don't worry, things will get better soon." She gave them a strained smile and leaned her forehead on her hand.

Chapter 7

"So *here* you are!" thundered a voice, making Eliza jump. Pierce Griffith loomed over their table. He looked muscular as a blacksmith in his worn shirt and gray-striped bib overalls. His fingernails were black with ingrained dirt. "Confound it, Eliza. Why weren't you at the depot?"

"Hello, Pierce. Nice to see you again. Since we didn't know when you would arrive, we went ahead and got something to eat."

"Hmmpf. I was plowing, wanted to finish the goddamn field. Well, you done here? I already got your trunks."

"Thank you."

He slammed his palm on the table, making the silverware jangle. "Well, get a move on! It'll be dark before long."

Pierce was twenty-eight years old, though he seemed older. He had an angular face with brown hair, light blue eyes, ruddy cheeks, and a bushy mustache. She thought her new employer resembled a walrus—a tired, hungry one. *I am having an adventure*, she reminded herself.

He led the way to a large wagon and helped the two older girls climb in beside the trunks. Eliza sat next to him on the spring seat, holding Irene.

The setting sun peeked through the clouds as the wagon bumped along the road heading west. The terrain was flat, and the powdery dust disturbed by the horses' hooves wafted into their faces. Small, cheeping birds flew up from the ditches at the sound of their approach. Irene fussed for a while, then fell asleep.

Pierce kept making sidelong glances at Eliza. "You look like a schoolmarm," he said finally, his eyes mischievous, evaluating.

"You think so? Well, you need someone to help take care of your boys, and I need to support myself and my children. So we'll team up and see how it goes."

"I see." His lips twitched into a hint of a smile, and he turned toward her, the shirt taut on his powerful frame. "Well, I'm glad you came. A bunch of dad-gum gold-diggers have been snuffling around, wanting the job, but I don't like having strangers in my home. I figured you'd be the perfect choice."

"Thank you." A shiver ran down her spine. *I think this job is going to work out.*

They sat quietly until Eliza broke the silence. "Don't you have any trees around here?"

Pierce puffed out his chest. "We got *lots* of trees. We'll be coming to some in a few minutes." A jackrabbit sped across the road in front of them and darted into the weeds.

"I'm just surprised. This area looks nothing like Lecompton. I can hardly believe all the thistles piled up in the ditches."

He changed to a more conversational tone. "You get more water back east. It's open prairie here. But the soil is good, rich black loam, up to four feet deep. Some farms even grow berries and salad vegetables for restaurants in Chicago." As they neared Pierce's farm, he indicated which fields he owned and where the neighbors lived.

"What kind of stock do you have?"

"Beef cattle mostly, six milch cows, a bunch of chickens, and a dozen hogs. I own the farm free and clear—no mortgage, I'll have you know. 135 acres under the plow, and the rest in pasture. I have a half section, and the north fork of the Solomon River runs along the south part of my land. We're two miles north and pert' near three miles west of Densmore. See those trees over there to the left? That's the river. This here's the county road, and my house is just ahead."

"Why do you say 'milch' cows?"

"Eh?"

"I mean, instead of 'milk' cows?"

He snorted. "Oh! It's a Pennsylvania Dutch expression, I suppose. You know the old joke: I'm going to throw the cows over the fence some hay."

As they approached Pierce's farm in the deepening dusk, it looked more desolate than Eliza had remembered. The small clapboard house was weather-beaten, with no porch or second story to relieve its squat features. To the north of the house was a barn, and behind it were some small outbuildings and a row of small trees. The farm looked completely different from her parents' big farmhouse, stone barn, extensive garden, orchard, and ten-feet-tall lilac bushes. *I expect he had to scrimp and save to get his farm going.*

"Okay, I got three bedrooms, one for me, one for my boys, and you and the girls can have the other one. I moved the hired man out to the buggy shed."

"Thank you."

Pierce inclined his head in the direction of the barn, where they could see a flickering light. "My hired man has started the milking, and I got to go give him a hand. You can help with milking, too, but not tonight. If you wouldn't mind, could you rustle up a bite for us to eat? We'll bring your trunks in later."

"I'd be glad to," she replied.

Pierce drew the horses to a stop in front of the house and helped Eliza and the girls get down from the wagon. There was a strong smell of manure. An iron mud scraper and a rickety stool were beside the front door.

They could hear the sound of children playing inside the house. Eliza's eyes sparkled. She brushed dust from her clothes and took a deep breath. The journey was over, and her new job was about to begin.

"Come on in." Pierce gestured for her to enter. "It's not much, I'm afraid." The kitchen was chilly, and it smelled of lard, pepper, and unwashed bodies. A kerosene lantern on the table filled the center of the kitchen with a golden glow. Three small barefoot boys in shabby overalls huddled together and stared at them.

"This is Ralph, he's eight, Ross is seven, and John is four." He turned to his sons.

"Now you boys do whatever Eliza says, or else you won't get any supper, you hear?" They nodded energetically. Pierce tousled Ralph's hair and smiled. "They're a little bashful." He turned and left, closing the door behind him.

"I'm so glad to see you," Eliza said in a soft voice. She smiled at the boys and shook hands with each one, saying their names. *What adorable little waifs.*

"I remember you from last year. These are my children," she continued. "This is Sadie, she's eight, like you, Ralph. This is Nellie, she's five, and Irene here is two. Pretty soon we'll know each other very well. Now, could you boys tell me where I could find an apron?"

They didn't have an apron, but they showed her the pantry. She rummaged around in the semi-darkness and found eggs, bread, and jam. No fresh vegetables except for one onion. Next to the door was a washstand with a basin, a towel, and a bucket of water with a dipper in it. She washed her hands and had the children wash up as well.

"You have any salt pork?" The boys didn't know.

"Well, that's all right, don't you worry. It will take me a day or two to figure out what supplies you have on hand. How about if I make some scrambled eggs for supper? Ross, you and Sadie may set the table. Where do you keep knives and forks?"

"In a drawer in the table." Ross had a cute face with a pronounced dimple in the middle of his chin.

"Okay, good. The girls and I have already eaten, so you'll want to set places for five people. Ralph, could you please tell me where you keep the butter and a skillet?"

Before long the room was filled with the delicious smell of frying onion. Eliza stirred the eggs with one hand while holding Reenie in her other arm. The floor was unpleasantly sticky. Mopping that floor would be high on her list for tomorrow. Nellie clung to her mother's skirt, sucking her thumb. When the food was done, Eliza moved the skillet off the burner and covered it with a lid. Irene had fallen asleep.

Eliza smiled. "Ralph, do you know where the girls and I are to sleep?"

"In the back bedroom, ma'am. I'll show you."

"Thank you, Ralph. I can tell that you know many things. I'm probably going to need you to give me a lot of advice." He raced ahead of her and opened a door. There was just enough daylight to discern where the bed was.

She paused. "Do you have a clean rug or something? You know, I hate to put Reenie down in the bedroom when the rest of us are in the kitchen. She might wake up and not know where she was. Thank you for showing me our room."

They returned to the kitchen, and Ralph found a couple of clean towels.

"Since you're such a helpful fellow, what I need you to do is to make her a little bed, somewhere out of the way, but not cold. Poor thing is all tuckered out."

Ralph spread towels on the floor of the pantry, and Eliza lay Irene down. The toddler did not waken. Hopefully, she would stay asleep until the rest of them were ready to go to bed.

"Thank you, Ross and Sadie, for setting the table. You did a very nice job. The scrambled eggs are done. And we have bread, butter, and jam. We're all ready now, and it won't be long until your father comes back in. Do you have a book you can show Sadie? She likes to read."

Ten minutes later the men came in the front door, carrying Eliza's trunks. "Something smells good!" said Pierce. They delivered the trunks to her room, then hung their caps and chore jackets on wall hooks beside the door and washed up.

"Come 'ere, string bean," said Pierce. "Eliza, meet Edwin McLung, my new hired hand. He's a young squirt, still wet behind the ears." He punched Edwin's shoulder good-naturedly.

Edwin spoke in a low, rumbly drawl. "Twenty-six next month, I'll have you know." He chuckled. Taller than Pierce, Edwin was rail-thin, with a shock of dark brown hair, an earnest face, strong, chiseled features, and soft brown eyes. He wore a plaid flannel shirt, overalls, and boots.

"Pleased to meet you, Mr. McLung." She shook his hand.

"Oh, you better call me Edwin," he replied with a grin. "If you called me Mr. I wouldn't think you were talking to me."

Pierce and the boys immediately sat down at the table and tackled their meal. Pierce leaned forward over his plate and brought his mouth partially down to his food, and the boys ate mostly with their fingers.

Pierce paused mid-bite. "Edwin, could you please do the separating now? You can show Eliza how to run the cream separator."

Edwin, who had been about to sit down, retrieved his jacket. "You might like to put on a wrap, ma'am. It gets cool of an evening." He picked up the lantern they had brought from the barn and held the door open for Eliza.

Pierce looked up from his plate and smirked. "Thanks, pal. We'll wait for you like one hog waits for another!"

Edwin laughed. "That's all right. I get to lick out the pan."

Eliza grabbed a shawl that was hanging on a hook by the door, put on her bonnet, and followed Edwin to the milking shed. They were enveloped by the homey aroma of warm milk as he explained how the separator worked.

With a thump and a splash, Edwin poured bucket after bucket of fresh milk into the metal bowl of the separator, closed the cover, and pushed the pole up and down to spin the centrifuge. Soon a stream of thick cream poured from a spout into a five-gallon cream can. The remainder, the skim milk, emerged from a spout on the other side of the machine and fell into a large container below.

Edwin wiped sweat from his brow with the arm of his jacket and banged the lid of the cream can tight with his fist. Then he tipped the cream can on edge and rolled it out of the way.

"That's how you do it. Slick as a whistle." He laughed amiably.

"Why do you roll the cream can?" asked Eliza.

"No need to pick up a heavy can when you can roll it," answered Edwin. "Completely full, it would weigh over fifty pounds. We usually sell half a can a week."

"Where do you sell the cream?"

"I dunno. Every Friday we ship it off on the train."

"Doesn't the cream spoil? How do you keep it cool?"

"It's best to keep milk cool, but cream, you don't have to. I guess because of so much butterfat. Pierce's milk cows are Jerseys, which give extra rich milk."

It was getting late. The lantern, which hung from a nail, was surrounded by a cloud of fluttering millers. Edwin began to dismantle the separator. "Next I carry the whole kit and caboodle back to the kitchen, wash all the parts, and rinse them in boiling water, ready for tomorrow morning."

"Tell me what to do," said Eliza. "I can finish this up myself." It felt good to be active after a long day sitting on the train. She helped him carry the parts of the separator to the kitchen. Then he went back for the bucket of whole milk that hadn't been put through the separator and which was intended for use in the house.

"We leave the skim milk in the barn," he explained, "and feed it to the hogs in the morning." He handed Eliza the bucket of warm milk.

"Thank you," she said. "Since the night is cool I'll set the milk right here next to the window. Now, for heaven's sake, Edwin, sit down and eat. I'll wash and sterilize the separator." She put water on to boil and then paused. "I'm not sure I made enough food for hungry men."

"I'll grab a sausage," said Edwin. He took a lantern and was back in a few minutes with a sausage around ten inches long.

Pierce was sitting at the table, arms folded, half asleep. "Don't use up all the sausage," he grumbled. "Got to last till fall."

Out of his employer's line of sight, Edwin raised his eyebrows to Eliza and cut off two slices of sausage, one for him and one he handed to Pierce, who ate it in a couple of bites. Eliza wrapped the end in paper and set it aside.

The hired man gobbled down his meal in silence, then put on his jacket and picked up a lantern.

"Good night," he said, touching his cap as he glanced toward her.

"Six o'clock," said Pierce. He belched.

"Yes, sir. Haying tomorrow on the south forty."

"Right. But first thing, I want you to hitch up a team and plant beans. After the sun burns off the dew, we'll rake the hay and haul it into the barn."

After Edwin left, Pierce stood up, scraping his chair on the floor. "Off to bed, boys. School tomorrow." They hugged their father and disappeared.

Pierce wound the clock, gave the embers in the cook stove a quick rake with the poker, scratched under his arms, and looked at Eliza. "You can use this lantern tonight," he said reluctantly. "We had a couple other lanterns, but they got broke."

"Thank you." Eliza went to get Irene, who was fast asleep. As she had expected, the towels under the toddler were sodden. She changed the baby's diaper without waking her and tossed the wet things on the porch to deal with tomorrow.

"Sadie, could you please carry the lantern for me? Be very careful." She picked up Irene and put an arm around Nellie.

The evening had gone pretty well, she thought. The Griffith boys were friendly and well behaved. Tomorrow, the combination of school and chores would help the children get better acquainted. Hopefully, after a few weeks of home-cooked meals, Pierce would be in a more cheerful frame of mind.

Although she was extremely tired, Eliza didn't feel sleepy, so she penned a quick letter to her parents. There was so much she wanted to tell them. For the moment, she just said that their trip had gone well, everyone was fine, and she was sure that soon she'd have things put to rights at Pierce's house. It was small and wouldn't take much time to clean.

Eliza turned out the lamp and listened to the girls' regular breathing. The smoke of the extinguished wick hung in the air.

The next morning, Eliza opened her eyes wide in the dark, disoriented. Then she heard Pierce bang around in the kitchen, stoking the fire in the cook stove. She leaped out of bed and felt around for her skirt and blouse from the night before. Irene was quietly talking to herself. Eliza picked her up, grabbed a clean diaper, and made her way to the kitchen.

To her surprise, the kitchen was lit only by the crackling fire in the cook stove. The gray light of dawn crept slowly through the window.

"Daggone it, you forgot the lantern." Pierce's touch on her arm startled her. "At the moment we only have two lanterns, and Edwin has the other one. I'm trying to shake down the ashes here and can hardly see what the heck I'm doing." *Apparently. he considers candles an unnecessary luxury.*

Eliza's nostrils flared. "I'll get it," she replied and dashed back to her bedroom. Sadie and Nellie had awakened. "Please put on your clothes from yesterday, girls. You can dress properly after breakfast."

Pierce handed Eliza a box of wooden matches. She carried the lantern to the window, removed the chimney, soaked the wick and trimmed it, struck a match, lit the wick, replaced the chimney, and put the lantern in the center of the table. Now the room was full of light.

"I'll put on water for coffee," she said, and he sat at the table to wait.

Reenie toddled around and tried to talk with Pierce. He ignored her.

"For Pete's sake," he said after a while, rubbing his chin stubble, "get that child a clean diaper, or it'll put me off my breakfast."

Really, I can't do everything at once. After the kettle started to heat up on the stove, Eliza poured a little warm water onto a rag, picked up Reenie, and knelt in a corner to change the toddler's diaper.

The kettle began to whistle shrilly. She made coffee and poured a cup for Pierce and one for herself. Then she bustled around making pancake batter. Pierce stirred sugar and milk into his coffee. As hot pancakes piled up one after the other on a serving plate, she set the table, with forks and knives for the adults and just forks for the younger children.

Reenie, now clean and dressed, tried to climb into a chair, but she couldn't quite manage it. She walked around and around the table, touching the edge of each plate. Pierce frowned and studiously looked away.

Edwin, coming in the door, stopped in mock amazement at seeing Irene. "Glory be, it's a little angel!" The baby looked straight up at the tall man and almost toppled over. They all laughed. After Edwin sat down at the table, Reenie crawled over and pulled herself up to stand at his knee. He reached down to pick her up, but she squealed and dropped back onto the floor.

When the other children came into the kitchen, Eliza brought pancakes and sausage to the table. The older ones added butter and molasses and began to eat, staring across the table at each other. Eliza cut sausage into small pieces for Johnny and Irene and rolled up their pancakes so they could eat them in their hands if they wished.

"Is there enough for me to have another pancake?" asked Ralph.

"Here's another one," she replied. "Eat as much as you want. I can always make more." She poured mugs of milk for the children and braided Sadie's and Nellie's hair as they ate.

"That tasted mighty good, Eliza," said Pierce. "Thank you. Now the way we're going to work this is that Edwin and I will do the morning milking. The kids have to walk to Reedy Schoolhouse, which is about a mile south. There's no time to dilly-dally, as the school bell rings at 8 a.m., and it takes forty minutes to walk there. In the evenings, though, I'd like you to help with milking, okay?" His resonant voice had a firm and manly sound.

"Sounds good." Eliza had no problem with that. She was here to work, after all, and she liked being busy. She did feel more relaxed, however, after the men left the house and she just had the children to deal with.

Chapter 8

"Wash your hands and faces, each of you," said Eliza. "And wash them good, not just give them a lick and a promise. Then go to your rooms and make sure you have clean clothes on when you come back. It is almost time for you to leave for school."

She looked at Ross, who was dribbling molasses from a spoon onto his plate. "Are you still hungry?" She put a hand lightly on his shoulder.

"Pitcher."

"You're drawing a picture with molasses? Well, please don't waste food. This afternoon, when you come home from school, we'll find some paper and you can draw a picture. Now go wash up." She patted his arm. "By the way, you have beautiful hair! I wish I had thick, shiny hair like you." He blushed and lowered his eyes.

A short while later Ralph, Sadie, and Nellie returned to the kitchen.

"Where's Ross?" Eliza asked Ralph.

"He don't like school. Sometimes he stays home."

"Dear me. Tell him to please come here." After a few minutes, the younger boy reappeared.

"What grade are you in, Ross? What friends of yours are in that class?"

"I'm still hungry."

"Here's a piece of bread to carry in your pocket then. There's no help for it, boy. You've got to go to school and learn that readin', writin', and 'rithmetic. Off you go!"

She gave her oldest daughter a kiss. "Sadie, darling, be a good girl and study hard. Ralph and Ross will show you where to go. When you come back this afternoon, I want to hear all about your first day."

"Goodbye, goodbye, have fun at school!" She stood in the doorway, holding Irene. "Wave, sweetie. Wave goodbye to the big kids!" Reenie stretched out an arm and opened and closed her little fist, then she wiggled to be put down and ran back inside. Eliza and Nellie stood and watched the older children until they were out of sight.

The colors of sunrise had faded, and the blue bowl of the sky was filled with sunshine. A bracing wind blew from the south. Eliza threw out her arms and took a breath of deliciously fresh air. She heard snatches of birdsong and wondered if the birds here were the same as those back home. So far, she had just seen sparrows and barn swallows, but she could hear meadowlarks close by.

Pierce's house faced toward the east, and the front door led directly into the kitchen. With several big windows, it had plenty of light, despite the dark brown woodwork. North of the kitchen was the front room, which had similar woodwork but looked darker due to the heavy curtains that were closed to keep out the cold. A hallway led from the front part of the house to the three bedrooms, and there was also a porch on the far side of the house where the wash tubs were stored. The furniture was old and plain but serviceable. Pierce's house felt a little cramped after living in her parents' spacious home.

Right outside the front door, there was a pump for getting drinking water, and on the north side of the house was a windmill that pulsed in regular beats, pumping water into the tank, from where it drained through a pipe to another stock tank in the corral.

Eliza checked to make sure that Nellie had done a good job of getting herself ready for the day. Then she went over to John, who sat on the floor, engrossed in making a fanciful structure out of twigs. *What a handsome child.* Without comment, she reached down with a wet cloth and gently washed his face and hands.

"I see you know how to amuse yourself, John."

"Me Yonnie."

"You'd like me to call you Johnny? Okay, I'll call you Johnny. My name is Eliza."

He looked up with a dubious expression.

"That's awfully hard to say, isn't it? You can call me Ann if you want. That's my middle name."

"Anna?"

"Sure, call me Anna if you like. I don't mind."

"Mama," said Johnny, looking at the floor.

Eliza squatted beside him, her eyes filling with tears. "I bet you miss your mama, honey. She's up in heaven, isn't she? But I am here now, and I will take good care of you, just like your mama did." She rubbed his back, and her eyes filled with tears. His face had a mournful expression, so she quickly pressed on.

"Would you like to draw a picture? Nellie, can you look for some pencils? I saw a roll of shelf paper in the pantry. You and Johnny can sit at the table and draw me a picture."

The morning went by quickly. While the children played around her, Eliza emptied the ash bucket, cleaned the fire tongs, and put a spoonful of vinegar into a pot of beans to slow cook for supper. Then she pumped a fresh bucket of cold, iron-tasting water and had a good long drink.

In the pantry, she found crocks and bowls, lard, flour, sugar, and a sack of tired-looking potatoes. There were signs of mice in the corners. The house had obviously suffered for some months from the lack of a strong feminine presence. Eliza wiped dust from the shelves and made a list of what she needed to get from the general store. Then she swept and scrubbed the kitchen floor, opened a couple of windows to circulate the air and let the floor dry, and sat down to rest.

The sun slanted through the window panes, making elongated rectangles on the plank floor. The curtains blew gently in and out. *Oh dear, I see there's cobwebs hanging from the ceiling. Well, tomorrow is another day.*

Through the kitchen window she looked eastward to the county road and the pasture beyond, where half a dozen horses grazed, tails to the wind. The house stood on a small plateau, and she could see far into the distance. Gusts whirled the loose dirt on the county road into dust devils. To the south was the river, hidden by trees. *Tomorrow I'll take a long walk around the farm and see everything.*

She noticed a gold band on the window sill, and smiled sadly. *I bet that's Nannie's ring.*

After the men had their noon meal, the wind blew harder. *I guess on the open prairie there's not enough trees to tone down the wind.*

Sadie, Ralph, and Ross arrived home from school at a quarter after four, hungry as bears. Eliza quickly picked through the potatoes for good bits and fried thin potato slices with bits of sausage.

Sadie had a lot to tell her mother. "The teacher is awfully nice, but the schoolwork is too easy. I did the same math last year. The teacher gave me a book to keep in my desk and read if I finished before the others."

"How many students are in this school?"

"Fifteen kids, all together. Most of them are older than me. Oh, and I share a desk with another girl. She's nine, and has a skipping rope; we played with it at recess. But tomorrow we have to bring food. All the other kids brought their own dinner bucket, but Ralph, Ross, and I had nothing to eat until the teacher shared her food with us. I was starving!"

"What? I'm so sorry, honey. I didn't think to ask if you needed to take a dinner with you. At your last school, the teacher served soup to the children at noon. I wish you had 've told me, Ralph. I would've fixed you kids some food to take."

"We never take any chow to school, ma'am. Dad says we have to wait and eat when we get home, but the teacher usually brings extra and shares with us."

"Well!" said Eliza. "From now on, you will each take your dinner to school, and tomorrow I will send along a sausage for you to give to the teacher. She deserves a nice gift for sharing her food with you these past months. Don't you think that seems right?" *Pierce can afford it. But I do think I'll give a sausage to the teacher on my own hook. No need to get him riled up by asking permission.*

Later, Ralph and Ross showed Sadie and Nellie around the farm, telling them the names of the horses, and that they shouldn't ever get in the pigpen because the pigs might eat them. Then the older girls played in the bedroom with their dolls. Johnny fell asleep on the couch, and Reenie took a nap as well. The older boys messed around outside. Eliza baked a pan of light cakes and patched a rip in a pair of Ross's overalls.

As supper time approached, she added sausage to the beans and made biscuits and gravy, while Reenie clung to her leg. *I'll need to start a garden,* she thought. *And they might have canned goods in the cellar.*

When the men returned at 6, Sadie stopped them at the door. "Halt!" she said gaily. "Who comes into Sherwood Forest without my pass?"

Edwin held up his hands and smiled. "What's this? Do we have to pay a toll?"

Pierce pushed from behind. "What the. . .? Horsefeathers! Let a body through. It's my own house, for chrissake." Sadie looked up at him timidly and shrugged.

At suppertime, she had lots of questions. "Can we ride the horses, Pierce? Why do you have so much junk around the farmyard? How come you don't have any baby chickens? Can we go to town sometimes, and do they have a candy store?"

"For crying out loud!" Pierce said. "You're a regular Little Miss Chatterbox! Better to be quiet and keep your eyes open. That will give you answers to most everything."

Sadie blinked.

Nellie snorted with laughter. "That shut her up."

Eliza scowled. "Nellie Jane! That's not a very nice thing to say." Nellie smirked.

Sadie leaned her head to one side. "Well, I like to know things."

"Curiosity got the cat," said Edwin, laughing.

"It's good to be curious," said Eliza, "but Pierce is right. Sometimes it's better to use your eyes and ears, and not talk so much."

"And no, you can't ride my horses," Pierce continued. "They are workhorses, not riding ponies."

After several days, life on the farm had settled into a new routine. Ross and Nellie fed sprouted oats to the chickens and gathered eggs. Ralph pumped buckets of water for the kitchen and filled the coal scuttle, Sadie carried in cobs and wood from the wood pile, and Johnny collected dry leaves and twigs for tinder.

The next week, the men found time to spade up a garden plot, and Eliza and the children planted potatoes. Soon it would be warm enough to plant carrots and cabbage. Eventually, Eliza wanted to plant some flowers. There were no flowers at the Griffith farm except for a honeysuckle vine that twined up the ladder of the windmill.

She cleaned the laundry bins and found the washboard, and the men restrung the clothesline. Pierce purchased some household supplies they had been lacking, including a couple more kerosene lanterns and some mouse traps, which Eliza baited with bacon grease. The mice situation gradually improved.

Eliza had never known anyone like Pierce. He was bold and boisterous and did whatever he wanted, regardless of the consequences. Perhaps it had something to do with the freedom of living on the prairie, with its vast horizon and endless pastures of bluestem and buffalo grass. *It feels good to be around a man with such vigor in his step.*

One day she mentioned to Pierce about seeing the gold ring on the window sill. "It was Nannie's wedding ring," he replied huskily. " Right where she left it the day she died." He blew his nose. "Besides, leaving it lie there tells me whether my housekeeper is a thief. You have to watch out for that sort of thing when you deal with other people."

"Well, you won't have to worry about me, Pierce," said Eliza. "I'm not a thief."

"From what I can see of you so far, you seem quite nice," he said, and he stroked her bottom.

"Now *that* I'm not going to put up with!" she said, scooting away from him.

He laughed. "I was teasing."

"I'm quite serious. None of that."

"Okay, okay."

"Just so we understand each other," she said firmly.

Her cheeks felt red and she walked quickly into her bedroom. She hid her face in her apron until her breathing calmed, then spent a few minutes straightening the girls' dresser drawers. Perhaps that was just a predictable moment of awkwardness between them, and would not happen again. *You have to get such things clear at the beginning.*

That night, however, as she lay down to sleep, her muscles were tense. She tried to get hold of herself. *Am I jumpy and thin-skinned because of what happened with Joe? I thought I was past that. It almost makes me wonder if there's something about me that makes men want to take advantage.*

One morning before school, Ross asked Eliza, "Why did you come to live with us? I guess you don't have a husband, huh?" He strutted around with his hands in his pockets, waiting.

"I used to be married, but now I am single. I support myself and my girls by working as a housekeeper."

"Ah, so you're a maid, a servant."

"Not exactly, I'm a housekeeper, and I will help take care of you."

"I don't have to do anything you say, you know. You're not my mother."

Eliza nodded. "I'm not your mother, but I am taking care of you now. Your mother is in heaven. Do you miss her?" Ross turned away and ran outdoors.

As soon as the children became acquainted, they got along more or less like siblings. Eliza kept a close watch to break up quarrels almost before they got started, mindful that she had brought the girls out to a new place and a new life they had not chosen.

"Where's *our* Papa?" Nellie asked her mother one day. "I don't like that Pierce man."

"Well, sweetheart, you'll learn in life that it's tempting to judge other people before you know them well. It's best to be generous and give people the benefit of the doubt."

Eliza paused. "Listen, honey, we had to leave Papa, but it had nothing to do with you." She touched Nellie's chin lightly with a forefinger.

"He *did* love you girls, but he became so unhappy that he was better off by himself." She winced. "I know that doesn't seem to make much sense."

"If Papa gets happy again, will we go back?" Nellie chewed on a fingernail.

"No, precious." Eliza gave her a hug. "He moved far away, and he has a different wife and family now."

"Oh." Nellie wandered off, and Eliza sighed. She hoped that simply being there as a consistent, loving, motherly presence would keep the girls from being harmed by the divorce.

Pierce came in the door. "I'm going to town this morning to do the trading," he said, handing her a gallon jar of cream, "as well as stopping by the blacksmith to get some horseshoes put on. Also, I want to pick up a batch of chicks." Eliza handed him her grocery list.

"I buy new chicks each year," he explained. "That way I have eggs to sell all summer, and then we can eat chicken through the winter–if the coyotes don't get them first."

Eliza poured the cream into the butter churn, and Johnny and Nellie took turns pushing the stomper up and down. Thump, thump, thump. After a while, the children opened the lid and wiped a taste of cream off the stick.

"Whoa, hold your horses!" Eliza said, her hands on her hips. "Don't put your fingers in the food, please. I'll get you something else to eat. You kids are always hungry." She brought them some bread, butter, and jam.

"Tell you what," she told them. "Tomorrow morning at breakfast I'll fry extra pancakes and leave them in the pie cupboard. Then if you get hungry in between times, you can grab yourself a pancake. Any that are left over can go to the chickens or the hogs."

After that, Eliza always had a plate of pancakes sitting on the middle shelf of the cupboard. She was pleased that the boys were starting to put a little meat on their ribs. They had been really too thin when she arrived.

She loved Pierce's old pie cupboard. The tin inserts in the doors were punched with ventilation holes in a hearts-and-leaves Pennsylvania Dutch design. Underneath the cupboard door was a rounded drawer to hold flour and a wooden pastry board that pulled out flat. Eliza usually had several pies sitting in the cupboard covered with a tea towel and ready to serve.

When Pierce came home from town, he said, "I shut the chicks in the brooder house. Two boxes, fifty chicks each. Nobody open the door, now! The chicks are shook up from the bumpy ride coming home, and need to rest and calm down. In an hour or two we can go out and dip their beaks in water, so they get the idea of how to drink."

Later, they all trooped out to the brooder house and sat or squatted on the floor. The children were excited to see the newborn chicks squirming around. Peep, peep! There were so many of them, and it was a warm and noisy place.

"Don't pick them up," said Eliza. "They are too delicate. Just watch them and see what they do. They need to be a week old before they're big enough to hold. No, Sadie! What did I say? You could squeeze them to death without meaning to."

"I was being real careful, Mama."

"Don't pick them up! See their tiny legs? It would take very little pressure to break them. You have to wait until they are stronger. Leave the chicks on the floor. Hold them around their belly with both hands. And put their beak in the water for only a second; otherwise they might drown before they figure out how to drink. See the teensy breathing holes on their beaks?"

94

Ross picked up a chick and started to put it into his pocket.

"No, honey. Put it back."

"I'm giving it a ride."

"Oh, dear! Don't do that, Ross, please. Baby chicks can get hurt very easily." said Eliza.

Pierce's hand flew out and slapped Ross's face. "Hey, lunkhead, put it back. You need to clean out your ears?"

"Okay, okay."

After supper, Pierce got down on the floor and wrestled with Ralph and Ross. Eliza wondered if he was being too rough with them, but the boys seemed to love it.

"Two against one!" they shouted. For a while, Pierce pretended to let them win, then he pinned them both to the floor. Eliza's eyes lingered on Pierce. *Such strong shoulders!*

"Do you say 'uncle'?" he asked. "I'll let you up as soon as you say 'uncle.'" The boys struggled to escape but, in the end, they had to admit defeat. When they went to bed, they were sweaty but smiling from ear to ear. Pierce had some coarse ways about him, but Eliza could tell he was a good-hearted man who loved his children.

Chapter 9

The weather that spring turned terribly dry. Pierce and Edwin worried about whether the pastures had enough grass for the cattle. And in a few weeks it would be time to plant summer crops. A desultory breeze blew the dust around. Then, for a few days, there was no wind at all, as if the earth were holding its breath, waiting for the wind and rain to come and sweep everything clean.

Pierce hadn't made any more passes at her, and Eliza gradually began to relax around him. *I guess he was just feeling his oats that night.* Hopefully he wouldn't spring that sort of thing on her again. She made an effort to put the incident firmly out of her mind.

Washing clothes was a weekly, all-day task. Eliza soaked everything overnight in a washtub with soda crystals and hot water, and the next morning she added warm water and soap. She rolled up her sleeves and scrubbed them on the washboard. Then she forked them out with a long stick and put them into the rinse water. Diapers, sheets, and good clothes got an extra rinse in blueing to counteract the yellow of the lye soap. The diapers and sheets were boiled before being put through the wringer and hung on the clothesline.

As the weeks went by, Ralph, Ross, Sadie, and Nellie spent more and more time outdoors. They played tag, cowboys and Indians, or hide-and-seek. They climbed trees and made grass whistles. They trekked through the fields and pastures, following well-worn cow paths or exploring the underbrush in the draws. They returned happy and tired, with hands full of scratches and socks full of cockleburs.

Eliza could see that this rough-and-tumble life was good for her girls. Sadie and Nellie roamed with Ralph and Ross farther than they would have on their own, and their arms and legs grew strong. It reminded Eliza of the freedom she had had as a child, following her brothers around their parents' farm. She didn't worry about the girls' safety because she knew the boys would watch out for them.

The two eldest children, Ralph and Sadie, were easygoing, sensible, and clever at thinking up games. Ross was a scrapper, a hothead, but smart. Nellie was an independent soul, content either as part of the group or playing by herself. She liked to ponder things. Johnny was a shy and dreamy child. He spent most of his time in or near the house, constructing pint-sized farms and railroads of twigs woven together. He often played with Reenie, showing her over and over how to roll a ball back and forth, trying to get her to focus on the task.

Eliza smiled warmly at him. "You are very good with babies, Johnny."

His eyes were suddenly sad. "*We* had a baby—w*onst*," he said. Eliza bent down, put her hand on his shoulder, and looked directly into his face.

"You still *do* have a baby sister, precious. She just doesn't live here anymore. Ruthie lives with your Gram and Gramps Thompson, remember? Let's ask your father if we can invite them to come visit us real soon."

Eliza went to sprinkle the clothes to be ironed. Tomorrow was bread-making day, and when the stove was at baking temperature, the irons would heat up quicker than usual.

The next day, the old cook stove kept acting up. By the time she got the fire hot enough for baking bread, it wasn't drawing properly. She opened all the windows and made a game of it. Nellie, Johnny, and Irene ran around flapping dishcloths to get rid of the smoke.

The children played in the front room so Eliza could have the table free. After she ironed shirts, dresses, and sheets, they remained slightly damp, so she folded them over the clothes horse to finish drying.

Later Sadie, Ralph, and Ross played in the front room, and the little ones were at the table talking with Eliza. When Pierce and Edwin came in for supper, the older children glanced into the kitchen and then continued with what they were doing.

"What the devil is with those boys?" asked Pierce in a plaintive tone. "Don't they know their own father anymore?" He stomped over to the washstand, washed his face and hands, and took a long drink of water with the dipper.

Wiping her hands on her apron, Eliza gathered up some drawings the children had made and dashed into the front room. "Here, go show these to your dad." she told the boys. "It can be his surprise." She didn't want Pierce to think that she had supplanted him in their affections.

That evening she asked him, "If you don't mind my asking, how often do Ralph, Ross, and John see their grandparents?"

He frowned. "They see my parents at Christmas, and once or twice in summer, like for the Fourth of July. That's more than enough, in my book."

"Even so, they live only two miles away. Surely the grandparents would love to see the boys."

Pierce interrupted. "For Pete's sake, woman, if my folks want to spend time with them, they can come over any time. I have no time for frippery. I'm not really close to my people, all right? It's more of a business relationship. When Nannie was alive, we did visit her relations some."

Eliza folded her arms. She could hardly imagine feeling like that about her relatives. Whatever their disagreements or tensions, her parents and her brothers and sisters visited each other often and, in times of trouble, she could count on them to stand by her side.

Every evening before the children went to bed, Eliza read aloud one chapter from a children's novel. She had a whole stack of books in her trunk. She had planned to read *Heidi* next, but now that she was reading to boys as well as girls she decided she'd start with *Treasure Island*.

All the children loved story time. Irene would play quietly on the floor while the others crowded near Eliza on the couch. Pierce sat some distance away, noting down the day's expenditures in his ledger. She had a hunch that he, too, was listening to the story.

Eliza admired Pierce for taking care of his money so carefully. That was how he could afford to purchase so many head of livestock. The farm was doing well, she could see that. And Pierce was easy to work for because he was methodical in his habits. As long as his needs were met, he allowed her to do as she pleased.

Pierce is a rougher sort of man than my father and brothers but, after all, there are different kinds of people in the world. And he is interesting—complex.

"What we need around here is a cat," Eliza remarked one day to Ralph.

He cringed and collapsed into a chair.

"What's the matter, honey? Don't you like cats?"

The boy covered his face with his hands. "Blackie died," he stammered.

She put an arm around his shoulder. "I'm sorry, Ralph. You must've really loved your kitty."

His face was wet with tears. "Dad shot him. Because Blackie kept crying around the house. After Mama died. He shot him over and over. Blackie ran around the yard. He tried to get away, but he got dead."

Her eyes brimmed as Ralph sobbed against her apron. *It's good that I am here to comfort these motherless children.*

After putting a couple of apple pies in the oven, Eliza sat down to darn Pierce's socks. Sadie set the table while the other children did the outdoor chores.

Ralph carried the kitchen scraps out to the pigs. "Here, sooey, sooey!" he called.

Ross and Nellie gathered the eggs and herded the chickens back into the chicken house. "Here, chick, chick!" They had around two dozen laying hens right now. The eggs were be packed into a special wooden crate that held twelve dozen eggs. When the crate was full, it would be taken to town and sold to the general store.

Johnny played a lot with Reenie, which was a big help to Eliza. Otherwise, the toddler needed to be watched every moment. The sound of happy squeals came from the front room, where the two children had built a train out of chairs and blankets.

"Could you keep an eye on the stew, Sadie?" she asked. "I want to whip up some apple 'crispet' real quick."

Eliza beamed at her oldest daughter. "You're getting to be a real help around the house, sweetheart. I'm proud of you! We make a good team."

Around 9 p.m., when all the children were in bed, Eliza sat at the kitchen table in the light of the lantern, sewing rickrack along the frayed edge of an old apron. She realized with a start that she hadn't gone anywhere since she had arrived at Pierce's farm. She needed to find a way to make friends with women in this community.

Pierce, reading a newspaper on the other side of the table, crumpled the paper and flung it down. "The men running this county are a bunch of dad-blamed idiots!" he grumbled. "I could tell those tin-horn politicians a thing or two.

He stood up and stretched. "I got to go to the barn and look at that Jersey heifer. She's acting real restless, so I shut her in a stall."

When he returned, he told Eliza, "She's about to calve, all right. She's pressing her head against the wall and stretching out her back legs, but don't worry. With a first calf, a cow's labor can last several days.

Edwin and I spread straw around the stall. She'll probably have it tomorrow. I'll check her again in the night."

In the wee hours, Eliza woke as someone shook her shoulder. Pierce whispered, "Wake up! I need your help in the barn. We got to pull that calf." She dressed and hurried to the kitchen.

"You carry the lantern," said Pierce. He opened the front door and filled a bucket with water from the stock tank. The air was chilly as they walked to the barn.

"Looked like heifer has wore herself to a frazzle," he said as they strode along. "I don't know if her calf is breech or just extra big, but we have to get it out of there or the cow will die, and the calf too."

Edwin met them at the stall and hung up the lanterns to have plenty of light. The heifer lay flat on her side with her eyes closed, exuding warmth but making no sound other than her labored breathing. There was a sweet smell of hay mixed with scents of leather, harness oil, and manure. Edwin held the cow's tail out of the way while Pierce splashed water on her hind end.

Eliza petted the heifer's neck. "Don't you worry, mama," she said. "We're going to help you." The cow rolled her eyes, frightened.

"Okay, listen, Eliza," said Pierce impatiently, "Here's what I want you to do. Ease the calf out with your hands when we pull, but don't get in our way. Savvy?" He got on his hands and knees and reached his arm deep inside the cow's uterus. "It's not breech, because I touched the head."

Edwin handed Pierce a couple of pieces of rope and gave the cow a couple of good thwacks on her side. "Let's go, mama. Give us another try." Edwin prodded the cow's flank, and Pierce gave her an enormous push. The heifer humped her back and strained.

"If the calf comes out a bit further, I'll grab the feet," shouted Pierce. Edwin pushed rhythmically on the cow's side. The cow groaned. Something black started to bulge out from the slimy opening.

"Got 'em," said Pierce. He knotted each of the pieces of rope to the calf's front hooves, then tied the ropes to a thick board and wrapped them around it several times.

"Move in close, Eliza, and help the calf squeeze through. Don't be squeamish, woman. Get your hands right in there."

He glanced at Edwin. "Ready?"

Both men grabbed the board and pulled hard. Eliza held the cow's tail out of the way with one hand and, with the other, she massaged the lip of the opening from which the calf would emerge. The calf's feet would come out a few inches and then slide back inside. The men tried again and again.

Finally Pierce swore, and they stopped for a moment. The calf's feet stuck out about four inches from the opening, and they could also see its tongue.

"I saw the tongue move," panted Pierce. "It's still alive." The two men sat on the floor, braced their feet against the cow's hindquarters, and pulled on the board again. After a few minutes, Pierce stopped and hurled the board onto the floor.

"Goldurn it!" he said. His face was haggard. "It's not working. And the calf's feet have got cold. A bad sign." They paused to take stock. Dust motes shimmered in the air and floated slowly downward. Pierce took off his sweat-stained shirt.

Seeing Pierce standing there bare-chested gave Eliza a momentary ripple of sexual desire. She averted her eyes and stroked the heifer's head and neck. The cow's large, protruding eyes were glassy.

"Don't be scared," she said. "We're helping you."

Pierce snapped his fingers. "Again!" he ordered, and moved decisively to the cow's side. Eliza leaped back into position.

"This time had damn well better do it," he said through clenched teeth. "If the head comes out, the rest'll pop like a cork." He and Edwin braced their feet against the cow and pulled. The effort was visible on their faces. The cow moaned weakly.

After ten seconds, the dark blob gradually oozed forward. The cow's bowels emptied. Eliza put her fingers into the lower opening and tried to stretch the skin so the lumpy parts of the calf's body could pass through. The calf moved out a bit farther and then, suddenly, its entire body emerged in a spurt of blood and slime. The calf lay flat on the floor in a shapeless heap, its front feet ahead of its body and its back feet stretched out behind.

For a moment all was quiet. Then Pierce hunched over the calf and began to rub it aggressively. "We got to stimulate it to start breathing!" he shouted. As Pierce rubbed its chest, Edwin got a piece of straw and poked its nostrils. After a few minutes, the calf jerked, twitched, sneezed, and started to breathe.

"Oh, man!" said Edwin, coughing and laughing. "I was spooked there for a minute."

"Yah, it was a close shave," muttered Pierce. The men massaged and slapped the calf until it was breathing evenly on its own.

"Rub the heifer down with a burlap sack, would you, Eliza? Her body has had a shock, and she mustn't get a chill." She rubbed the cow until the animal's sweat dried.

"Now let's let the calf alone for a few minutes," said Pierce. "It needs a bit of time to recover. But we have got to get that cow up, or she'll have a prolapse." He hit the heifer's legs with his fist. "Come on! Stand up, you dad-blamed critter!" The cow protested loudly.

Eliza grabbed the calf by its back feet, slid it out of the way, and wiped slime from its face. It was a healthy-looking bull calf. Pierce and Edwin slapped and kicked the cow until she rose clumsily to her feet, trembling. She snorted and swished her tail. The men offered her a drink of water from the bucket. The heifer paused a long time, then leaned down, sniffed at the water with her rubbery muzzle, and began to drink in big gulps.

"Son of a gun, she's going to be all right," said Pierce.

He dragged the calf back next to the heifer. She stared blankly at it, then hesitantly sniffed the calf and began to lick its wet body. After a while, the calf held its head up. The cow was calmer now. She made little grunting noises and continued to sniff and lick her calf.

Edwin patted the cow's neck. "When we come out in the morning to do the milking, I bet that calf will already be having breakfast."

They trudged back from the barn. "Thanks for your help, Eliza," Pierce said. "You really knew what to do. You must be an old pro at this."

Her eyes were shining and her night braid disheveled. "Actually," she said, "I never saw a calf born before. With so many brothers around, my help was never needed. But I've had children myself, and it's not all that different. Such a cute little calf! It has a sweet face."

"Well, for a woman you are pretty darn tough. I'm glad you were here."

"Thank you, Pierce. That's a very nice thing to say." *Sounds like he's beginning to see I could be useful around here.*

One day, after Ralph, Ross, and Sadie had left for school, Eliza was thinking about how on her parents' farm the chicks had had a small yard to run around in. The baby chicks were more active now, and growing fast.

Carrying Reenie, and with Nellie and Johnny trailing along behind, she investigated the entire farmyard. It was entirely different from her father's farm, which had tidy paths, well-built sheds, and doors with functioning hinges. Pierce's outbuildings were made of reclaimed lumber and repaired with mismatched pieces of wood or tin. There was a corn crib, a hog shed, an icehouse, a flimsy, open-walled wagon shed, and the buggy shed where Edwin had his small room.

North of the farmyard, she could see a pasture with a small herd of Herefords—shaggy white-face steers that were sold for beef. Pierce kept back one a year to butcher for the family's use. In the south pasture were the horses and the milk cows. Farther west there was more grazing land, and close to the creek there was a bean field and an alfalfa field.

The large post-and-beam barn had a central alleyway with stalls and storerooms on either side. The three overhead lofts were filled with hay, alfalfa, and straw. In the tackle room there were horse collars and tools, curry combs, coils of rope, tools, buckets, and pieces of scrap metal. Bridles and harnesses dangled from ceiling hooks, out of the reach of mice and rats. One stall was boarded up to be a granary, and another held a bunch of culled lumber. *Maybe I could use some of those boards to build a fence.*

Stopping at one stall, Eliza looked over the half-height door at the heifer and her calf, which now seemed strong and healthy. The mother was licking it and lowing happily.

Then Eliza and the children checked on the baby chicks. She helped Nellie, Johnny, and Reenie each hold one, and she let Johnny measure out the right amount of feed for them. She could have done it much faster herself, but it was good for him to do it. He was meticulous. Then she got the watering can and let Nellie pour water into their V-shaped trough, narrow so that chicks would not fall in and drown.

When Pierce and Edwin came in for dinner at noon, she asked, "Pierce, could I have some scrap wood? I want to fix a little pen so the chicks can run around in the fresh air."

"There's a pile of old lumber in the barn. Be my guest."

After the men were back at work and Irene was taking a nap, Eliza went out again and selected several long, thin boards about four inches wide, pried out the nails, and straightened them. She considered the task a while, then sawed each board into equal lengths. Having watched her brothers do that sort of thing, she figured she could do it too. However, by the time she had cut four boards, she was getting a blister on her right hand. No matter. She could work on it a bit each day.

When Pierce came in for supper, he teased her. "Wasn't that hard on your lily-white hands? Looked to me like you could use some help."

Eliza lowered her chin and raised her eyes. "I would appreciate that, thank you." It embarrassed her that she so obviously needed help.

"In a few days, I might be able to spare some time. Pass the potatoes."

She pressed her lips together, saying nothing. *What a strange fellow.*

The next day, when she went to the brooder house to feed and water the chicks, she saw a pile of short boards around two feet long stacked neatly by the door. Pierce had done that yesterday, after all. She scrutinized the boards. *Aha,* he had chopped them into lengths with an ax, much quicker than sawing them. *Wish I had come up with that idea.*

Eliza settled the children in the front room with some toys and told Nellie to watch Reenie and Johnny, then she set to work. She didn't know how to build a fence, but it seemed like it couldn't be too hard. She dug a shallow trench with the hoe, propped the boards up in a row, and then filled in the dirt again. It was still wobbly. So she found some rope and began to tie them together.

Pierce came up behind her and touched her lightly on the shoulder. She flinched.

"Skittish, aren't you?"

"Sorry." She laughed. He didn't move away, and her skin began to tingle. Her heart was beating fast. *How annoying.* It was hard to concentrate with a virile, attractive man just a few inches away.

"What in Sam Hill are you doing?" He grinned. "Sheesh, that fence looks like a goddamn chimpanzee built it!"

Eliza was startled for a moment, then she inspected the unevenly leaning boards and began to chuckle. "You're right. It looks terrible." Their eyes met, and then they both doubled over with laughter.

"As you can tell, I have no notion how to build it," she admitted.

"Well, at least I was able to make you laugh. Why are you so serious?"

Eliza shrugged. "I don't know. I guess I'm sort of reserved."

He stared at the boards. "Well, what I might do for a fence is to put up chicken wire, then fasten boards to the bottom holes, so the chicks can't wiggle through. Let me help you."

"That would be great. And thanks for cutting the boards. Right now, though, I've got to get back to the house and start dinner."

"That little fence will work well enough for a few weeks," Pierce explained later, "but then the chicks will need to go into the more secure chicken house. During the day they can scratch around for bugs and seeds. Grown chickens take different feed, but not as much, because they find most of their food by themselves. The problem with them free-ranging is that coyotes and hawks get quite a few."

Chapter 10

A few days later Eliza heard a big commotion outside. Pierce and Edwin had roped a bunch of calves and tied them behind the wagon. Then Pierce stuck his head in the front door.

"Hey, I'm going over to my father's to brand and cut the calves. If you want to come with me, hustle!" Eliza called the children, and they all climbed into the wagon.

The farm belonging to Pierce's father was two miles northwest. John Griffith came out to greet them when they arrived. He had a slim build, intense brown eyes, and erect posture. Coming along behind him was Pierce's sister Mollie, twenty-two, and Pierce's brother Frank, who was seventeen.

"This is Eliza, my new housekeeper, Nannie's cousin from Lecompton," said Pierce. "Eliza, my father." They shook hands.

"John Griffith. Pleased to meet you, ma'am." Pierce had told her that his father had served in the Civil War, then left Pennsylvania with his wife and children to homestead in Kansas.

"Mollie, take Eliza and the children to the house. I'm sure Mother would like to see them." Mollie smiled and took Johnny and Nellie by the hand and led them inside.

"Come on in," said Pierce's mother, Binnie, who was wearing a long gray gown. "Hi, Johnny, how's my boy?" She reached out and patted her grandson's head. Mollie had on a shorter, flowered dress with a dark brown apron.

"Excuse the soap smell," said Binnie.

Mollie dished out coffee, milk, and some Pennsylvania Dutch custard pie. "You came at just the right moment," she said, giving the children a wink. "We just finished doing the wash and were ready for something to eat."

"Why on earth did Pierce pick today for you to come visit?" Binnie complained. "Cutting calves is no place for women or children." Then she chuckled. "Oh, my! Just see the curls on that baby! She's quite the picture." The older woman reached out to pat Irene, who drew back and buried her face against her mother. Eliza introduced Nellie and Irene.

"Yesterday I was to town," said Binnie, "and I heard that pox has broke out recently in some parts of Kansas. Thank goodness, not anywhere near here."

"Smallpox is a terrible disease," said Eliza, picking at her food. "Years ago, I lost a baby to that. Wasn't nothing we could do."

"Tsk, tsk." Binnie was sympathetic.

"Well, he's up in heaven now, and I have three beautiful girls. The oldest, Sadie, is in school right now. She's in third grade, same as Ralph."

Johnny got up and started to walk into the front room.

"Just where do you think you're going, young man?" called Binnie.

"I didn't touch anything."

"Well, you skedaddle out of there anyway. You don't have no business in there. Just sit on your chair and be a good boy." He came back and sat down.

Binnie wrote out the recipe for a favorite Griffith family dish, dandelion greens with warm bacon dressing, and gave it to Eliza.

Edwin poked his head in the door. "I'm to take you and the kids back now. Charlie's here and they're ready to start. Pierce and I will eat supper here. Binnie's going to cook mountain oysters."

110

Charlie, Pierce's tall, soft-spoken older brother, thirty-one years old, had a farm a mile northeast of Pierce's. The father and brothers often worked together when a group of men was needed to do farm jobs.

So those are Pierce's parents. Although younger than her own parents, John and Binnie seemed elderly and stern, although pleasant.

After Eliza got home, she went to the brooder house to see about the chicks. "Oh, no!" she gasped, squeezing her eyes shut against the sight. Several chicks lay on the ground, limp. Some chicks were missing as well. "A dog or coyote must've jumped over the fence. I guess we should only let them out of the brooder house when we can be right there to watch them."

What sort of animal had gotten in and eaten the chicks, the children wondered. Then the older ones came home from school, and the misfortune had to be discussed and exclaimed about all over again.

When Eliza cooked, she often let Nellie and Johnny measure, stir, and taste. It kept them occupied, and it was indeed a help for her because she had to hold Reenie in one arm to keep her from getting into everything. The toddler was quiet as long as she could see what was going on. Then while they waited for the men to come in, Eliza and the three little ones played Ring-Around-the-Rosie.

The next day at breakfast Pierce said, "I never thought your fence idea would pan out."

Eliza leaned back and crossed her arms. "If you got a dog, maybe that would keep the wild animals away."

"I used to have a darn good cattle dog, but he got kicked by a horse and had to be put down. One of these days I'll get me another dog."

A few days later a breeze came up, and it really blew hard. In the afternoon, tired of listening to the wind howl, Eliza decided to explore the storm cellar in the afternoon. At least it would be a little quieter down there. She tidied up the house and put a pot of beans in the warming oven ready for dinner. She gathered a few toys into a basket and lit a lantern, then called the younger children to come outdoors.

Eliza pulled hard on the iron ring of the cellar door and lifted the door up and over. It flopped face down with a loud clatter. Johnny peered down the stone stairway and began to cry.

"Don't shut me in there!"

"Sweetie, I would never do that. We will all go down the stairs together." She put an arm around his shoulder.

His eyes were frightened. "But when we're down there, someone might come and shut the door and put a big rock on it, and then we couldn't get out."

Eliza thought for a moment. "This might be a secret cave, you know, like in the story of Aladdin. Remember, he found jewels in the cave? There's no telling what might be down there, and I am going to find out."

She held the lantern high and descended the stone stairs purposefully. The flickering light threw eerie shadows on the rough cement walls. The children followed hesitantly and gazed around wide-eyed.

The cellar had been dug into the side of a hill, and it had a dank, musty smell. Rickety wooden shelves three tiers high lined the dirt walls, and under the lowest shelf were wooden baskets of potatoes, onions, and turnips. She could use some of these right away. Pierce had occasionally carried up onions and potatoes for her, but this was the first time that she had seen the cellar for herself.

On the shelves were jars of tomatoes, pickles, catsup, piccalilli, plums, peaches, and jam. Two-gallon crockery canisters held wheat. Eliza looked with satisfaction at all that food. Nannie had been busy, *bless her heart.* No one would go hungry in this house.

Eliza shoved several canisters into the center of the room. "Here, you can use these for pretend chairs."

"Let's have a tea party," said Nellie, digging into Eliza's basket of toys. "I'll be the mother."

Once the children were playing, Eliza took an inventory of the cellar's contents. Each time she moved a crockery jar or canister, it made a loud grating sound.

When the children started to get bored, she opened one more thing, a wooden crate sitting in a far corner. At the bottom, under some old dishes and ceramic beetle traps, she found a box with a tiny tea set. The girls would adore playing with that! Eliza knotted the little box carefully into her apron. She wanted to be alone when she unpacked it.

They had just gotten back into the house when there was a flash of lightning. The wind rose higher. The windmill banged and clanged as its massive head swung back and forth. The pump rod jerked up and down, and a steady stream of water splashed into the tank and flowed over the rim. There was a patter of rain on the glass panes and on the roof. Eliza checked through the house to make sure all the windows were closed. She noticed an old water stain on the ceiling in the boys' room.

Looking outside she saw Pierce and Edwin's wagon on the county road, approaching the farm at a pretty good clip. The horses' coats were dark with rain, and their hooves splashed in the water-filled ruts. The men drove directly to the wagon shed, cared for the horses and then, shoulders hunched, they ran to the house.

"Whoo-hoo!" said Edwin. "It's rainin' to beat the band!"

"A gully-washer!" agreed Pierce.

"I'm afraid you might have a leak in the roof over the boys' room," Eliza said as she poured coffee for the men. "It's not leaking now, but the ceiling looks like the water comes in there sometimes."

Pierce raised one eyebrow. "Is that right."

"Well, you hadn't mentioned it."

"I'll get to the dad-gum roof when I can afford it."

That evening the sound of quarreling came from the boys' room.

"You boys pipe down," yelled Pierce. "What the heck is going on in there?"

"He's hogging more than his share of the bed," whined Ross.

"Quit squabbling, or I'll give you something to cry about," shouted Pierce, turning back to his newspaper. The boys lowered their voices but continued to quarrel.

Eliza went to their room and asked if they wanted back rubs. She sat on their bed and rubbed their backs, then tucked them in. "Snug as a bug in a rug," she said. "Good night, sleep tight, don't let the bedbugs bite!" The boys giggled.

When she came back to the kitchen, Pierce looked up with a lopsided grin. "You spoil those kids to death."

Eliza laughed. "Well, I can't settle properly for the night until I know all the children are fast asleep."

They sat together at the table in the light of a lantern. Eliza mended some shirts, and Pierce paged through the local newspaper, reading aloud items he thought were interesting.

"You sure have a lot of funerals in this community," Eliza remarked.

"Well, between sickness and accidents I suppose it adds up."

Pierce seemed to be in a good mood, so she broached a subject she had been wondering about.

"I enjoyed meeting your parents. How many people are there in your family?"

"I have two sisters and two brothers. I'm right in the middle. My father never had much to do with me, though. He favored the other kids."

"Are you closer to your mother then?"

Pierce drummed his fingers on the table and spoke in a resigned tone of voice. "She's all right, but the fact of the matter is, when I was growing up I never got a fair shake. Charlie was the golden boy and got anything he wanted. My older sister Laura used to take me under her wing sometimes."

"Sounds like a sad situation."

Warming to the topic, he continued, "You could almost say I raised myself. I was out on my own by age nine."

"Nine years old? That's awfully young. What did you do?"

"Worked as a servant."

"How could your parents turn you out like that?"

Pierce lifted his hands weakly. "My father is a hard man. He went out as a servant himself at a similar age, and so I guess he thought that it would make a man of me."

She tilted her head to one side and sighed. "I'm really sorry. Sounds like you had a tough childhood."

His gaze shifted inward. "Some of the people I worked for were pretty handy with a belt. If I didn't do things right, they let 'er rip. It was almost as bad as being home with my damn dad." He looked down at his hands, which were lumpy and muscular, with bruised fingernails. Then he turned his hands over and held up his palms. She could see scars underneath his calluses.

"Good heavens! That's terrible! I remember when Joe was mean, those last few years that we were married. At the end, it was almost like being around an animal out of its cage. And I thought I couldn't leave. But then I did."

"Sure. Sometimes you can't change a situation except by running away. But enough of such talk. It does no good to wallow in the past. Look forward, is my motto. Speaking of which, time to hit the hay." He slapped his knees and stood up.

The weather was warmer every week. Eliza baked a bread pudding and two apple pies and set them in the cupboard, then she and the children went outdoors to work in the garden. She wanted to plant onions and sow lettuce seeds. Next week she would plant cucumbers, snap beans, and set out the little tomato plants she had growing on the window sill. It wouldn't be too long till they had salad greens—if the deer or the rabbits didn't eat them.

She dug long furrows in the soil with a hoe, then squatted down. "Pinch in a few tiny seeds at a time, like this," she told Nellie. Then she asked Johnny to cover the seeds with dirt. "Just cover them lightly. They are still asleep."

"Night-night?"

"That's right, punkin," said Eliza, amused. "Tuck them in and tell them good night. In a week or so they will wake up and push their little green heads out of the covers."

"That's ridiculous," said Nellie. "Plants can't hear anything."

"Well, it does no harm," replied her mother, straightening up. "If he wants to talk to them, he can." She smiled and patted Nellie's shoulder.

The garden was about twenty feet away from the windmill, and next to the windmill was a stock tank with a wooden cover on it to keep the water clean. A pipe led downhill from the tank to another stock tank in the corral where the cattle and horses drank. Eliza lifted the cover, filled the watering can, and carried it to the garden.

She let the children take turns using the watering can, keeping hold of the handle so they didn't flood the seeds out. The garden patch was on the sunny side of the house, where the seedlings would grow well. Eliza stood back and put her hands on her hips to admire their handiwork.

Later the children were busy drawing at the table, and Eliza smiled. *I feel like a mother hen with all those adorable little heads sitting close together, bent over their work.*

She slipped into the front room and unwrapped the miniature tea set. It had two cups and two saucers and a teapot with a lid. Each delicate china piece was golden brown, with a couple of violets painted on it. The underside of the teapot was stamped 'Made in Japan.'

She lifted the lid of the teapot and saw a scrap of paper folded inside. Using her little finger, she managed to extract it and read the penciled words "for Ruthie." *How sweet.* Nannie had planned the tea set as a surprise for her baby daughter when she was older. Eliza wrapped it back up and set the box on top of the cupboard until she could return it to the cellar. Then she tidied the house and put pork chops on to fry for supper.

Sadie kept the others entertained while her mother cooked and Nellie set the table. "Mama." Nellie looked troubled. "Pierce hits the boys. I seen him."

Eliza turned. "Oh dear, that's not good. Well, they are a different family, and used to different ways. Without a mother in the house, it must have been hard for him to handle the kids. Well, there's no need for him to do that any more. I am taking care of most situations now. But if he ever hits one of you girls, come and tell me. I won't put up with that."

That evening, when Pierce handed her the week's salary, he asked, "What are you doing with all this darn money, Eliza? You are costing me a pretty penny and, let's be honest, you don't need most of it. You and your girls get room and board for free."

Eliza took a step backward and clasped her hands behind her back. "Half of my earnings, I lay aside to go back to Lecompton and visit my parents." She kept the bills and coins in a tin on top of her dresser.

He snorted. "To tell you the truth, I thought you'd turn down the salary. I'm practically your relative, you know, and I doubt your parents paid you a salary when you lived with them, hmm? I figured it would be enough if I just paid for anything you needed, such as clothes or travel."

Eliza folded her arms in front of her. "Perhaps that's what you thought, Pierce, but it's not what you offered me in your letter. I do appreciate having free board and room, but also I like having money of my own. If I didn't have a salary, I'd have to beg you for every dime."

"By the way," she continued, "those steers in the north pasture would do better if you'd move them to fresher grass."

Pierce raised his eyebrows. "Why in Sam Hill do you say that?"

"They aren't moving as a herd anymore. It's each man for himself. When cattle are grazing on good grass, they all move the same direction."

"Hmmpf. Very observant. I'll check on them tomorrow."

The wind rose again during the night, and when Ralph, Sadie, and Ross left for school the next morning, it was blowing around thirty miles an hour.

"Just a prairie breeze," said Pierce, putting on his jacket and cap.

"Watch this, Eliza!" called Ross. "If I spread my jacket out, the wind blows me along. Whee! I'm a kite."

When the men came to the house for dinner, they paused by the front door, slapped dust from their overalls, and studied the sky. There were only a few scattered clouds, but the wind was growing stronger and the air was chilly.

"We're going to have some weather," said Pierce. "We better move the cattle into the corral. They need to be close to water in case the dirt starts to blow." After a quick meal, he and Edwin went to saddle their horses.

Eliza followed them out, her apron flapping in the wind. "Pierce, shall I fetch the children from school?"

He paused for a moment. "Naw, don't go. From the look of that sky, I bet the teacher lets school out early, and you might miss each other along the way. Ralph's got a good head on his shoulders. He'll make sure the others get home." He squinted at the sky again.

"Do you have dust storms often?" asked Eliza.

"Every few years," said Pierce. "There was a real bad one last year about this time. They don't seem to reach the eastern part of Kansas. It's more of a prairie phenomenon." He snapped his fingers. "I gotta get going." He and Edwin disappeared in the direction of the barn.

Throughout the afternoon Eliza kept looking out of the window to watch the sky. She shut the chicks in the brooder house, shooed the chickens into the chicken house, and fed the pigs. She weighted down the rain barrel with an iron so it wouldn't blow over.

Then she showed Nellie and Johnny how to play tic-tac-toe on the slate. Listening to the wind moan, they kept losing track of whose turn it was to play. Finally, they gave up the attempt and pushed their chairs next to a window where they could watch the direction from which the older children would be walking.

Russian thistles tumbled along and slammed against the house with a scratchy thud. The house creaked and groaned, and the windowpanes rattled. Eliza covered the bedroom windows with sheets, as the storm was blowing in from the west.

Irene was cranky and wanted to be held all the time. Finally, Eliza deposited her on the floor next to Johnny and Nellie and snatched up a shawl, disregarding the toddler's wail. "Okay, you guys, don't let Reenie follow me outside."

The wind was blowing a gale, and the air was filled with dust. The road and the pasture were visible only in between gusts. Eliza pulled the tail end of the shawl over her nose and mouth and ran a few hundred yards along the path the children walked to school. The wind flattened her clothes against her body, and dirt stung her face. She called the children's names. There was no answer but the whistling of the wind. Her teeth felt gritty, and the sky was growing dark.

Suddenly, she saw a wall of whirling gray-brown dust surging toward the farm like an enormous ocean wave. She rushed back to the house and slammed the door behind her, gasping for breath.

Chapter 11

Eliza heard cattle bawling. The men must be herding them toward the corral. Ten minutes later, Pierce and Edwin opened the front door and tied one end of a rope around the doorknob.

"That's so we can get to and from the barn if it gets worse," said Pierce. "It probably won't, but it's already pretty dang bad." He tested the knot with a yank. "Got a cup of coffee for us, Eliza?"

The men sat at the kitchen table to wait. Eliza was glad for the task, as she was so worried she could not sit still. Nellie and Johnny stared at the men, then went back to looking out the window, although almost nothing could be seen. Irene had fallen asleep on the couch. Dirt and pebbles blew noisily against the side of the house. Several flies buzzed around the room. Pierce drummed his fingers on the table.

Eliza wiped a film of dust from the table and handed the men their coffee. Then she set a pan of eggs to boil for deviled eggs. *The children are in danger.* She stood at the stove watching bubbles rising in the pan as the water boiled. There was nothing visible outside but clouds of dust.

She sprinkled damp tea leaves on the floor, which enabled her to sweep up some of the dust without flipping it into the air. Then she got a cup of coffee for herself and sat at the table.

Johnny came into the kitchen and leaned against her chair. Wordlessly she set aside her mending basket and lifted him onto her lap. She put her arms around him, and he buried his face in her neck.

After a while, Eliza got up, put a pan of scalloped potatoes into the oven, and sliced some bacon to fry, along with a few limp carrots that needed using up.

"Will we have to go down to the cellar if the storm gets worse?" she asked.

Pierce scowled. "We might if it gets really bad. Though in any case, we'll stay right here 'til the kids get back. One good thing—I didn't see any funnel clouds."

Edwin agreed. "The sky doesn't have that funny yellow cast it gets before a tornado. It just looks dark. Still, there's so much dust in the air that you can hardly breathe."

Another half hour passed. At last, there was the rattle of the doorknob, and Ralph, Ross, and Sadie fell into the room.

"The Lord be praised!" exclaimed Eliza.

"Where the devil have you kids been?" asked Pierce. "You're late." Sadie glared at him.

"We got lost coming home," explained Ralph. "Then we found the way again."

"What happened?"

"With all the dust blowing," said Ralph, "we couldn't see the path. Then Ross lay down and cried and wouldn't get up. By the time we made him go on, we had got turned around and didn't know which direction to go. Sadie had the idea that we should climb a tree, so when we came to a tree I clumb up to where the dust was thinner, and I seen where we were.

"Then she gave me her underskirt to cover my nose and mouth. I kept walkin' the right direction. Sadie followed me and held onto Ross by his jacket. It was easy once we got to the pasture fence."

Eliza hugged each of them, one by one. "You did just right, and I'm proud of you."

Pierce nodded and said, "Go get cleaned up now, and have something to eat."

As Nellie silently set the table, Eliza lit another lantern and lay supper on the table. She called Ross to her.

"It was hard coming home today, wasn't it?" she said. The boy nodded. She put one hand on his shoulder, and as she heated up the food they stood like that for a long time, without speaking and without looking at each other. Then he went to sit at the table with the others. The whole family was exhausted and thankful to be together. Edwin lifted Reenie onto his knee and began cutting up her food.

All at once, there was a banging on the side of the house. The adults rose simultaneously. Before they could reach the door, it burst open, and a short, bandy-legged man with a gray beard staggered inside. He was covered with dust and in his arms he carried a limp dog.

"Evenin', folks," he croaked. "Ain't fit out there for man nor beast. Can you take pity on a poor peddler? I could use me some grub and a place to hole up till the storm passes." Eliza ran to fill another plate and get him something to drink. The man lay his dog gently in a corner. The children crowded around the skinny animal.

"What's his name?" Ralph asked.

"Champ," said the old man. "I don't know if he'll make it, though. The dust really got to him."

The peddler stood at the washstand, splashed water on his face and hands, and wiped them on the towel. The children stared somberly at the motionless, medium-sized dog. Nellie seemed the most affected, and she remained kneeling beside it after the others had wandered away to hear the old man tell about his travels. After a while, she brought a rag and wiped the dog's nose. It coughed and sneezed.

"He's going to live," Nellie declared. She washed the dog all over, then rubbed it dry with a towel. It was so thin that its ribs were visible. "He's too tired to eat," she said, "but I'll put a dish here with water so he can get a drink soon's he feels like it."

"You make a darn good nursemaid, young lady," said the peddler. "Tell you what. If Champ pulls through, you can keep him. He's a good dog, and I never have enough to feed him properly."

"Oh boy, a dog!" exclaimed the children, and they ran over to Champ. Despite the noise of the children's chatter, the dog had not stirred.

Get back," ordered Nellie. "And don't yell. Champ is in his sickbed and can't have visitors yet." There was a note of authority in her voice, and the other children held back. Nellie gazed at the dog and petted its head.

The peddler chuckled. "You tell 'em, Nursie! Poor old Champ's already walked enough miles to last him a lifetime. He'd probably rather stay here with you kids than tramp around with me."

"And you better check him for ticks," the old man added, between mouthfuls.

Pierce groaned. "Lordy, that's all we need. . ." Edwin squatted next to the dog and used hot match heads to remove several ticks.

The next day the wind decreased to some extent. Eliza swept the whole house and cleaned up the piles of dust on the window sills. The children did not venture out but instead played with Eliza's private stash of rainy-day toys. The peddler slept in the barn for a couple of days, and Eliza washed his threadbare clothes. As soon as the windstorm ended, he retrieved his cart full of pans and spoons for sale. Then he ate one last meal with the family and said goodbye.

"Time to mosey on, folks," the peddler said, "Thank ye kindly for your hospitality." He looked over at the dog, which lay on a blanket in a corner of the kitchen.

"So long, old pal!" He bent down and rubbed the dog's ears. The dog licked his hand. "You're a good dog, and I'll miss you."

Pierce went out early to look at the livestock and walk the fences, seeing if they needed repair. He took the older boys with him, saying,

"Right after a windstorm is the best time to hunt for Indian arrowheads."

Champ had begun to drink some water, although he still refused to eat. Nellie lugged him outdoors and told him about everything on the farm. She explained to him where he could go and where he could not go. She made him a bed next to the house, behind a bush that was her private fort. The scrawny dog was too weak to walk more than a few steps at a time, but Nellie assured the others that Champ would be good as new in a few weeks.

"What kind of a dog is he?" Nellie asked the men one day.

"A mutt!" said Pierce.

"A peddler's dog. A junkyard dog. Mixed breed," said Edwin.

"I mean, what can he do? Some dogs are cattle dogs, or sheep dogs, and some are bad dogs and eat chickens, and some dogs do tricks."

Edwin took the question seriously. "Only Champ knows what kind of a dog he is," he told Nellie, "and so you'll have to ask him."

"Dogs can't talk!" she said, rolling her eyes.

"Of course they don't talk in words like people do. They talk to you by what they do, by their actions. You have to watch Champ carefully and see what he does in different situations, then you'll know what kind of dog he is." Edwin smiled. "Who knows? Maybe he's a circus dog, a lion tamer dog."

Nellie needed a special friend, Eliza thought, so she didn't allow the other children to feed the dog. Besides, since Champ didn't do anything other than sitting on his haunches or sleeping, the others didn't find him much fun to play with.

The dog gradually recovered his health and appetite. He slept under a bush and would sometimes slink around the farm, limping. Nellie tried to teach Champ to fetch a stick, but he wouldn't do it.

"What kind of dog is Champ, Mama?" she asked Eliza one day. "He didn't tell me yet."

"He's a really dumb dog," broke in Ross. "He lays around all day and don't even know his name."

Eliza pursed her lips. "Well, I can tell that he likes you taking care of him so good. Maybe he's a companion dog." Nellie nodded.

"He's a loyal dog," suggested Sadie. "Like Greyfriars Bobby."

Eliza was glad to have a dog on the farm. Although Champ wasn't very energetic, it made her feel safer just having him out there in the yard.

One Saturday morning Pierce's older brother Charlie came over for a discussion. Eliza put out apple pie, Cheddar cheese, and coffee for the two men and retreated to the bedrooms with the younger children. She changed sheets, straightened bureau drawers, and swept floors while the children played. She didn't pay much attention to the men until the voices from the kitchen grew loud.

"Pull in your horns, Pierce!" said Charlie. "You like to speculate, I don't. Yah, well, no need to get all het up."

"Get out of my goddamn house, you miserable, tight-fisted schmuck!" shouted Pierce. *Is it necessary to be so belligerent?* Eliza thought. But she understood. *Pierce views life as an obstacle course, and he throws himself into everything with all his might.*

After his brother left, Pierce stomped around the room with clenched fists, cursing and ranting. "Charlie heard that a cattle drive is coming up from Texas next week, see, and he thought I might be interested," he explained to Edwin and Eliza. "It's exactly the sort of investment opportunity I like, but right now my money's tied up. I tried to persuade him to go in on it together, but he refused. What a fool!"

"Why not talk to your dad?" asked Edwin. "He's got plenty of dough."

Pierce slammed his fist against the door frame. "For chrissake! I wouldn't ask that man for a rope if I was in a goddamn sinkhole."

Eliza decided it might be a good idea to take the children elsewhere for a while.

"Why don't we go fishing?" she asked. "When I lived on the river we ate lots of fish. Any fishing poles around here?"

"We used to," said Ralph. "I'll check in the barn." The other children followed him eagerly and they returned with a pole, a spool of fishing line, and a net. Eliza put baked potatoes in the warming oven for the men's dinner and made a picnic lunch for herself and the children. It was a chilly day, so she told them they could not wade in the water, just play with stick boats, the rope swing, or go fishing.

"What kinds of fish do you have here in the Solomon, Ralph?" she asked as they walked along the path to the river.

"We got bluegill, crappie, channel cat and, if you're lucky, largemouth bass. But you have to dig for green worms first."

"Where do you get those?"

"I forget."

Eliza laughed. "No matter. We'll see what we can find for bait." As they walked toward the river, a hawk flew low overhead.

"Probably hunting for mice," she said. They passed a draw where there were a lot of tall weeds and a tangle of bushes. A pheasant scurried into the underbrush as they approached.

Eliza's eyes crinkled with contentment as they reached the river. She drew in a deep breath. "Each river has its own special smell, doesn't it?"

They stood at the edge of the water and looked at the impressions of cow hooves in the soft mud. The river made a quiet rippling sound as it rushed over rocks and branches. They walked farther until they found a place in a bend of the river where the bank was steep. Although the water was clear, it was clogged with weeds and submerged branches.

"This spot looks like it has lots of hiding places for fish. We know their secrets though, don't we?" She found a flat spot near a clump of Johnny-jump-ups (wild pansies) and spread out an old blanket to sit on. Several hours later, they went home with sodden clothes and three catfish, which Eliza fried for supper.

Easter came early in 1900, on April 15. Eliza was used to combining an Easter celebration with her birthday, which was April 11. This year she was going to be thirty-four, and she thought that Easter would be a splendid time to celebrate their new, combined household. She decided to invite the Thompson grandparents and to give each of the children a present.

She wanted to make a knitted purse for Sadie and a rag doll for Reenie. She decided to buy colored pencils for Ross, a ruler for Ralph, two tin horses for Johnny (a little one and a big one, because he liked babies), and a set of hair barrettes for Nellie.

"What the hell is this namby-pamby stuff, Eliza?" asked Pierce, glancing at her shopping list. "Yarn, toy horses, colored pencils. . ." He adjusted the crotch of his overalls. "Think I'm made of money, woman?"

She folded her arms behind her and smiled. "Don't worry, Pierce. I'll give you money to buy gifts for the children. I thought I'd surprise them with Easter presents—you know, to celebrate the fact that our two families are living together now. I've chosen things that will last, by the way, not cheap cardboard Easter baskets that fall apart. The vanilla is so I can make a 'specially nice cake for the holiday. See if you can get the good vanilla, not the watered-down stuff they sometimes have."

"Hell, I don't do the shopping. I just hand your list to the storekeeper and pick up the box later. What do you need colored pencils for?"

"That's for Ross because he likes to draw."

"Nothing for him. Ross is a lazy son of a gun, always trying to get out of work."

"Well, he seems interested in art. Maybe he has some talent in that direction."

"Hmmpf."

"I've also been thinking that Easter would be a good time to invite the Thompsons over. Would that be all right? I'm sure they would like to see their grandsons, and Johnny has been feeling lonesome for Ruth."

"Pretty soon you'll be urging me to attend church and sing hymns! Who's in charge of this family, eh? You or me?"

"You are," she replied evenly, standing up to clear the dishes.

"I do not take orders from a petticoat! Remember that, will ya?" He snatched a pancake from the cupboard and tromped outside, slamming the door.

Eliza smiled to herself. She had learned not to take Pierce's irascible moods personally. He was a good man at heart, she knew. Also, regardless of how much he grumbled, whenever she needed or wanted anything, there was always enough money to buy it. How different from how her life had been with Joe!

On Easter Sunday morning, the children were astounded to find a gift lying in their bed next to each of them when they awoke. They brought their gifts to the breakfast table to show the others. Eliza stowed the new things temporarily on top of the cupboard so they wouldn't get misplaced in the turmoil of the day.

Jake and Mary Thompson arrived not long after breakfast, bringing the boys' younger sister Ruth, cute three-year-old with dimples in both cheeks. Pierce shook hands with the Thompsons and held out his arms for little Ruth, who went to him after a tentative peek.

"Whoa, Ruthie! Look at you. You little scamp! You're getting to be a big girl." The pudgy toddler wriggled to be put down, and his face fell. He kissed her quickly and let her slip to the floor.

"What kind of baloney is this? I can't tell whether she remembers me or not."

Gram touched his arm. "Ah, Pierce, pay that no heed. Ruthie needs a while to warm up to people, and it's been some time since she's seen you."

Ruth was the same age as Irene, and after some initial bashfulness, the two toddlers were shrieking and laughing and chasing each other around like playful puppies. Later Eliza sat on the floor of the front room and helped them roll a ball back and forth.

Gramps reached into his pocket and brought out two wooden and metal tops, one red and the other yellow with blue stripes.

"Ruthie's not old enough to play with these, so you older kids might as well have fun with 'em," he said.

It was almost like Christmas with so many new toys. Gramps knelt on the floor and showed the children how to wind the string around the top, hold it with one finger, and then pull the string with the other hand. The top would hum and spin around in a circle, and Eliza and Gram made sure the toddlers didn't grab them.

"This is great!" said Eliza. "You folks should come over again real soon. How's Ruthie doing these days?"

"I think she's adjusted well to living with us," the grandmother replied. "She's a hale and hearty child. The last few weeks she's even been stringing a few words together."

"The boys remind me so much of Nannie," said Eliza. "She was such a sweet person, and they miss their mother, of course. They are brave and good boys, and I love them so much."

Ralph came over to Gram's chair and leaned his head against her shoulder. She reached up and patted his arm. "How you doing, honey?"

"Eliza's nice," he said. "When you talk with her, she hears what you mean."

"I'm thankful that you boys have a woman's influence in the home again. It's much better."

"Better cooking too! I was getting tired of sausage and grits."

"Things must seem different around the house, eh, Pierce?" asked Gramps.

"Good Lord, with so many kids running in and out, I feel I'm living in a goddamn anthill!" They all laughed.

"Do you boys have a toy box?" asked Eliza. "We could put it right here in the front room."

"Wait!" said Pierce, "I don't want toys lying all over the floor."

"I'm sure the boys are responsible enough to pick up their toys," she replied. "You can ride herd on the younger ones, can't you, Ralph?"

Ralph nodded and jumped to his feet. "I'll get the toy box. It's a wicker basket with a lid."

"Aren't you boys too big for toys?" asked Pierce, as Ralph dragged in the toy box.

"Oh, boy, our blocks!" exclaimed Ross. "I almost forgot about them."

Eliza had prepared a dinner of chicken and dumplings, asparagus, pickles and, for dessert, lemon cake with boiled icing. Then the older children played outside while the women washed the dishes and got the toddlers down for naps.

After a while, the older children came back in. "We been out and seen the chicks," reported Nellie.

"They go peep, peep, peep, all the time," said Sadie to Gram, laughing, "and you have to teach them how to drink. And they have special food, and they run around so fast, sometimes they run into each other and fall over!"

Later in the afternoon Eliza made coffee and served rhubarb pie.

After a while, Gramps stood up. "We'll have to head home shortly, Mother," he said, "And those dark clouds look like rain. But Pierce, I'd like to take a look at your cattle first. How much acreage you got in pasture?" The men disappeared.

The children built a corral in the front room with blocks and galloped Johnny's toy horses around the corral. "A mama one and a baby one!" Johnny sighed happily.

"With so many boy toys around," said Gram, "you better watch out, Eliza. Sadie and Nellie are going to turn into boys!"

"Oh, don't you think all kids like blocks and tops?" Eliza replied. She helped the younger ones take part in the toy corral project without messing up what the other children had done. By the time the men came back inside, all the toys had been put away.

At bedtime, Eliza wrote a long letter to her parents, telling them that things were going well. She had put in a garden, Pierce's boys were wonderful, Sadie was learning to embroider, Nellie helped her a lot in the kitchen, and Irene had just cut her last baby tooth.

Chapter 12

A mist-like rain began to descend and by the next day, it had become a driving rain. The roads were mired in mud, and the children were chilled to the bone walking home from school.

As Ross was getting ready for bed, he came back out to the kitchen. "Hey, Eliza! It's raining into our room."

"Is your window closed good and tight?" she asked. She went into the boys' bedroom, and Ross pointed to the ceiling. Sure enough, there was a dark splotch. Rain was starting to seep through the wallpaper.

"Hoo boy!" she said, with an infectious laugh. "Thanks for letting me know. I'll fetch a bucket to catch the drips. I better check all through the house." There was another leak in the front room, probably because the rain was coming down so hard.

"It's been a month since you came," Pierce said to Eliza one evening as he handed her $5. Bending down to take off his boots, he spoke from below the table. "Don't get a swelled head but, in my opinion, you are doing a damn good job as housekeeper."

"Why, thank you." She sat down to crochet an edging for a pair of pillowcases. "I think this has been a good move for my girls and me, and I really appreciate your making us feel welcome. I *would* like to make one request if I might. Please don't swear so much. I'm afraid the children will pick it up. It's a pleasure to take care of your boys though. They are very intelligent."

"You bet my boys are smart," he said. "All three of them. Smart as all git-out. And as soon as they finish grade school, they can begin to earn their keep."

"Oh, I expect Ralph at least will go on to high school, don't you? He is the best in the whole school at ciphering."

"I can't afford for him to go to any high-falutin' high school. What am I supposed to do, buy another saddle horse so he can waltz into town and back every day? All I got was the eight grades, and if it was good enough for me, I reckon that's good enough for Ralph."

"Well, Pierce, if he just works on the farm after he graduates from country school, he'll know nothing other than how to farm. But if he goes on to high school, he can either farm or do some other career, depending on what he wants to do."

"For crying out loud, the poor kid's only in third grade! Lots of time to decide. In any case, it's nothing to do with you. Someday I'm sure one of the boys will take over the farm, and I'd like to buy more land for the others as well. That's one reason I'm working so hard. It's a sight more help than I got from my father, who put me out to work at age nine."

Eliza said, "I know, and that's awfully young. I can certainly see how hard you've worked to get this farm going. You can be proud of what you have accomplished. But you'd be doing your boys a big favor if you let them go on to high school. I certainly would like my girls to get to go to high school."

Pierce gave her a stony stare and stood up. "If I want your opinion, woman, I'll ask for it, all right? See you in the morning!"

Arrogance and bluster were part and parcel of Pierce's personality. Eliza had a hunch that, with time, he would probably let at least his oldest boy go to high school, after all. She thought that Ralph was exceptionally talented, and she was determined to stick up for him as much as she could.

She missed her parents, who were generous and who took into account what their children wanted to do with their lives. If she had wanted to continue her studies past grade school, for instance, they would have found some way to arrange it. And now that more high schools were opening around the state of Kansas, Eliza wanted to see all six of the children under her wing get a good education. If they weren't inclined in that direction, that was their choice, but she felt they should have the chance.

Pierce wanted to do right by his family, she knew. She could only imagine how it must have worn him down to be forced to earn his keep at nine years old! That was the same age as Ralph was now. She had heard of children in poverty-stricken families starting to work at age ten or eleven, although never younger. Ralph was a sensitive boy. She could not imagine letting him go out on his own in the world, and perhaps be mistreated by a harsh employer. It might harden him against life and against other people.

Eliza recalled that when she left for this housekeeping job, her father had said that if it didn't work out, she could always come back home. She was grateful for him giving her that option, but after a month here—*Had it only been that long? It seemed like several months!*—it would be unthinkable to go back home. She had taken Pierce's boys into her heart. It almost felt like they were her own children. She had no desire to quit her job. She had found her footing in this new household, and it had become her life.

One evening Eliza was washing dishes and Sadie was drying them. Sadie asked, "Mama, I've been wondering. Why don't we ever see Grandma and Grandpa Vaughan?"

"They live in Topeka, darling. That's pretty far away."

"But when we lived closer we didn't visit them very often either."

Eliza nodded. "That's true. Not the last few years anyway. Would you like to write to them? I'm sure they would love to get a letter from you."

"And what about Papa? I don't just forget about people."

"Do you think of him sometimes?"

"Yes, and he's in my good-night prayer, like always."

Eliza discarded the dishwater, wiped the pan dry, and took off her apron. Then she sat at the table and eased Sadie onto her lap. Sadie put her arms around her mother's shoulders.

"Some things are really sad, aren't they?" said Eliza. "If life had been different, we might still be on the island and living with Papa."

"He scared me," said Sadie. "But before that, he was nice."

"I know, precious. When Papa started hitting us, we had to go live with Grandma and Grandpa. Otherwise, we might have gotten hurt. It's never right for someone to act like that, and I don't understand why he did it."

"Do parents sometimes stop loving their children?"

"Sweetheart, I will never stop loving you."

Later, Eliza sat down and wrote to her parents, expressing her appreciation that they had given her such a happy childhood.

One afternoon Eliza was working on some dresses for Sadie and Nellie, letting down the hems and opening the gussets to widen the bodices. Ralph came into the room and sidled over to her chair.

"Say, Eliza! Anything I can help you with?" All three of the Griffith boys had blue eyes, and Ralph's eyes were the brightest blue.

"No, not right now." She smiled. "How polite of you to ask."

"I could sweep the floor or wash dishes."

"I believe I have things pretty well in hand, honey. Why do you ask? Is there something in particular that you'd like to do?"

Ralph scuffed his shoe on the floor. "I thought that if you had too much work to do, you might get tired of being here and leave."

"That's a new wrinkle!" she exclaimed, amused. "You're a thoughtful boy, Ralph. I like you to help me sometimes, but I'm not overworked. Don't you fret about that! I am happy here. You and your brothers are very dear to me, and I expect to stay here a long time."

"Good," he replied. He held onto the back of Eliza's chair and began to test how far he could hop away from it on one foot without falling down. "Did you know I can run very fast? If a bull ever chased me, I would run so fast I'd be gone before he knew where I went off to!"

She gave him a quick hug. "I've seen you. You run like a deer." Ralph giggled and bounded away.

Eliza smiled to herself. She could picture Nannie's boys growing up to be fine men. Pierce would teach them the masculine skills, and she would make sure that the gentle part of their personalities was not pushed aside.

She felt that her life was back on track now. She was supporting herself and her family financially. *No more potato-peel soup for my girls!* Her daughters had adjusted well to the change of environment, and Nannie and Pierce's sons were good boys. Eliza made no distinction between their two families. She treated each child like her own.

The problems she had had with Joe—his violent streak, and being so terribly hard up for money—were gone forever. She had pressured Joe to do what he should and, worse than not accomplishing that goal, it had driven him to resentment and rage. She would not make that mistake again. A man had to have the freedom to choose what he did in life. Otherwise, he felt fenced in. Of course, she had the same desire herself.

It was raining again. The garden would have to wait. Eliza sorted through the carpet rags and started braiding them together to make a rug.

Pierce had butchered a pig, and she had the meat soaking in buckets of brine. When it had finished, they would rub salt on the hams and the sides of bacon and hang them in the milk house. Pigs matured quickly, plus they ate almost anything. As long as pigs stayed healthy, you got more meat for your dollar with bacon and ham than with beef.

A few days later Ralph and Ross came indoors after a long walk.

"Where's Johnny?" asked Eliza. "I thought he was with you."

Ralph replied, "He was with us at first, but he couldn't keep up with us. I told him to go home."

"He's a slowpoke!" said Ross. "He's too little to keep up with us big boys." He snickered.

Ralph said, "I'm beat. We walked really far." He flopped onto the couch.

"You boys weren't over by the train tracks, were you?"

"No, ma'am."

"Well, that's one good thing." She stepped outdoors and called Johnny's name over and over, then came back into the house.

"Johnny's not here. He must've got stranded somewhere, or lost. Remember, your little brother's only four years old. Where were you when you separated?"

"Huh? I'm too tired to hunt for him. I told him to go back home, and he said he would." A whine had crept into his voice. "Besides, I wouldn't even know where to start looking for him."

"You have more excuses than Carter's has pills, Ralph, my boy. Come on, let's go! You're the oldest, so you were responsible."

Ross laughed unkindly. "You're in for it now, Ralph!"

Eliza frowned. "Enough of that talk, Ross. It sounds too uncharitable for a nice boy like you."

138

She took hold of Ralph's shoulder. "Put on your jacket again. You and I have to hunt for him. I'll just go tell Sadie and Nellie that we're leaving."

Ralph and Eliza tried to retrace the boys' footsteps. Ralph lagged behind, while Eliza flew from place to another, checking all the byways and calling Johnny's name. Her brow was furrowed, and her hairpins were coming loose.

"Keep a good eye out, Ralph," she said. "He might have wandered off the path." They walked for about an hour, through the pasture and a stubble field and past a thicket. They had almost passed by a clump of bushes when Johnny called out to them. Like a timid bird in its nest, he had wedged himself under the bushes and fallen asleep. He scrambled out and rushed into Eliza's arms.

"Mama!" he said, his lower lip quivering, "I knew you would find me." He pressed his cheek against her skirt and yawned. Eliza dabbed away a tear, picked him up and kissed his cheek, then put him back on his feet.

"I couldn't find my way back," he mumbled.

Ralph hovered one step away. His shoulders drooped. "I didn't remember it was this far. Maybe you walked the wrong direction, Johnny."

Eliza bent down and looked right into Johnny's face. "We were worried about you, sweetie, and we would've hunted until we found you." She held each boy by the hand as the three of them walked slowly back to the house.

"You made a mistake, Ralph. Everyone makes mistakes, it's part of being human. But I think you can see that sometimes small mistakes have big consequences.

"As your punishment, Ralph," she continued as they neared the house, "you may not go out of the yard for the next two days, other than to school and back. And please pick the sand burrs out of Johnny's pants and socks for me. Tonight, you must tell your father about what happened. Maybe that will help you remember to take good care of your brother." He turned his face to the floor and nodded.

Eliza slipped into the bedroom to fix her hair, then finished cooking supper, which was pot roast and vegetables, with rhubarb cream pie for dessert.

That evening she said to Pierce, "I hope you don't think I was out of line for disciplining Ralph. Though if I'm in charge of the children, I do need to be able to correct them."

"To my mind, you're way too lenient. I would have given Ralph a good whipping. But when I'm not there, it's up to you, Eliza. If he learns his lesson, that's the main thing."

Eliza used a lot of cream and butter in her cooking. She packed butter and cream into old coffee cans and put them in a barrel of water to keep fresh, or if the weather was really sweltering, out in the icehouse.

The icehouse contained blocks of river ice that Pierce and a hired man had cut during the winter. Every year Pierce would haul them home and packed them in layers of straw, and they would last all summer. The ice was used to cool watermelons and to make ice cream. When the family wanted clean ice for drinks, such as lemonade or iced tea, they bought that from the general store, which had an ice machine.

Life was going well. Reenie was learning to dress herself, Sadie was practicing cursive handwriting, and Nellie was teaching Champ to "sit" and "go lie down." The boys rolled a hoop with a stick and made darts out of wooden shingles. The darts were like arrows with a notch for a string to hook onto. With a string on the end of a stick, they could shoot a dart in the air a hundred feet high.

One morning, it struck Eliza that Ross was no longer reluctant to go to school. He simply got dressed and left with the others as a matter of course. She asked him about it, and he said, "Well, Sadie has been helping me with my letters, and besides, I like the onion bread you put in our dinner bucket."

Sadie explained that she had shown Ross how to sound out words by getting a stick and drawing large letters in the dirt. "I told him that each letter was an animal that made a different sound and that if you remember the sound each one makes, they will tell you stories."

"How clever! You are an inventive teacher, Sadie," said Eliza.

"I'm not as bad at reading as I was," Ross said. "The teacher makes me sit up front, so as I don't watch the others."

"I'm very glad that school is going better for you."

"But anyway, Eliza, my feet hurt all the time."

"Let me see your shoes, honey. Maybe there's a nail in there, or a pebble." He took them off. The leather was thin on the toes, and the heels were worn down on the outside. Reaching in, she could not feel any rough places. She put one shoe next to his feet.

"My stars and body! No wonder the shoes bother you, Ross. They are too small. You just as well go barefoot in the house. For school, we need to buy you some bigger ones." That night she mentioned to Pierce that Ross needed new shoes.

"He can wear Ralph's old ones," grumbled Pierce. "I can't afford new shoes right now. Maybe after harvest. Buying groceries and paying your damn salary uses up all our cream and egg money."

During the next few days, Eliza did a complete review of the children's clothing. The boys' overalls were frayed, and some of their shirts were tattered and had buttons missing. All six children were growing fast and would need new clothes, coats, and shoes. It wouldn't be fair if she bought new clothes for her own children and Pierce's boys went around in old and patched ones.

Eliza decided to earn extra money by raising geese. Hens' eggs sold for twenty-two cents a dozen but goose eggs, which were larger, brought in a quarter apiece. She could also sell the geese for meat at Thanksgiving and Christmas. That would surely supply enough money to buy clothes for all the children. Other than that, she would mend and "make do."

She asked Pierce to buy five fertilized goose eggs from one of the neighbors. The lady told him that they would take a month to hatch. Eliza kept the eggs in a muffin tin under a dishcloth. Four times a day she turned them and sprinkled them with warm water. The children could hardly wait to see the goslings hatch. Eliza promised them that the minute one of the eggs started to crack open, she would tell them.

Pierce's birthday was the following week; he was going to be twenty-nine. Eliza asked Edwin what he thought Pierce might like to have for a gift, and he suggested a belt. When the men took the wagon to town the next time, Eliza asked for ten yards of cord. That was the cheapest way to make a belt. Edwin managed to buy a brass belt buckle without Pierce noticing, and the secret project began.

Eliza tied the buckle to a bedpost in her bedroom and cut the cord into equal lengths. Then she tied each of those into the belt buckle with a loop. Thus there were eight strands of cord fastened to the belt buckle. After that, it was a matter of braiding. The children took turns working on the belt, under her supervision. Even Reenie was allowed to help. Eliza watched to see that the children followed the pattern correctly and kept the cords pulled taut so the belt would fit inside the belt loops of Pierce's good pants. After the braiding was finished, she sewed the cords together to form a tongue, cut off the ends, and closed the raw edges with an overhand stitch.

Pierce was quite surprised when he received the gift. "Well, if that don't beat all! I thought birthday presents were just for kids."

"We made it ourselves," bragged Ralph.

"I imagine you had a little help," he said, winking at Eliza.

"Edwin got the buckle, Eliza showed us how to do the braiding, and we kids did the rest."

"I really like it. Thank you." For the birthday dinner, Eliza made a chocolate cake, Pierce's favorite. She usually had some sort of pie in the cupboard, but for special occasions she liked to bake a cake.

One day Ralph, Ross, and Sadie came home from school with some news. "Hey, guess what?" said Ralph. "We're going to have a spelling bee the last Friday in April. The parents are s'posed to come and be the audience."

"Each of us has to memorize all the words on our spelling lists," added Sadie, "and if we want, we can also learn other words, for instance from a book or newspaper."

Eliza nodded. "Good idea! And you have plenty of time to prepare. After you have learned your words, we could have our own spelling bee at home to help you practice for the big day."

Ross shrugged and opened his box of colored pencils. "I can't spell," he said. "It's different for Ralph. He's good at spelling."

Eliza rubbed his shoulder. "You're a smart boy too. Use your noggin. Why don't you and I practice your spelling words while you draw?" she asked. "Make hay while the sun shines. Let me see your list."

While Eliza chopped vegetables for stew, she called out letters to see if he could recognize the words: A-C-O-R-N. R-I-V-E-R. C-H-I-C-K-E-N.

"Hey," said Ross. "That last one's not on my list."

"See? You recognize your words already."

Chapter 13

One warm spring day Pierce announced, "For the next few weeks, I don't want any of you kids going barefoot outside, no matter how warm the weather is. It's rattlesnake season."

Edwin nodded. "Those critters'll bite you before you know what's what."

"Naw, I would run away very fast," said Ralph.

Eliza folded her arms. "Ralph, mind your father. Keep your shoes on until he tells you different."

Sadie looked puzzled. "I thought rattlesnakes gave a warning first by making a rattling sound."

"They might or they might not," said Pierce. "You can't count on it. They might forget." He paused. "Sometimes they lose their rattles and then they *can't* make any sound. This time of year, best not to walk through tall grass or weeds, and keep a sharp look-out wherever you go. Remember, snakes are about the same color as the brush and weeds around them.

"Yesterday I saw a big old rattler sneak into the corn crib, probably to hunt rats. In the pasture, the snakes go after prairie dogs. They have one big meal, and then don't eat for days. When they're hungry, though, they move lightning fast. And if they bite you, you're deader than a doornail."

The discussion about rattlesnakes made Eliza uneasy. Living on the open prairie was more dangerous than she had realized. She wasn't used to watching for snakes and wasn't sure she could kill one if she saw it. Around Lecompton, almost all the snakes she had seen were garter snakes.

One night Eliza woke with a start. Bang, bang! Someone was at the door. "Griffith! Wake up! Every man on his feet." Pierce and Eliza ran to the door. It was a neighbor.

"Fire at Hiram's place! The family got out, but the house is a goner. We're trying to save the barn. I'll send the wife and baby over to your house." Pierce lit a lantern, put pants and jacket on over his nightshirt, pulled on his boots, and ran outside.

"I'll make a pot of coffee," Eliza called after them into the darkness. She lit another lantern and got dressed. By the time Hiram's wife Bernice arrived with their baby, the kitchen was warm. The neighbor woman was wearing a coat over her nightgown. Bernice told her several times how they had just barely managed to escape. "We moved into that house only four months ago!" She began to shiver, and Eliza wrapped her in a blanket.

Nine-month-old Evaline jumped up and down in her mother's lap, enjoying the unusual excitement. Eliza could tell that Bernice needed time to recover from the shock, so she picked up baby Evaline. The baby protested at being held by a stranger, but Eliza distracted her by sprinkling drops of water on her little hand. She changed Evaline's diaper and put one of Irene's old dresses on her. Then she dandled the baby on her knee, swinging her arms and saying, "Bouncy, bouncy!"

When the children rose for breakfast, events were in full gear. Bernice, wrapped in a blanket, was eating scrambled eggs and biscuits, and five tired men in disheveled clothing stood around drinking coffee. Eliza was at the stove, holding the neighbor's sleeping baby.

"Darn, I missed all the fun," said Ross. The men laughed.

"You wouldn't have wanted to be there, boy," one man said.

"Could you carry a full bucket of water and run with it?" asked another man. Then he looked at the other fellows and twisted his cap in his hands. "The only thing I can figure is a rug or something must've got too close to the stove."

"Either that or the chimney was fouled," said Pierce, "as quickly as that fire spread."

"I hate living in the country," moaned Bernice. "I haven't been so scared in all my born days. We should just move into town with my parents. Hiram can still go out and farm if he wants to."

The men stared at the floor for a few minutes. "Well, I better be getting back to home," said one.

"Rotten luck, Hiram," said another. "A damn shame." They left, one by one, slapping Hiram on the shoulder as they headed for the door.

"Thanks all," he said. "You've done us a huge favor, saving the barn and the livestock. I don't know how I can ever repay you."

"Don't mention it," they mumbled as they shuffled out the door.

Pierce shook Hiram's hand. "Out here on the prairie," he said, "we stick together. If you decide to rebuild the house, just say the word, and we'll help you put up the frame."

One day a fat package arrived for Eliza from her sister Mate. "Sorry this is late for your birthday," the enclosed note read. "I saw these yard goods and thought it would make you a pretty summer dress." There were several yards of white fabric featuring a multicolor design of flowers and red ribbons. Maybe she could find a local dressmaker and have a dress made.

The children were practicing for the spelling bee. Ralph had memorized all his assigned words and reviewed them every few days. Sadie had learned additional words as well; she wanted to win. Ross studied his spelling list only if someone sat and worked with him.

Eliza decided that the next time Pierce went to town, she and the children should go along. She hadn't left the farm since she had arrived, and was feeling a bit stir-crazy. Although she was an employee, she wanted to go out and make some friends with women in the area.

After she turned over the goose eggs one morning, Eliza thought that this might be an excellent day to re-stuff the mattresses. She cleared and washed the table to get ready for that project. All at once, she heard an odd sound. She put down the dishcloth and listened. What was it? Hmm, nothing, apparently. She dried the table with a tea towel.

She heard the sound again, louder, an agitated rumbling. What on earth?

Looking out of the kitchen window, she saw a wild-eyed steer run by, shaking its head. She could hear the rest of the herd now, groaning and bellowing. Oh, no, the cattle were out, and Pierce and Edwin had gone to town. She would never be able to chase them back in by herself. She was even a little reluctant to go out into the farmyard. *For goodness sake, where are Nellie and Johnny?* She stepped outside and called them.

More steers ran through the yard, snorting and bawling. She grabbed up Reenie and ran outside to hunt for the other two children. Nellie and Johnny were squatting beside an anthill.

"Come inside, this minute," she said. "The cattle are out. It's not safe. They might step on you."

Nellie peered desperately in all directions. "Wait!" she yelled. "I have to find Champ. I want him to be safe too."

"We can hunt for Champ after bit," said Eliza, reaching for Nellie's hand. "Come on, kids! Into the house, right now. It's dangerous with the cattle running around like this. Let's go inside, and have some gingerbread." Nellie screamed angrily and began to run away.

"Nellie Jane! Where's my big girl?" Eliza lunged forward, grabbed Nellie's wrist, and pulled her toward the house, panting with the effort of doing that without dropping Reenie. Johnny glumly walked toward the house beside them.

Nellie tried to twist from her mother's grasp. "I have to save Champ! The cows might step on him. He's little, and they wouldn't see him. He could *die*!"

Once they were inside the house with the door shut, Eliza said, "Champ is probably safe and sitting in your fort."

From some distance away came the sound of barking and growling. "He's out there, and he's in danger!" moaned Nellie.

Eliza peered out of the window. She dared not leave the house, as the children would have followed her. Just then Pierce's team and wagon rattled into the yard and stopped in front of the house.

"What the hell's going on?" demanded Pierce, as he opened the door.

"I don't know. The cattle are running around like chickens with their heads cut off."

"First time they ever broke through a four-strand fence." He rushed outside, slamming the door behind him.

He was back in a few minutes. "Damn dog is fighting a rattler out in the corral," he said. "Got to get my gun."

"Don't hurt Champ!" screeched Nellie.

"Get that blasted kid away from me," snarled Pierce. "I got to load my gun."

"Let's go to the bedroom," said Eliza quickly. "Maybe then we can see what is going on." Nellie ran to the bedroom as fast as she could, and the others followed, their attention riveted on the drama at the corral. Eliza pulled up the sash, and they huddled together on the floor, looking out the window.

They could not see the dog anywhere. Cattle milled around the yard, vocal and jittery, as if they hardly knew which way to run.

"Champ, come back!" Nellie called as loud as she could, her voice tense and strained.

"Hush, child," said Eliza. "Champ is in a fight for his life, and he has to concentrate." Nellie's face turned pale. She threw herself on the rug, her shoulders heaving with quiet sobs.

After a few minutes, a gunshot rang out. They held their breaths. Nellie and Johnny began to cry. That frightened Reenie, and she started to cry as well.

Later the family gathered in the farmyard and Pierce explained what had happened. "After I shot the rattlesnake, by gum, that sucker wouldn't let go. Champ had the snake's head clamped in his jaws and kept shaking it." He grinned and shook his head.

"So I got a monkey wrench and clamped it tight around the head of the snake, then took my knife and hacked the head off. At that point the dog let loose, but he kept on growling at the motionless head and the twitching body." He shook his head. "That dog is smart, he knew that the fangs could bite even after the snake was dead."

"Can I have the skin?" asked Edwin. "I'd like to make a belt out of it. You can eat the meat also."

"Not me," said Pierce. "It's all yours. I *would* like to keep the rattles, though. That rattlesnake was darn big." The two men discussed different techniques that could be used to clean and stretch the snakeskin.

Then Pierce went over to Champ and examined his fur. "Eliza, I can't tell whether the dog was bit or not," he said. "Don't let the kids play with him for a couple of hours. If he doesn't seem sick by then, he probably didn't get bit. Douse him in soap and water though, in case he got some venom on his fur.

"But the first order of business is to get these dad-blamed cattle back in. Come on, Edwin." They saddled up and left.

Later, Edwin buried the snake's head in a deep hole behind the barn and poured ammonia on the spot so no animals would smell the meat and dig it up. The venom remained poisonous for a long time.

When the older children came home from school, the others told them the story of the rattlesnake and how Champ had saved the day. Eliza put a washtub out in the yard and filled it with warm, soapy water. The dog was asleep behind Nellie's favorite bush and inclined to stay there, but Eliza pulled him out.

When he realized what she had in mind, the dog tried to run away. She picked him up and half-dragged him, squirming, to the washtub, and with the older kids' help, she gave him a thorough bath. Champ emerged cleaner than he had been in some time, smelled better also.

"It was brave of him to attack the snake like that," said Eliza. "He probably kept it from getting close to the house."

"So now we know what kind of dog Champ is," said Nellie, beaming. "He's a protecting dog. A hero dog!"

"That's right, he's a hero dog. He's also an old dog and sleeps a lot. But when he sensed danger he was on the job, and he protected us." Eliza beat a raw egg into a cup of milk and put it in front of Champ. "Here's a special treat for you, boy. Good dog!" He lapped it up eagerly, sliding the cup along the floor as he ate.

It was almost time for supper. Earlier, Eliza had made a couple of pumpkin pies, which she now put into the oven. She set the irons on the stove so she could iron a few shirts while the stew was simmering. Sadie kept an eye on the supper, Ralph fed the pigs, Ross and Nellie gathered eggs and shooed the chickens in for the night, and Johnny took care of Reenie.

Pierce and Edwin did not get back to the house until dark. Besides chasing the cattle back into the pasture, they had to fix the break in the fence. When the men finally sat down to eat, Eliza thought that Pierce looked tired and worn. *At least these days he doesn't have to worry about the children,* she thought.

When the school held the spelling bee, both Pierce and Eliza were on hand to watch. The teacher called out the words, and each of the schoolchildren did their best to spell them. The winner was Sadie, who spelled L-I-C-E-N-S-E correctly after the runner-up, a sixth-grader, made a mistake. She received a peck of apples as her prize. Ralph came in third and got a certificate.

The last Saturday in April, Pierce took Eliza and all the children to Norton, the county seat. The plan was to go to the general store so Eliza could buy sewing patterns and notions, then the family would go to the baseball game.

"Can we get hot dogs, Dad?" asked Ross.

"You bet! They always have hot dogs at ball games."

Around ten o'clock that morning Pierce brought the wagon to the front door and gave a loud whistle. Eliza and the children donned jackets and hats and tumbled out of the house. Edwin stayed at the farm to do chores. The children sat on straw in the back of the wagon, and Eliza sat on the front seat with Reenie on her lap. The sun was hot, but there was a gentle breeze.

As they drove along, she watched Pierce in profile. His body was strong and masculine, his movements precise and efficient. *This family is in good hands.*

The general store, a long, narrow brick building with a large plate glass window, was packed to the ceiling with shelves of things to buy. It smelled like sawdust, coal, apples, onions, and peanut brittle. A couple of old men were playing checkers by the stove. When the family came in, the old men clapped Pierce on the shoulder and asked if he wanted to have a drop to drink at the saloon.

"Back in half an hour," Pierce said abruptly as he stepped out the door.

Eliza and the children stood by the wooden counter and looked around. The counter had a scale, a roll of brown wrapping paper, a ball of string, sacks, and a large cash register, plus a rectangular box filled with order pads for charge purchases. The rest of the room had shelves full of merchandise.

"I know it's fun to see everything," she said to the children. "Just look with your eyes and not with your hands. Sadie, could you take Reenie? If she gets fussy, bring her back to me."

By the time Eliza had chosen some dress and blouse patterns, Pierce reappeared and was chatting with the storekeeper's daughter while her father was in the back room unloading boxes and hammering wooden crates together.

Slap! "Stop it, Pierce! Behave yourself."

"Aw, I'm just teasing you."

Although she caught only a fleeting glimpse of what was going on between Pierce and the storekeeper's daughter, Eliza decided to finish up her shopping right away. She bought patterns, thread, buttons, a tin wind-up chicken, and a box of Tiddledy Winks. She always kept a few new toys in her trunk for rainy days. Then they all climbed into the wagon and drove to the baseball park.

At the hot dog stand a slate listed various foods for sale. Pierce announced, "I'll be damned if I'm going to stand and wait while each of you decides what your hearts desire. I'm buying a hot dog and a root beer for each of you."

"I hate root beer," said Nellie.

"Well, drink out of the dang water pump then." Pierce paid for the food and distributed it.

Eliza edged close to Pierce and held her hands behind her. "While you have your billfold open," she said quietly, "you could give me my $5 for last week. It's a few days late."

He sputtered. "Oh, you want money, do you?" He leaned back. "You're a money-grubber after all. Not so saintly as you make yourself out to be." He returned the billfold to his pocket. "In my opinion, you and I are about even by now."

"It's the wage you offered me for this job," she said matter-of-factly and held out her hand. Very slowly, Pierce removed his billfold again and put a dollar bill in her hand.

She waited. His mouth twisted into a smile. "Oh, you want more?" He gave her another dollar bill and started to put away his billfold. She continued to hold out her hand. *I hate to haggle, but fair's fair, right?*

Pierce grimaced and rubbed the back of his neck. "Eliza, be reasonable. I feed you and your kids and give you a place to live. And look, I'm treating you and the girls to a baseball game and the whole shebang. You can't keep on asking me for money. Pretty soon I won't have even a tail feather left!"

Eliza sighed.

"I need to talk to a guy over there," Pierce said, and walked away. Eliza pocketed the two bills. *I have to just let this go.* She got the children settled on wooden bleachers to eat their hot dogs.

The baseball game didn't start until one o'clock, so there was some time to kill. After the children had eaten, they wanted to play on the bleachers.

Eliza divided them into pairs. "Ralph, would you take Johnny? Nellie, you want to go around with Ross? Sadie, you can help with Reenie."

"I'm not going anywhere with Ross," protested Nellie. "He tries to peek up my skirt."

154

"Ross, you mustn't do that."

"Aw, heck, it's funny to watch her get mad! And it don't hurt nothing."

Eliza put her hands on her hips. "Well, stop tormenting Nellie. Be your best self. Why don't you stick with Ralph then, and Nellie, could you and Johnny go together? Stay with your buddies now, all of you."

The older boys ran up and down the bleachers, and Nellie and Johnny practiced walking backward. Reenie, demure in her little dress, squealed as she walked along the lowest tier of bleachers, holding onto Sadie's hand.

"I'm here if you need me," Eliza called after them.

The sun was hot, and Eliza wished she had brought a sunbonnet. What she wanted most, aside from a few calm minutes to herself, was to see what style of clothes women in this part of Kansas were wearing.

"Mama, Mama, help!" Nellie's voice was frightened. *What now?* Eliza heard Johnny screaming and ran over to check. Sadie and Reenie went over, too. Johnny had fallen between the bleachers and had got caught on one of the crossbars.

"Oh dear, let me see if I can boost you up." Eliza crawled under the bleachers through a narrow space covered with dirt and cobwebs. She pushed Johnny up until he was able to slip between the supports and crawl back onto a seat.

"There you go!" said Eliza. The boy started to calm down. " You aren't hurt, are you?"

"I'm okay."

"No harm is done then," she said, with a twinkle in her eye. "A little dirt is good for you."

Nellie made a wry face. "Ugh, that Johnny is a heap of trouble."

"Actually, he's a normal child of that age," said Eliza, stifling a laugh. "You got into lots of trouble yourself when you were four years old. Now you are older, and you think before you act. You did just right though, Nellie, by calling me when you needed help. Now, let's get all you kids gathered up. The game is about to start."

The baseball game lasted all afternoon. Pierce leaped up and caught one of the foul balls, and children were thrilled to learn that they could keep the errant baseball. As they walked back to their wagon to start for home, Pierce swung Johnny up onto his shoulders. The little boy crowed with pleasure, and Pierce and Eliza shared an amused glance.

Chapter 14

"Well, hello, Missy! What do you think you're doing out here in your nightgown this time of night?"

Eliza jumped. After getting ready for bed she had slipped back into the kitchen for a minute, and Pierce had come silently up behind her in a nightshirt and bare feet.

She blushed. "I had to punch down the sourdough for tomorrow's biscuits."

"You look pretty with your night braid," he said, coming closer.

"Well," she stammered. "See you tomorrow." She backed up and turned away.

"What's your hurry?" Pierce reached forward and slipped an arm around her waist, preventing her from leaving. "You've been working very hard lately, and I have too. How about we have some fun?"

"No! Let me go! I'm going to bed now." Eliza tried to twist out of his grasp.

"Relax, kitten. Come to me. I won't hurt you." He forced her to face him and held her fast with one hand. With the other hand, he massaged her back. "For Pete's sake, all I want is a little loving."

"Stop it! Let me go!" Her face clouded. "Have you been drinking?" His breath did not smell of alcohol.

"Come 'ere, beautiful dark eyes! It's been too damn long since I've had a woman, and isn't it around two years since you left Joe?" He stroked her cheek. "I can tell you want it."

Eliza put both hands against his chest and pushed. "No, leave me alone! I'm not a loose woman."

"Pshaw. A single woman, a single man, living in the same house? It's simple human nature. You wouldn't 've moved in with me, Eliza, if you hadn't thought that this might happen."

She shrank away from him.

His smile vanished. "Come, Eliza. I want you. Having an attractive woman parading in front of his eyes every day makes a man feel frisky."

She tried to resist, but he forced her into his bedroom. It was a small, plain room with a bed and a chest of drawers. A painting of hunting dogs hung on the wall. The room smelled of leather, hair pomade, and dirty socks.

She was no match for his strength. Pierce pushed her onto the bed, held her arms, and let himself down slowly on top of her, his body insistent. After the situation reached a certain point, Eliza realized that there was no point in struggling. She was loath to make noise and wake the children.

Afterward, he said, "That wasn't so bad, was it?"

She grabbed a pillow and pushed her face into it to muffle the sound of her sobs.

He caressed her back and spoke softly. "For chrissake, don't get upset. What we did doesn't hurt anybody. You're a beautiful and desirable woman. Having your full breasts and round hips in front of my eyes day after day, I couldn't help but want you.

"But if what we did is a problem for you, hell, pretend this never happened. Fine with me." He blew out a puff of air and turned onto his side, pulling the covers over his shoulder.

She fled from his room.

The next day Eliza hardly spoke to anyone. What to do. What to do. *If only I could talk the situation over with Mate, or one of my girlfriends back home.* Out here on the prairie, she had no women friends as yet.

Although she was so upset she could hardly breathe, she went through the motions of cooking, cleaning, and milking. She hoed in the garden with ferocity, muttering to herself. The children sensed something amiss and trailed along behind her. The men kept unnaturally quiet, sensing that she was angry.

If Nannie had not died, she would not be in this predicament. And if she were to get pregnant? As a single woman, that would be a disaster!

It felt impossibly awkward to continue living in Pierce's house, but how could she uproot her children again, six weeks after their big move and before the end of the school year? Nellie would never forgive her if they left Champ behind. If she took the girls back to Lecompton, could she find another well-paying job?

And it would be a shame for Nannie's boys to feel abandoned once again. Would Pierce make Ralph give up his dream of going to high school?

Things had been going so well. She had even appreciated Pierce more recently. She was starting to understand him. They could have gradually become fonder of each other and—who knows?—maybe eventually gotten married. But now he had spoiled everything!

Should she return to her parents and surrender her newly-gained independence to salvage her self-respect? Perhaps she could renegotiate her relationship with Pierce. She had a feeling that he wasn't truly dangerous or malicious. He was emotionally immature—careless with other people's lives.

She needed trees. As soon as the older children left for school she took Nellie, Johnny, and Irene down to the river. She got them busy building something with sticks and mud and leaves, then she walked a little ways away and threw her arms around a big Dutch elm tree. She pressed her forehead against its rough bark. Sunlight filtered through the thick branches. Tears ran silently down her face. Squirrels scrambled up and down the tree trunks and chittered among the branches.

A flock of geese flew high overhead, going north for the summer nesting season. She listened to the hoarse hark, hark sound as they called to each other.

That tree, stalwart and patient, had stood there for a hundred years. It and the others around it had seen generations come and go. Standing among those big trees comforted her. Gradually her breathing returned to normal.

Eliza decided to confront Pierce directly. Perhaps he would have a twinge of conscience and even apologize. She pondered for several days how to approach the topic, mentally rehearsing what words to use.

After a few days, she started to feel queasy and extra tired. Though she tried to mentally prepare to have a big talk with Pierce, she didn't feel like thinking; she just wanted to lie down and sleep. *Maybe I'm coming down with the flu.* No harm delaying the discussion for a few more days.

By the next week, her stomach upset had not gone away. When she had a few moments for herself, she put her face in her hands and moaned, trying not to panic. Then when her "days" didn't come on their regular schedule, she realized she had to take action.

As the men came in for supper that evening, Eliza took Pierce aside. Seeing the grim expression on her face, he tried to shove past her and into the house. Ignoring the belligerent jut of his jaw, she said, "You and I need to talk."

He scratched his armpits. "Pffft! Some other time, all right? I've had a hard day."

"Even so. After the children go to bed."

He blew his nose, walked into the kitchen, and sat down heavily.

Later that evening, when they were alone, Eliza came right to the point. "I don't believe I can keep on working here at your farm, Pierce. I think I'm in the family way, and *you* are the reason why."

His mouth twitched into a smile. "What do you know!" His eyes darted around the room. "Although it does create a predicament, doesn't it?"

Her eyes were hard. "It's possible I could find a job keeping house for another family around here. Although, once it's clear that I am going to have a baby, I'm afraid they might turn me out. I expect most people wouldn't want to have a fallen woman in their home."

"You're probably right about that," Pierce replied, squirming in his chair. "Also, we'd miss you. You are a good worker, and great with the boys. It wouldn't be the same around here if you left." He coughed. "But I agree, we can't leave things the way they are. I have my reputation to consider."

She looked at him, aghast. "What about *my* reputation? I could probably go live with one of my sisters. Mate would take us in, I'm sure."

Pierce sighed. "Blast it! Why don't you and I get hitched! Make it legit. That would solve the problem, wouldn't it?"

"And you think I'd *want* to marry you?" She spat out the words. "Why marry someone who doesn't treat me with respect?"

"Listen, Eliza. We could make a go of it." He leaned closer and spoke directly. Her heart beat faster. "If you're worried that I might act like your first husband, you can rest easy. I would never hit a woman."

He looked at her with a tender expression. "Listen, I need a wife, and my boys have taken a real shine to you. You need a husband to support you and your children. It's the perfect solution. What I had hoped for all along."

"What?" She looked away with a horrified expression and wrung her hands.

Pierce reached across the table toward her. "You're a fine woman, Eliza. I've been thinking for weeks of asking you to marry me."

She crossed her arms in front of her. "Well, that was sure a pig-headed way to declare your intentions!"

"Forgive me, Eliza. What happened between us the other night seemed very natural to me. You have to admit that in many ways you're already acting like a wife." He cleared his throat. "I know that's a poor excuse. I'm sorry for making such a mess of things."

She pouted her lips. "All I know is how to be a wife and mother."

"You're a fine woman and a good mother. Please, please stay. Will you consent to marry me?"

She gasped for air. "I don't know."

Pierce drummed his fingers on the table, then scooted his chair back a few inches. "For crying out loud, it's not that strange. Nannie and I got married when she was pregnant with Ralph, and my parents got married when my sister was on the way. Happens all the time."

Eliza looked daggers at him. "It may be common in your family, but it is *not* common in mine."

She took a deep breath. "I love your boys, and I am fond of you, or at least I *was* before now. If you treat me well, I might learn to love you. But I am not willing to marry you just for the sake of my reputation, or yours. It would have to be a genuine marriage. Otherwise, I'll take my girls and move back to eastern Kansas, come what may."

"Eliza, don't leave. I'll be good to you. Please stay and be my wife." He looked at her desperately, then stared at his feet. His brow glistened. She pressed her lips firmly together and breathed rapidly.

After some minutes, she said, "Well, give me a day or two to mull things over, then I will give you an answer."

I managed to deal with a maniac who had a screw loose, so surely I can handle a small-town bully. Besides, if she left and word got out about why she had gone, it's possible that no other housekeeper would be willing to work for Pierce either, and then the boys would be left alone much of the time or sent to an orphanage.

That night, she could not sleep. The moon was bright, her stomach was upset, and thoughts raced through her mind. She stood for a long while in her bedroom, watching the pure, innocent faces of her three daughters as they slept.

She crept to the boys' room and peeked in. Ross was a restless sleeper; he turned this way and that with snuffles and groans. On the other side of the bed, Ralph snored softly and had an arm around Johnny, who was cuddled up against him like a cherub. *How could I leave these poor motherless children?* They needed her to be a stabilizing presence in their lives.

Her parents would not be overly glad to see her back under these circumstances, she thought. They had grown older and were probably less able to tolerate a houseful of children. Also, her mother believed that female virtue was a woman's responsibility, regardless of the circumstances. She remembered back to how protected and loved she had felt when her father was near. Now, however, she had to fend for herself.

Perhaps true happiness was not in the cards for her. She had sometimes dared to dream of marrying a man who would love her and treat her well. On the other hand, perhaps it was her destiny to marry Pierce and take care of his children. Why not make the best of this situation, and accept responsibility for her life as it was, not as how she wished it to be? *Lord have mercy, Pierce is nothing but a moody, overgrown teenager!*

The next evening she told him, "All right, I will consent to marry you, on one condition. You seem to have an eye for anything in a skirt, and before long, my girls will be growing up. Promise me faithfully that you will never lay a hand on them, never bother them in a sexual way."

With a grim expression Eliza folded her arms. Her eyes drilled into his.

Pierce's relief was palpable. "I promise. Absolutely. I would never interfere with your girls. Oh Eliza, what a wonderful, warm-hearted, forgiving woman you are!" he said in a husky voice. "God knows, I don't deserve a gem like you." He reached across the table toward her. Gently evading an embrace, Eliza took his scarred and calloused hands in hers. He continued, "I will do my goddamn best to be a good husband to you."

She stared at their clasped hands. "You understand, it may take me some time to adjust. . . I wouldn't be surprised, though, if in time we can grow to love each other." *Pierce is a proud man, but if he treats me well, I don't mind playing second fiddle.*

"Do you want a wedding ring, Eliza? Or how about a nice gold necklace?"

"No need for that," she replied. "I'm not one for fuss and feathers. Your word is good enough for me. Just be kind to my children. However, it would be nice to have a buggy and a gentle horse so I can go places on my own."

"Whatever you want." He looked happier than she had ever seen him.

"And also. . ." She held her arms behind her. "We have to get married right away. People talk, and when a baby is born to a new couple, as you know, they always count the number of months since the wedding. I am a woman of virtue, and I shall endeavor to stay that way."

"We could go to the justice of the peace tomorrow if you want."

"Let's do that."

The next day Pierce and Eliza gathered all the children together and told them that they were going to get married. The children said "Yay!" and hugged them both at once. *I feel swept along by events beyond my control, but I believe everything will somehow work out for the best.*

The next morning Eliza wore her plum-colored skirt and a brooch and took extra time arranging her hair. Pierce rubbed soot on his good pair of shoes to hide the scuffs. They got a marriage license and were married by the Justice of the Peace. After the brief ceremony they had a wedding photograph taken, and the whole family had dinner at a café downtown. It gave Eliza an odd feeling to suddenly be his wife but, 'in for a penny, in for a pound,' as the saying went.

"We're a real family now," said Sadie, hugging her mother. Pierce smiled broadly, leaned over to Eliza, and kissed her lightly on the lips.

"I was so hoping that you and Dad would get married," said Ralph.

"Mama," said Johnny, leaning close to Eliza.

"Yes," she said, "I'm delighted to be your mama." She pulled him onto her lap and rested her cheek in his hair.

Ross was quiet at first. Then he said, "You're not my *real* mother, you know." He curled his lip and looked away.

"Of course not, honey. Nannie is your real mother, and you will never forget her. That's only right. But I hope you and I can love each other in a different sort of way."

"I don't have to do what you say unless I want to."

"Well, your father and I are married, and I'm not an employee anymore. I'm your stepmother."

"My evil stepmother."

Pierce spoke up. "Well if *you* aren't full of piss and vinegar! Treat her with respect, son, or I'll tan your hide!"

Eliza reached out to Ross. "I can understand how you might be worried, honey. But you and I are friends, aren't we?" She regarded him with a twinkle in her eye.

"Before you came, Dad was gone a lot, and we did whatever we wanted."

"I know, but please, let's do our best to get along."

Eliza wrote to her relatives to tell them the news. She was a little nervous about whether her parents and sisters would approve of her marrying Pierce, so she kept a close eye out each day for their reply. As time passed and no letters came, her heart sank. She began to resign herself to having a more distant relationship with her relatives.

Eliza puttied windows, scrubbed and sanded the scratched woodwork, papered the front room, and painted the porch. She planted iris along the south side of the house. Pierce burned the rickety old outhouse and built a new two-seater next to where the other one had stood.

Since she wasn't feeling well, Eliza tried to relax and take extra good care of herself. She stopped wearing her corset and gave it away. To soften the roughness of her hands, she made some cold cream from white wax, almond oil, and glycerin. She was extra gentle with the children to help them adjust to this significant change in their lives.

Late one afternoon Alexander, Elizabeth, Alpha, and Mate with her husband and baby, suddenly appeared at the Griffith farm. They had hired someone to drive them out to where Pierce and Eliza lived.

Eliza ran to meet them, exclaiming in surprise. "My word, I had no idea you were coming!" She burst into tears of joy.

"Land sakes, haven't seen you folks in a coon's age!" said Pierce. "Come right on in. Let me help you with your trunks."

"How've you been?" asked Alexander, shaking hands with him.

"Still above ground, far as I can tell!"

Elizabeth looked from Pierce to Eliza. "We had figured someone would meet us at the train station." She brushed dust from her clothes. "Didn't you get our letters?"

Eliza gave a tearful hug to each of her relatives. "No, I didn't get any letters, and I was afraid. . ."

"My dear," said her father, understanding. He patted her hand.

Later, when Eliza was making beds on the rug in the front room for the children, Ross said "Here!" and thrust several letters into her hand. Ralph glowered silently from the doorway.

"Thank you, Ross," said Eliza, seizing him by the wrist. She brought her face down to his and spoke quietly. "That was a cruel thing to do, hiding my letters. It caused me a lot of heartache." She let go of him then, and stood for a minute, holding her hand over her eyes, getting control of her feelings. *What sorrow that child must be going through to have done that.*

Chapter 15

"I am delighted to see you settled at last, sweetheart," said Elizabeth the next day. "You live far from the taint of that first marriage, and you have a trustworthy man who can support you and the girls. And at the same time, Nannie's children are well provided for. Everything worked out in the end."

Eliza swallowed hard. "Yes, I think, all in all, that it was good to come out here."

Alexander changed the subject. "Pierce's plans to enlarge the farm are very impressive." He steepled his fingers together. "As for me, I am getting ready to retire in a few years and am having a new house built in Lecompton, one that will be big enough for our whole family to come to visit."

"Splendid idea!" Eliza exclaimed.

She was grateful to have the other women's help with cooking and cleaning and taking care of the household. Her mother supervised the kitchen, and all of the Glenn sisters had a nice way with children.

At the beginning of her pregnancies, Eliza typically was sick to her stomach. The others could see that she was having difficulty keeping up, and were glad to help. Her sister Mate, to whom Eliza had confided the full details about her sudden marriage, was very sympathetic.

"You are very brave to marry Pierce after all that," Mate told her in private. "At least he doesn't drink! Not to speak of, I mean."

The relatives stayed for two weeks. As they were getting ready to return to Lecompton on the train, Mate offered to take Sadie and Nellie home with her for several months.

"Oh, boy!" cried the girls, jumping up and down.

"You'd miss a few weeks of school, Sadie," said Eliza.

Ross spoke up, "On the last day of school they have foot races, and prizes, and a picnic, and sometimes a watermelon feed. It's really fun. And then you get your report card and see if you passed."

"Going to Aunt Mate's would be more fun, I think," said Sadie. "I can't bear the thought of giving up an adventure. Anyway, I know I passed."

"Can I bring Champ?" asked Nellie.

"No, precious," said Mate. "They wouldn't allow dogs on the train."

"He would miss me."

"Well, cutie-pie, it's up to you," said Eliza. "You are welcome to go with Sadie to Aunt Mate's house, or you can stay here, whichever you want."

It was a hard decision for Nellie, but in the end, she said, "I want to go to Aunt Mate's house." Eliza nodded gratefully. Four children were plenty to take care of when she wasn't well, and she knew the older girls would have a good time at her sister's.

"Champ won't forget you," she assured Nellie. "When you come back, he'll be so tickled to see you he'll hardly know what to do. You girls be good and help Aunt Mate take care of little Earl. When our baby is born, I'll need you here to help me."

"Just don't have it till I get back," said Nellie.

"I won't."

A couple weeks later, Eliza alerted Irene and the boys that one of the goose eggs had a crack in it. Rushing into the kitchen, they could hear a gosling pecking its shell from the inside. In several hours, all the goslings had hatched. They went cheep, cheep and were fluffy and yellow, like baby chicks, but with much bigger feet.

Eliza kept the goslings in a box in the kitchen until they had learned to drink water and walk. Then she brought them outside for a little excursion. They nibbled at weeds and followed her around, chattering to each other and to her. Then she put them in the empty brooder house to stay safe until they were bigger. The chicks had meanwhile grown large enough to be in the chicken house.

When the goslings were several weeks old, Eliza thought that they were probably old enough to swim. When the goslings were put into the water tank, they swam around and around, paddling their feet and commenting noisily. They turned somersaults in the water, dove to the bottom, and popped up again like air bubbles. They chased each other on the surface of the water, flapping their wings.

"The oil on their feathers keeps them afloat," she told the children.

The next month was a busy time on the farm, with harvesting peas, cultivating beans, and dehorning calves. Eliza worked in the garden, with occasional help from Ralph and Ross. She stripped herbs and dried them. She bought a second-hand treadle sewing machine and made maternity smocks and baby clothes, as well as white flannel drawers and chemises for the girls.

The first week of July, all the wheat in the neighborhood turned at the same time. The nut-like scent of ripe grain filled the air. Pierce hired an enormous crew to gather in the harvest. Horses and mules pulled headers which cut off the heads of the grain and elevated them into a header barge, which hauled it to the stack. With a pitchfork, Edwin and some other men stacked it in a particular way so it would shed rain.

Later, other men came and pitched the wheat into a threshing machine run by an enormous steam engine. A team of horses pulled a water wagon hauling water to the engine. There was a long flat belt going from the engine to the separator, which extracted the grains. Eliza loved cooking for the big crowd of workers.

"The wheat is threshing well," said Pierce. "Probably 40 bushels to the acre, with low moisture. That golden grain pours out of the machine like honey." He smiled broadly.

Pierce sold many wagon-loads of grain at the elevator and scooped the rest into a storage compartment in the barn. Then he and Edwin gathered the wheat straw and stored it in the haymow. They had a bumper crop of new calves and shipped several carloads of steers to Chicago.

After harvest, things slowed down a bit. Eliza made a lot of jam and pies to preserve fruit that was plentiful this time of year, such as strawberries, peaches, and plums. One neighbor gave her a bucketful of gooseberries.

"This should be interesting," she said. "I never cooked gooseberries before. It must take a lot of sugar. Maybe a smidgen of nutmeg? And I wonder if sour cream would make it not so tart." No matter how she dolled it up, however, the boys would not eat gooseberry pie.

"Hurray! More for me!" said Pierce, which made the boys laugh.

After the first months of pregnancy had passed, Eliza felt wonderfully healthy. Irene was in bed by 7 p.m. The boys ran around outside, playing hide-and-seek and trying to catch lightning bugs. Eliza and Pierce would sit on the front step until twilight, talking and watching the stars come out in the vast sky, one by one. They listened to the frogs and the crickets and the coyotes. An owl hooted down by the river.

On Sunday afternoons, Eliza and Pierce strolled around the farmyard arm in arm, admiring the garden, surveying recent improvements on the farm and planning for the future. When he leaned over and nuzzled her neck, her cheeks became rosy, and she grinned at him like a mischievous elf.

Eliza began to relax. *He really loves me*, she thought. *We have weathered the storm.* Regardless of the hubbub of children around them, Eliza and Pierce could exchange a glance across the room, and each know what the other was thinking. Day by day their relationship intensified and deepened.

At night, when all the children were asleep, Eliza and Pierce forgot the world outside and made love with a passion she had never experienced before. Pleasure filled her whole body. Afterward, they lay breathless in each other's arms, smiling at one another in the golden light of the lantern, which was turned down low.

Eliza rolled onto one elbow. "You make me so happy, Pierce. It feels as if some inner part of myself is awakening. I was not unhappy before, but now I feel filled with joy. It is almost like I am becoming more and more myself."

Pierce fondled her breasts. "Just behave and do whatever I say, and we'll get along fine," he joked.

"You silly man!" she said, as they embraced again.

In the mornings, she lingered over the breakfast dishes. The stark shabbiness of the furniture was beautified by the sun's rays, and the dust in the air sparkled. *I love my life again.* She made sure to remember interesting things that happened during the day to tell Pierce when he came in. Life felt more vivid than before.

Pierce and Edwin reroofed the house and the barn and painted the outside of the house. Eliza deferred to Pierce on most things, but if there was something she felt strongly about, she went ahead with it in her quiet way. He was more patient with the boys and did not appear to resent the extra mouths he was now responsible for.

The sunflowers in the fields and ditches grew tall as corn, and the air was filled with milkweed fluff. Eliza sat on a chair in the yard and took part in games of pretend with Johnny and Irene. She showed them how to make a "buzz saw" by twisting a button in the middle of a long loop of string.

In September, Alpha brought Sadie and Nellie back on the train so they could start school. The girls had lots to tell their mother about their adventures at Mate's house. Nellie would go into first grade, and Sadie was in fourth.

"The whole family is together again," said Eliza, giving the girls a big hug.

Late in the fall, a group of neighbors gathered to shuck corn. The men competed to see who could keep one ear of corn in the air at all times. There was a big team of horses and Pierce installed high bump boards on the sides of the wagons to stop the ears from spilling out. Eliza served a big meal of fried chicken, potatoes and gravy, cole slaw, pickled beets and onions, with strawberries and cream for dessert.

Pierce and Edwin occasionally went down to the river and spent a couple of days felling cottonwood trees with the two-man saw and chopping them into smaller lengths for firewood.

Johnny and Irene liked to touch Eliza's expanding waistline, trying to feel the baby inside. Irene chattered on and on about all the things she would do to help with the baby.

"Can the baby hear us in there?" asked Johnny.

"Yes, I'm sure the baby listens to everything we say."

"Well then, you better read it baby storybooks."

On Christmas morning, Eliza made flannel pancakes, which were light and less filling, because they'd be having a big meal later. The children crawled out from under their quilts and comforters and came into the kitchen to get warm. Johnny and Irene sat on the oven door. They were about ready to go get dressed when the older kids reminded them that it was Christmas, and then they all dashed into the front room to see their presents.

Ralph got a pair of stilts that Pierce had made, Ross got a bow and arrows, Johnny got a wooden wagon. Sadie got a stack of books and a yo-yo, Nellie got a scooter, and Irene got a dollhouse.

"You can make tiny furniture for it out of cardboard or wood, if you like," Eliza told her. "Use flour and water for the glue. Let me know if you want help."

In the middle of the morning, the Thompsons and the Griffiths (except for John Griffith, who rarely came to events at Pierce's house) arrived with good things to eat for the big holiday dinner. Eliza was heavily pregnant but still energetic, and the house was spic and span.

"Eliza, you are a wonderful wife and mother!" said Gram. "I can hardly wait to see this new baby! It will be a blessing that brings the whole family together." She lifted her eyebrows and smiled kindly. "I must say, Pierce seems absolutely devoted."

"He's so good to me. I couldn't ask for more." She wiped her brow on her sleeve and reached for a shawl. "Just a minute, I have to go out to the cellar and get a jar of pickles."

"It's nippy out there," said Gram. "Let me do it for you."

"Oh, I don't mind. I like winter. I like to brace against the wind and feel how strong I am."

"But you're in your felt slippers, sweetheart, and you shouldn't lift that heavy door anyway. I insist."

Soon they all sat down to Christmas dinner, and even Binnie got into the holiday spirit and told a few stories about her childhood in Pennsylvania. She also explained to Eliza how to make the Griffith family version of chicken and dressing. "As the old saying goes," Binnie said with a laugh, "'Kissin' wears out, cookin' don't.'"

1901 (the next year)

Their baby girl came into the world on February 14, 1901. Eliza and Pierce named her Enid, after Pierce's ten-year-old niece, Laura's girl. To the new parents, having a baby born on Valentine's Day was a perfect symbol of their love for each other.

Pierce knelt beside the bed and caressed Enid's soft head. "What a beautiful baby, honey. Those dark eyes! She's you all over again. God, I'm a lucky man." Her eyes full of happy tears, Eliza clung to his arm.

The other children could not get enough of looking at baby Enid's bright eyes and her fleeting expressions. "She's so tiny!" They took turns holding her and seeing if she would grasp their finger. Ralph, in particular, was eager to help take care of her. He was willing to change diapers and to walk the floor with her when she cried. The Lecompton relatives sent little crocheted sweaters and baby blankets with lace edging.

When Pierce went to town, Eliza asked him to buy more heavy white cotton flannel for more diapers. He also brought home a wooden cradle with painted flowers.

"This," he said, running his hand across its smooth surface, "is one top-notch piece of furniture."

"It's lovely! But darling, isn't it awfully expensive for something we'll use only a few months? I don't mind using that one up in the attic."

"Dearest Eliza." He reached for her hand and kissed her palm. "The money is not important. You are the best doggone thing that ever happened to me." As she pulled him down for a kiss, she smelled the sweet, familiar smell of his hair. *My heart is overflowing with love.*

Pierce said, "Would you like a nice gold necklace, honey? I know women like jewelry."

"Listen, sweetheart, I have enough necklaces. My treasures are the children."

Her sister Alpha came to stay for a whole month, giving Eliza time to rest up and enjoy the new baby. Eliza napped when the baby slept, and she was able to bathe the baby leisurely in a dishpan on the kitchen table. It was lovely to experience once more the softness of babies and how it felt when they nestled against her skin.

In a few weeks, some churchwomen came to call. They admired the baby and said they hoped the family would soon start coming to church services.

"I've been wanting to do that," Eliza replied.

"Well, since you're a new member of the community, this would be a good time to get acquainted. We have a women's charity organization, the Dorcas Society, which meets weekly, and you are most welcome to join. We help families who have suffered misfortune or infirmity, and sometimes we also go into their homes to cook and clean. Then there's also the Willing Workers quilting club. Once a month the hostess provides materials to make a particular quilt pattern. Each of us sews one block, and that gives us a pattern to make that quilt later if we want to."

When the weather warmed up and the baby was somewhat older, Eliza occasionally attended Sunday services. She helped cook and serve at church dinners and fairs and visited other women in the neighborhood. Her new friends admired baby Enid's sweet face and exotic dark eyes. The other women also gave Eliza cuttings for various kinds of houseplants, and she grew them in clay pots on windowsills in the kitchen.

There were many families with children living nearby, so Johnny and Irene had lots of playmates. The older children were busy with school, chores, baseball, horseback riding, and fishing. They waded and swam in the river and pretended they were beavers building dams. The neighbors gave Eliza a couple of kittens and after that, the Griffiths always had a bunch of cats, and the farm's problems with rats and mice were a thing of the past.

Eliza had continued the tradition she had begun years ago of reading aloud one chapter of a book every night and, in addition, Sadie had gotten into the habit of telling stories to the younger children. She liked doing it and always had a willing audience. When Sadie couldn't think of a good topic, the other children would call out suggestions. "Tell a story about if chickens went to school!" "Tell a story about a train going to the mountains and getting stuck in the snow."

Life had fallen into place in a way not unlike what she had known as a girl in Lecompton. Eliza wrote to her parents that she was content. "People out here on the prairie basically live and let live, and I have found good friends. My mother-in-law is a real character! The other day she was holding Enid and said, 'Fat little rat, ain't she?'"

With things going so smoothly, Eliza and Pierce considered bringing Ruth back into the family. However, since the four-year-old was happy living with her grandparents and the Thompsons were still willing to keep her, Pierce decided not to change the arrangement. Ruth had a quiet, contemplative personality, and life in a more tranquil household probably suited her better.

"How about if I buy a rocking horse for Enid?" asked Pierce.

"Oh, I wouldn't think so," replied Eliza. "She'd outgrow it pretty fast. Besides, she's an even-tempered child. When she's a little older, I'll try her on my horse, Star."

That Christmas Elizabeth, Alexander, and Alpha traveled out to western Kansas by train. Ten-month-old Enid was handed from one set of adoring arms to another. During the relatives' visit, it rained for days, and the dirt roads became almost impassable. The women thought up games and activities to keep the children occupied. They molded holiday candles and baked dozens of cookies.

On Christmas Eve, Eliza read aloud *The Night Before Christmas,* and everyone went to bed early. The adults slept in the beds, and the children spread out on blankets in the front room.

Christmas Day dawned clear and cold. The ditches were strewn with crusty, dust-covered snow, and the roads were threaded with iron-hard ruts. Frost pictures covered the windowpanes. Eliza got up at five to put an enormous roast into the oven. She also lay each child's presents on a chair covered by a cloth with their name on it, along with small bags containing peanuts, jawbreakers, jellybeans, gumdrops, licorice, and corn candy.

When the children woke up, they exclaimed over their presents and played until Eliza chased them out to get dressed. By then, the grandparents were drinking their morning coffee. Everyone had a bowl of steaming oatmeal, along with bacon, toast, and tangerines.

Alexander presented the children with a wooden sled he had brought with him on the train. "It's a humdinger!" he told them. A tiny bell hung between the front part of the sled's cutters, and there was a painting of a dog on the seat. The children cheered.

He grinned happily. "Get dressed, and you can try it out. See if it works." The children rushed through breakfast and bundled up. Despite the lack of fresh snow, they found patches of ice to slide the sled on.

Later, they had a festive meal with a nice beef roast with all the trimmings. For dessert there was dried apricots, prunes, and dates, and they took turns cracking English walnuts. Baby Enid wore a red velvet dress with a lace collar.

"I think she is going to be dark complected like you and Nellie," remarked Elizabeth.

"She's my papoose," said Eliza, with a smile, supporting Enid so she could stand up. "My sweet little papoose. And as for temperament, I think she's more of a Glenn. The Glenns tend to be quiet, gentle people."

"That's true, they are, and my ancestors, the Zinns, are people of firm principle."

Chapter 16

The day after Christmas, the men and the two older boys went hunting, and Sadie and Nellie played on the rug with the younger children, making a miniature town with playthings from the toy box. the women set up quilting frames in the front room. Eliza was thankful for their help; she had pieced several quilt tops, but hadn't had time yet to finish them.

Eliza told her mother, "I am forever grateful that you and Father taught us the principles of good character. Now that I am caring for so many children myself, I can imagine what an enormous task that must have been for you."

"Why, thank you, Eliza Ann," said Elizabeth, looking up. "I appreciate you saying that. And I'm glad that you finally have yourself a real man." Alpha glanced apprehensively at her sister, but Eliza was unruffled.

Elizabeth sewed a few more stitches, and her eyes narrowed, "You and Joe were just playing house. It worked well enough during the easy years, then when hard times came, you didn't have a firm foundation." She wound thread around her needle to make a knot, then snipped off the surplus and poked the knot inside the quilt. Eliza listened with a deliberately bland expression. "Anyway, that's what I think!" her mother said with a flourish.

Eliza fumbled to find the right words. "Joe got frustrated and wound up."

Her mother replied with some asperity, "It shouldn't be a wife's job to calm a man down. A husband is like the leader of the pack. It's his job to be strong, and to protect and take care of his wife, who in turn bears his children." Eliza didn't argue. Her mother clearly believed in the old-fashioned-style marriage, which placed less emphasis on the friendship between a husband and wife. To be sure, Alexander had turned out to be a sterling husband who loved Elizabeth dearly.

"Pierce seems to be a steady man," said Eliza, "and we're never hard up for money. He treats me well, and sometimes he even helps me take care of the baby, nights."

Suddenly the door flew open. "It's Ralph!" Pierce called. "He's hurt!"

Eliza ran to the door, recalling the .22 rifle that ten-year-old Ralph had just gotten for Christmas. She saw Edwin and Alexander walking slowly toward the house, carrying Ralph between them. The scattering of hard-frozen snow crunched under their feet. The boy's face was chalky white and he was moaning softly.

Eliza seized Pierce's arm. "What happened?"

"He slipped on the damn ice and fell into a ravine. Landed hard on some rocks. His right arm is broken. It's really boogered up and hurts like the dickens. I got to get the doctor." Pierce ran to saddle a horse.

In a few minutes, Ralph was lying on the couch with pillows. Eliza brought him a cup of milky coffee and covered his wound with a clean dishtowel. A piece of bone had broken through the skin, but it didn't bleed much.

"I better bring in some ice," said Alexander, putting on a heavy jacket. "He's still in shock. Once that arm warms up here in the house, it might start to bleed. Also, it will hurt a lot more."

It was a long day for those at the Griffith farm. The sky was overcast, with snowflakes flying here and there, and by three o'clock it was dark enough to light a lamp. It was terribly cold. Wind scoured the bare earth. For a while, it was sleeting. Inside the little house, the adults took turns sitting with Ralph, who faded in and out of consciousness, panting and in a lot of pain.

Late in the afternoon, Pierce came back with the doctor, both of them on horseback, their faces and hands almost frostbitten in the frigid air. The doctor hadn't wanted to risk taking his buggy out with the fierce wind and the torn-up roads.

"Froze my tail off!" boomed the doctor, taking off his wool cap with ear flaps. "We even ran into some sleet. A norther's blowing in, for sure." He removed his coat, hat, and scarf. The smell of damp wool filled the air. Edwin jumped up to see to the horses.

"Everyone out but the men," ordered the doctor gruffly. "I don't want no one keeling over." From the kitchen, the others could hear Ralph screaming as the doctor set the bones in his arm. The other children cried, and the women tried to comfort them. Then Ralph was silent. The ordeal was over at last.

"He should sleep a good while," said the doctor, packing up his bag. "I've given him a shot of morphine, and I'll try to come again tomorrow. Part of the bone was shattered. I set it the best I could, but I expect it will never be quite as strong as it was before. He'll need to wear that sling for six weeks. At this point, frankly, all we can do is pray that infection don't set in."

Pierce, his face taut and gray, rubbed bag balm on his hands, which were cracked and sore from being out in the cold. Then he pulled a chair next to the couch and sat beside his oldest son. He looked grimly at Alexander. "Ralph—he don't look so good." Pierce's voice had a catch in it. He leaned his head on his hands. It was snowing harder now, and the wind whistled as it swept past the house.

Alexander stroked his mustache. "What would you say to a drop of whiskey, Pierce?" For the rest of the afternoon, the two men sat next to a bottle and kept an eye on Ralph as they discussed the progress of the new house Alexander was building.

There was a brief knock at the front door. Edwin slipped in and handed a pan to Eliza. "Here's the rabbits we got this morning, soaked in salt water and ready to go." She thanked him and picked up the skillet to start making the evening meal. Edwin went back to the barn to milk the cows.

That night Eliza woke, hearing a call of "Mama! Mama!" Her heart beat faster, and she ran into the front room.

"Oh, precious, your mama's up in heaven." She touched his forehead. It was warm.

"I wanted *you*," said Ralph. "*You* are the Mama now. I feel hot." His fine-textured hair was sticking to his forehead. Eliza got him a drink of water and bathed his face and neck with a cool cloth.

"Please," begged Ralph. "Don't go, Mama. Sit by me." Eliza brushed his hair back from his face and held his hand until he fell asleep. For the rest of the night, she sat beside him, listening to the tick of the clock, the howl of the wind, and the tiny creaks and clicks of their wood-frame house. Whenever Ralph stirred in his sleep, she rested her hand on his chest, a gesture which soothed him.

The following day his fever had risen, and she made him drink beef broth and eggnog. After a week, the doctor said Ralph was doing reasonably well.

"The wound is healing, and his color is better. He's young, and I believe he's thrown off the infection. You've been very, *very* fortunate."

At first, Ralph was quiet and undemanding, then as he began to feel better, he complained more. "Mama, my arm hurts." "Mama, I'm bored." "Mama, could I have a cloth for my forehead?"

"Time for you to get up and move around," declared Eliza. She and Alpha helped Ralph stand up and walk to the kitchen.

"I'm dizzy," he said.

"I expect you are," said Eliza. "High time for you to start walking around." She had him sit next to the cook stove with a long-handled fork so he could toast himself a slice of bread.

After a few days, Ralph was ordering the other children around, asking them to bring him the things he wanted. In truth, he only needed special help when getting dressed. By the time Alexander,

Elizabeth, and Alpha traveled back to Lecompton, the boy was well on the road to recovery.

The next Monday, Sadie and Ross walked the path to school by themselves. "Lucky dog!" said Ross. "He gets to do anything he wants, all day long." Ralph, however, wasn't having much fun. Eliza got him busy pasting things into a scrapbook. Of course, then the younger ones wanted to help, which made the project more like babysitting.

"Mama, bring me my arithmetic book," he asked one day. It seemed a long time since he'd worked on those problems. After a few minutes, he tossed the book down. "I can't do them anymore. Besides, writing with that hand makes my arm hurt."

Eliza sat beside him and considered the problem. "Tell you what, why not start back at the first page, and do the problems again? You'll probably be able to do them faster this time. Try to figure them out in your head instead of on paper, and just write down the answers. It's good discipline and will make your brain smarter."

He sighed and chewed his lower lip. "It's like in Robinson Crusoe. I have to look more upon the bright side of my condition, and less upon the dark side."

"That's right, honey."

Sadie and Ross brought home assignments for Ralph which the teacher had sent. That evening he did his homework, and Sadie wrote down his answers. During the day he worked on arithmetic, doing the problems mentally.

"It was hard at first," he said, "but I'm getting the hang of it."

After a couple of weeks, Ralph was feeling chipper enough go to school, though he was careful not to bump that arm. The injury healed well, although that arm gave him an occasional twinge. Other than heavy lifting, he could do most things.

Once in a while, Pierce would tease Ralph. "Let me feel your muscles," he would demand. "How are you going to pitch hay next summer with only one good arm?"

1902 (one year later)

It was Saturday, sale day at the county seat. Pierce and Edwin came back from town early, with groceries. They had heard that several people in town had come down with smallpox. Better to go right home and not contract that terrible illness. They could spend the day fixing fences.

"Where's my goddamn fencing pliers?" Pierce muttered as he pawed through the clutter on top of the sideboard. Edwin came back from the barn carrying the post-hole digger and a roll of barbed wire.

A few days later, Pierce was later than usual with the morning milking. "Edwin took sick in the night," he told Eliza. "His head hurts and he aches all over. He said it wasn't that bad and he could still work, but I told him to stay in his dad-gum bed. We got a baby in the house." During the day Edwin developed a fever.

"Let me take him his meals," said Eliza. "If it's smallpox, I won't catch it. I've already been exposed." She did take special precautions in order not to bring the illness back to other members of the family. She put on an old coat and slippers whenever she took care of him. Afterward, she left those clothes in a corner of the buggy shed, then washed up with a quarter cup of bleach in a bucket of water. On the third day of his fever, Edwin broke out with smallpox pustules.

Pierce worked shorter days and temporarily took over all the milking duties so that Eliza had time to care for Edwin. The hired man had an itchy rash for two weeks. As he got better, he became restless and anxious to return to work, but Pierce sent him broken harnesses to repair and did not allow him to leave the shed until all the scabs had fallen off. Fortunately, Edwin had had a mild case of the disease, and no one else in the household caught it. By the twenty-fourth day, the scabs were gone, and he had completely recovered.

Eliza was doing well with her project of geese-raising. She learned how to catch a goose if she wanted to, and how to grip a goose's neck to keep it from biting. Pierce and Edwin built a goose pen with woven wire held in place with stakes and weighted it down with big rocks so the geese couldn't push under the fence and escape. During the day, the geese were let out into the farmyard, eating seeds and insects and squabbling among themselves. The gander kept the flock together and chased anyone who came near, except for Eliza.

She ended up with quite a large flock of geese, and she would pluck the down off their bellies to make pillows and feather beds. One unexpected benefit of having geese was that, when they were out in the farmyard, they protected the chickens. No hawks, foxes, coyotes, or raccoons dared approach the farm when those big, noisy geese were close at hand.

Meanwhile, back in Lecompton, Alpha had gotten married, and Alexander and Elizabeth's new house in town had been completed. The older couple had some health problems and, even with hiring a housekeeper, they found that their big new house was too much for them to take care of. Jane, an unmarried daughter in her thirties, moved in with her parents to help manage the household.

1903 (one year later)

In September, Edwin got married and moved to another county. As a wedding present, they gave Edwin the horse he had ridden when he was there, along with its saddle and tack. Pierce, Eliza, and the whole family missed him, for he had been like one of the family.

Despite advertising for another hired hand, Pierce was unable to find a reliable person to replace Edwin. Since his sons weren't old enough yet to work as hard as men, Pierce shifted his main crops from grain to the less labor-intensive legumes.

Eliza and the children also shouldered a more significant share of the farm chores. Sometimes Eliza saddled her horse, Star, and helped Pierce herd cattle.

One morning Pierce asked Eliza if she could check on the windmill in the west pasture. A month ago they had transferred a bunch of steers over there for finishing, and he wanted to make sure water was flowing well into their tank. He explained how to check whether the machinery was in good repair. As it was Saturday, Sadie was home and could watch the younger children.

Eliza saddled Star and rode over to the west pasture. It was like a little vacation to go out riding by herself. She had come to love this piece of land which sloped down to the river: the fields of grain, the paths through the pastures, the low hills from which one could see for miles. At the edge of the horizon, the land looked a silvery blue.

As she approached the windmill, she slowed the horse to a walk. Her gaze swept over the land that lay before her, grasslands as far as the eye could see. The gray-green buffalo grass was thick, its roots extending deep in the fertile soil.

There was a fitful breeze, and the head of the windmill swayed back and forth with a rusty screech. The metallic clang of the pump shaft rang regularly as a heartbeat. The cattle ambled over a distant hill, coming to get water. They walked in single file along the narrow cow path, their heads bobbing up and down and their tails swishing back and forth.

Eliza dismounted and dropped the reins. Squinting in the bright sunlight, she climbed the metal ladder and examined the windmill's gears and locknuts. The mossy stock tank was full and running over, and the water gushing from the iron pipe was cold. All was well. She leaned down and drank water from her hand.

After supper Pierce leaned back his chair on two legs and stretched. "You're getting to be a darn good ranch hand, Eliza!" he said.

"I mostly try to keep up with you," she said with a smile, stroking his arm. "I like riding my horse and working with the cattle. Besides, I'd much rather do a job myself than ask one of the children to do work they are not old enough or strong enough to do."

That year, they bought new furniture for the front room: a black horsehair couch, chaise longue, easy chairs, and wall sconces with glass reflectors. "It's about time we made the house comfortable," Eliza said. They also got a bench with a mirror and hat hooks and a sturdy kitchen table with three extra leaves. Roller window shades were installed to keep out dust on windy days, and they bought a Franklin stove for the front room. Some of the ramshackle farm buildings were replaced as well.

"Let's plant a row of trees close to the house for a windbreak," Eliza proposed, "at least a few, to shelter the flowers. My poor roses are blown to pieces almost before I get a chance to see them bloom. It would feel homier if I could put a few cut flowers on the table." To her, the farm looked bare with so few trees. She had loved the big trees on her parents' farm, and the swing, and the cool shade on summer days.

The windbreak never materialized, but Eliza planted iris in front of the house. She put pink, blue, and white bachelor's buttons next to the clothesline and several rows of sweet peas on the south side of the house. Because the farm was located on a flat section of land somewhat higher than the surrounding area, they had a long, splendid view, although that also meant that the house bore the brunt of the wind.

They didn't have many fruit trees—too messy, Pierce insisted—so Eliza and the children made jam from ground cherries, wild plums, and crabapples that they picked along the river. What they didn't eat right away, she canned. She also put up many jars of pickles, which added variety to the canned vegetables they ate through the winter.

Ralph, Sadie, Ross, Nellie, John, and Irene roamed through the pastures and fished in the river, coming home with grimy hands and wind-blown hair. They were tanned during the summers and rosy-cheeked in the winters. Getting together with the neighbors, the family enjoyed ice skating parties and taffy pulls. The children picked wild berries in the thickets, had sword fights with dry cornstalks, and hunted for Indian arrowheads in freshly-plowed fields.

Eliza would ask, "What did you see on your wanderings today?"

When the six older children were in school, it didn't take Eliza long to get the house in good trim. If the weather was good, she saw no need to stay cooped up in the house and yard. She would pack up little Enid, and they would wend their way among the open fields and pastures, finding out which wildflowers were blooming and seeing how the trees looked different from the last time they saw them.

Sometimes, she and the baby went out early in the morning, when everything was silvered with dew. Enid was a real daughter of the prairie. She learned the names of the herbs and wildflowers. She learned to recognize the bob-white, bob-white call of the quail and the whistled melodies of meadowlarks, robins, and red-winged blackbirds.

As the boys got bigger, they took over much of the caring for horses and mules. They liked to shinny up the support posts of the barn and climb on the rafters. "You're going to fall and break your necks!" Eliza complained, but they just laughed.

Pierce said, "Let them do it. Better than them getting up to some other sort of deviltry. If they fall, they'll know what not to do next time."

During a thunderstorm, Pierce taught the children to count the number of seconds between the lightning flash and the thunder to figure out how close the strike was. The air always smelled wonderfully fresh after a storm.

On windy days, Russian thistles tumbled by, rolling across the pastures and fields, collecting in large numbers against the fences and filling the road ditches. On quiet summer nights, the whole family sat on the back porch for endless, leisurely conversations. Eliza loved to gaze at the stars floating up there in the dark like other worlds. The children caught lightning bugs and kept them in a jar until bedtime.

Once a week, Eliza took baby Enid and spent the day helping a friend who was a widow with four children, one of whom couldn't walk because of a fall from a horse. The woman was dependent on her elderly parents and an alcoholic brother-in-law for support. *There but for the grace of God go I.*

She and Pierce didn't plan to have more children. The farm was becoming more and more prosperous as they concentrated on raising livestock. Less heavy toil was required, and Pierce shifted naturally into the next stage of life, training the boys for farm work and seeking out leadership roles for himself in the community. *Our lives are complete*, Eliza thought. *Now if I can just avoid getting pregnant.*

Chapter 17

Regardless of how hot the summer day, Eliza usually had something bubbling on the stove—cabbage, tomatoes, pickles, or jam. She made sauerkraut in a washtub and root beer in a ten-gallon crock.

As Eliza worked in the kitchen, she could hear chickens talking in a conversational tone: pok, pok, aawk? Pok, pok. On warm days several of the chickens would sit on the step, right outside the front door, smoothing down their feathers and resting. They had to be shooed away when anyone went in or out. *Those silly hens! I don't know why they park themselves right in front of the screen door.*

At the county fair, the boys tried their luck at the shooting gallery, and once Ralph won a funny cone-shaped hat, which he wore for years. The boys practiced throwing knives at a target on the wall of the barn.

Irene enjoyed making the house prettier by putting around doilies and knickknacks. She experimented with different ways of doing her hair, like weaving a ribbon into her braids. Sadie helped Irene make paper dolls and furniture for her dollhouse with cutouts from the Sears catalog.

By this time the children had taken over the milking chores entirely, and each had their favorite cow. When they didn't have chores to do, the children roamed the countryside. They picked ripe cactus pods and cut them open; the inside tasted similar to green beans or asparagus. The children seined minnows from the river for bait and went fishing. They laid pennies on the railroad track to see what happened when the train ran over them. In winter they ice-skated on the river.

Eliza made laundry soap for the laundry from wood ash and lard. She boiled the mixture on the stove, and cut it into blocks when it began to harden. Then she spread the blocks of lye soap on newspaper in the cellar for four to six weeks to cure. For washing dishes, Eliza used washing soda and, if something needed scouring, she added some fine sand.

On long, peaceful walks, Eliza and Enid explored the pastures and the river banks. Every season had its own special beauty. Enid would sit by herself for a long time, playing with sticks and grass or watching the birds. If the toddler was absorbed in something, her mother took care not to interrupt.

The neighbor women told Eliza what the wild plants of the area were good for. There was devil's claw that caught in her stockings, good-smelling clover, soapweed (yucca), goldenrod, musk thistles, pigweed, and sunflowers in the ditches and draws, milkweed with its sticky sap and, early in the spring, for a few days only, wild violets that grew in the mud along the edge of the river.

1904 (one year later)

Early in 1904, Eliza became pregnant again, and this time her sisters were unable to come and help. Mate was busy with her three youngsters, and Alpha was herself pregnant.

Eliza struggled to lift a full pail of milk onto the table, a task that would have been no problem a few months earlier. *I'm too old for this*, she thought, pressing her palm into the small of her back.

The first several months of Eliza's pregnancy were a real slog. She simply had no energy, and it took its toll on her usual good humor. She kept meals going in a perfunctory way. She often served leftovers or hot graham mush (cracked-wheat porridge). The breakfast dishes did not get washed until the older girls came home from school. Sadie took care of Reenie and Enid whenever she could. *Has my body given out at age thirty-eight? Maybe Mother was right, a woman does require extra consideration.*

Her physical health improved later in the summer, but still she tired easily. She cooked more greens, ate liver and onions, and baked molasses cookies. Nothing helped.

The garden had only a few tomatoes and some vegetables that had come up volunteer. The children did not seem mature enough to

194

organize the garden by themselves. Sadie took over more of the housework. The essential tasks moved along well enough, but whenever Mama slowed down, the others in the family did too. Eliza had been an engine that kept everything rolling.

A couple of women from the Dorcas Society started dropping by once a month to help her clean house, bake, and catch up on the ironing. It bothered Eliza to accept their help, but she could not manage any other way.

Pierce lost weight and began to look gaunt and strained. *It wears on him, I know, when I am not well.* He would look at Eliza and run his fingers through his hair. He was impatient with the children, especially if they had sniffles or coughs. Once, Pierce stepped on a metal top left on the floor and got so mad, he tossed it through a window. When Nellie talked back to him, he would fling out a hand and slap her face without thinking.

"Don't treat the children like that, sweetheart," Eliza coaxed. "Talk with them."

"Confound it, kids shouldn't need to be told more than once. If I tell them to do something, they should mind."

Eliza sighed. "You can't force anyone to behave. All you can do is make it easy for them to be good."

Nellie told Eliza that she was scared of him. "He's so big," she said.

"He's more bark than bite, I think," her mother replied. "He just wants to be the biggest toad in the puddle. Sometimes people do and say things they don't really mean. Try not to provoke him, sweetie."

Sometimes Pierce would grab Sadie and say, "*You* aren't afraid of me, are you, big girl? Come on, give me a kiss!"

"No!"

Eliza observed this with a pained expression. "Pierce, stop it, please! Don't tease the girls like that. They don't like it, and you are setting a bad example for the boys."

Eliza sometimes caught sight of her husband sitting by himself, slumped in a chair. These days he seemed so distant. Pierce seemed to view her as too delicate to hold, as if their happiness could not last. She had a feeling he was remembering his first wife, who died during pregnancy. *It must have broken his heart to lose Nannie.*

She was aware that there was a lot of pressure on Pierce, supporting seven kids and a pregnant wife, with no hired man to share the work and talk to. He didn't have any close male friends, and the experiences of his youth had taught him to trust no one but himself.

Some days Eliza was compelled to stay in bed. She could not do any of outside chores now, and had occasional spells of feeling blue. Sometimes when she was achy and exhausted, she spoke sharply to the children and had to apologize later.

Pierce tried to cheer her up by bringing little surprises for her from town. Once he came home with a camera. "What a perfect gift, sweetheart," Eliza said. She sat on a chair in the yard and tried it out, taking a couple of pictures of the children playing. "In a couple of months, when I am feeling better, I will really enjoy this. Thank you."

No matter how tired she was, Eliza kept up the evening book reading. They read and reread the books in her trunk, such as *The Merry Adventures of Robin Hood* and *Little Lord Fauntleroy*. In the afternoons, Eliza played card games with the children, even if she had to do it lying in bed. As her body became larger and more cumbersome, she dragged herself around. Her eyes were sunken with fatigue.

The boys' sister Ruth occasionally came to visit. Being used to a quiet household, though, she found the boys too rowdy, especially Ross. Ruth played only with the girls.

When Eliza was brushing her hair one morning, Ross came into the bedroom and sat next to her. "I'm glad you're having another baby, Mama," he said. "Johnny had Reenie for his special baby, and Ralph plays with Enid and carries her around on his shoulders. I need a baby for me."

"Ross, honey, have you been feeling left out?" She touched his arm. It was true that he had not formed a special bond with any of the other children. Nellie, the one closest to him in age, was no playmate. Their personalities were like oil and water, and the two avoided doing anything together.

"Well, when the baby is born," Eliza told him, "I'll need your help for sure. Babies need a lot of care."

"I think it'll be a boy because then I could play with him all the time."

"Well, it might be a boy, or it might be a girl. Either way, I expect that you and this baby can be special friends." She smiled and patted his shoulder.

December was a month of cold rain, a month of scarves, sweaters, and long johns. The winter wind made the windows rattle. The landscape was empty, silent. Snow softened the sharp edges of buildings and trash heaps and dead vines in the garden. Colors dissolved into shades of gray, and on clear nights the stars looked very near.

Eliza loved to look out at the snow, especially on moonlit nights when she was unable to sleep. Coyotes yipped and bayed to other coyote bands a few miles away. To avoid drafts, Eliza put rags under the door and inside the window sills. The family slept under heavy wool comforters.

Eliza's water broke early on the morning of December 6, 1904. The weather was cold and windy, but no rain. Sadie and Nellie stayed home from school to take care of the younger children, and Pierce brought the midwife out to the farm.

After some hours, the midwife called Pierce into the bedroom. "It's not going well. Her pains are irregular and just wearing her out."

"Blast! Should I get the doctor, sweetheart?" He leaned over the bed and gripped her hands tightly.

"No, I believe things are all right. I didn't have no trouble with my other babies. It's just going slowly. Perhaps if I could manage to get up on Star and ride a bit, that might do the trick." She heaved herself to her feet, and everyone put on coats, hats, and scarves. With the help of Pierce, Nellie, and the midwife, Eliza climbed onto a stool and mounted her horse.

Nellie rode another horse and held Star's lead rein and kept the two horses ambling at an even pace. Pierce walked beside Eliza, one hand on the saddle. They made big circles around the farmyard, over and over. Clip, clop, clip, clop. Nellie kept looking back to check how her mother was faring.

After riding for an hour, Eliza's labor was better established, and she wanted to lie down. She almost fainted as she dismounted, but Pierce and Nellie held her upright. Although Eliza was determined to walk back to the house, in the end Pierce had to carry her the last part of the way into the bedroom. She lay down on their bed and began to sweat and pant.

Now her time was close at hand. Her face took on a mask-like quality as her body geared up for its supreme task. Pierce shooed the children out of the room and shut the door.

In the early evening, the lusty cry of a newborn came from the parents' bedroom. Eliza gave birth to a strong, healthy boy—Alexander Glenn Griffith, named after her father. She held the new baby in her arms and caressed him gently as he slept.

After the first couple of days, however, the baby bellowed night and day, wah, wah, wah. Eliza didn't have enough milk for him, and cow's milk gave him colic. For a couple of months they had to walk the floor with him continually. They rocked baby Glenn, they gave him warm baths, and nothing seemed to help. Finally, they bought goat's milk from a neighbor. Eliza slept only in snatches, and it was difficult also for Pierce, who couldn't stand noise or commotion.

For the two weeks of her lying-in Eliza left most domestic chores to Sadie and Nellie. It took her a surprisingly long time for her to recover her strength.

Eliza showed Ross how to burp the baby and change his diaper. But he handled baby Glenn awkwardly, and the baby often cried when Ross was holding him.

"There, there," Ross would say, trying to pat the baby's back the way Eliza had suggested, but Glenn continued to cry and flail his tiny fists in the air.

"He doesn't like me," said Ross.

"You're his big brother," Eliza told him. "Of course he likes you. Don't worry, babies cry a lot. It takes them a while to get adjusted to being in the world. The important thing is to hold Glenn in a way that he doesn't get scared. Support his little head and cover up his toes, so he doesn't get cold."

Irene helped care for the baby, too. Although Glenn's ears stuck out, he had a cute face, with soft brown eyes and a rosebud mouth. The baby was a pretty heavy load for an eight-year-old girl, but Irene liked to carry him around on her hip, and she was good at thinking up ways to amuse him.

Eliza was also teaching the older girls how to sew with the sewing machine. Irene was quite interested, as she liked to wear pretty clothes.

When the weather grew warm, the kids played baseball, fished, hunted, and swam in the river. If the boys were riding horses and Pierce wasn't around, they would try to get Captain to jump ditches. They tormented the birds with their slingshots. The younger kids would push the screen door open and then ride it back as the tight spring pulled it closed.

The boys liked to roughhouse with Pierce and with each other. Nellie would sometimes join in too; she was strong for her age, and she enjoyed wrestling. Sadie was willing to arm-wrestle, but only if she thought she could win. Irene had no interest in that sort of thing. If the kids' physical play got loud, though, Pierce would put a stop to it or send them outdoors.

1905 (one year later)

Pierce spent more time with Eliza and the children after Glenn was born, often remaining in the house for an hour after lunch. At first, Eliza thought it was because he was proud of having another son. Later, she decided maybe he stayed for the company, as he no longer had Edwin to talk with.

As Reenie walked by, he would reach out an arm and say, "Come 'ere, snickelfritz! I'm going to get you! I'm going to get you!" Reenie would laugh and speed up. It was a fun game, but Pierce kept it up too long, and after a while Reenie avoided him. He tried to play-box with mild-mannered Johnny, and he teased Nellie that she was getting fat.

One thing that Eliza appreciated was that Pierce would distract Enid when it was time to feed the new baby. He would scoop up Enid and give her lots of kisses. "Yum, yum!" he would say. "You're my sweetheart, my little valentine, and I'm going to eat you up." Enid would chuckle and relax on his lap. She didn't seem afraid when her father was gruff.

"Don't spoil her," Eliza would say with an indulgent smile. Enid had a knack for how to warn Pierce when he was getting too rough without irritating him. Instead of crying or trying to get away, she would let her body go limp as if she were accidentally slipping off his lap, and he would stop and be more gentle.

During these years Irene and Nellie had the chore of doing the dishes. At first they took turns, but that caused so much friction between the

200

two girls about whose turn it was that Eliza told them they had to do it together. That actually worked much better. Nellie liked to wash because she could do it without giving the task much thought, and Irene preferred to dry because she could stack the dishes neatly. It exasperated her when Nellie shoved them into the cupboard any which way.

As Glenn got older, he followed Ross around. "I'm teaching him things," said Ross. He taught the toddler how to spit at people and how to make rude noises. Irene showed him how to play with roly-polys (sowbugs).

A month before Christmas, Champ died. There had been a hard freeze during the night, and Nellie found him behind her bush, lifeless. She ran to the house in a flood of tears.

"I should have made him a bed inside the house, so he wouldn't have got cold."

"It wasn't your fault, honey-bunch," Eliza told her. "He's a dog, and his fur coat kept him warm. He was used to being outdoors. But he was old, and his body was worn out. What's most important is that Champ loved you, and you made the last years of his life very happy." The children had a funeral and buried him, using a rock as a gravestone.

With no dog to annoy them anymore, the geese ruled the farmyard. Eliza eventually had five or six goose houses where the goose hens would hatch their eggs. When a goose went to get something to eat, the gander would sit on the eggs to keep them warm.

The old gander patrolled the area all day. If he thought any of the children got too close to his flock, he would nip them or beat them with his wings, making a loud, low-pitched sound: a-honk. Sometimes, he would even chase Pierce.

The female geese, although similar in appearance to the gander, had a quicker and higher pitched hink-hink-hink call. Eliza could pet them and feed them by hand. The goose eggs brought in extra money, and

Eliza served roast goose each Thanksgiving and Christmas. Those drumsticks were really big.

"Gol darn it, when are things going to get back to normal around here?" Pierce asked one day, punching Eliza's shoulder affectionately. She knew what he was referring to. In addition to not keeping up with housecleaning as well as she used to, she had not had marital relations with him since Glenn was born.

"I don't know why, Pierce, but I am bone-weary. Run-down. I can't seem to get my energy back after having Glenn. Maybe I should spend a few weeks at the hot springs."

"Why don't you go visit your parents, honey? I know you been through the mill the last few months. Get rested up. Recover your strength." He lay back on the chaise longue and sighed.

Eliza nodded. "That's a great idea. Mother and Father are anxious to see our new baby, and these days they're not up to traveling. Maybe Alpha and Mate can come to Lecompton with their kids and stay at the same time. After all, my parents' new house has plenty of room. Wouldn't it be nice, Pierce, if our whole family could go?"

"Doggone it, Eliza, you know very well I can't leave the farm. Also, I need Ralph and Ross to stay here. But take Johnny with you. He's of little use unless a person works right with him to supervise."

"Okay, I'll take Sadie, Nellie, Johnny, Reenie, and the two young'uns. I hate to leave you without a cook, but I can't spare Sadie. She's indispensable to ride herd on the younger kids. Besides, she has been wanting to see her grandparents."

"Recover your strength, that's the main thing," said Pierce, giving her a quick squeeze. "However long it takes. For Pete's sake, stay two months if you want."

"Well, we won't stay more than a month, for sure. However, darling, I have to tell you something. You and I need to stop having relations. That is not something I want to say, and I wouldn't say it except that I think I have to. The truth of the matter is, Pierce, that my body is simply not up to bearing any more children. I'm sorry, honey, but we've got eight children here to raise, and I need to stay alive and healthy."

"What the hell?" His jaw clenched for a moment, then he looked at her with a roguish smile. "Men have their needs, you know."

"Sweetheart, I love you. It is just that. . . we cannot risk another pregnancy. I might not survive it." She shook her head and stared at her hands. "God has given us two beautiful children, and we should not ask Him for any more."

"Well, if that's a fact, then we have to come to terms with it," said Pierce. He struggled to his feet and took his wife into his arms. "I wouldn't want to lose you for the world." She swallowed hard.

"Dearest Eliza," he said. "You're a good, good woman. Better than I deserve." They shared a tender kiss.

Chapter 18

When Eliza returned from Lecompton, Pierce greeted her with a big hug. "By golly, it was lonesome here without you!" He grinned. "Welcome home!"

"I missed you too, honey," said Eliza. "And it feels like a new beginning." They got two small bedsteads for their bedroom and switched around some of the other beds. Johnny had a trundle bed, which he would share with Glenn when the baby got older. Sadie shared a big bed with Nellie and Enid. Irene, who was a restless sleeper, had a single bed of her own.

Glenn was toddling around by then, and the other children said he was cute as a bug. He spent a lot of time holding onto Eliza's skirt. "The runt of the litter," Pierce called him. When Glenn walked by, Pierce would give him an affectionate spank on his diapered bottom.

Eliza was somewhat apprehensive that Pierce would insist on having intimate relations with her, despite having agreed to stop. However, he appeared to be resigned to her decision. *Besides, I doubt he wants to raise eight children alone, and with that big a brood he wouldn't stand much chance of remarriage.*

"We're like a team of old horses," he said with a rueful smile. "We're used to working together, mile after mile."

1906 (one year later)

Pierce learned to make wine and dug a new cellar. After all, it wouldn't do for the family's jars of canned fruit and vegetables to be destroyed by an explosion of fermented juice. Eliza and the girls picked wild grapes, chokecherries, and sand plums along the creek, and Pierce experimented with making different kinds of wine. Like many farmers, he also made hooch.

Eliza was too economical to put much cream into ice cream, but the children loved it that way, because then they could eat as much as they wanted. "Ice cream isn't a dessert—it's a food," the boys would say. In early summer they liked to climb up in the cherry tree and eat cherries with their ice cream.

The family attended church and school events more often. Eliza's pies won blue ribbons at the county fair. They played cards with the neighbors and went to dances at the old opera house. Eliza developed close friendships with many women in the community.

The main difficulty in the Griffith family during these years was that Pierce and Nellie could not get along. The two of them seemed to lock horns every other day. Nellie was chubby, with a square chin, thin lips, and prominent eyebrows that slanted toward her nose. Just to be around her made Pierce irritable.

When he laughed at her and called her 'Calamity Jane,' Nellie's stomach would boil, and she would say something tactless and defiant.

"I'm just teasing!" Pierce would retort. "Don't have a conniption." But before long they were going at it hammer and tongs. Nellie was also getting into fights at school. She was grumpy on the playground and inattentive in class.

"Mama, Pierce keeps tormenting me. Everything I say or do just sets him off."

"I'll speak to him," said Eliza, "but you also need not to keep the pot boiling. It seems to me though that the two of you could use a complete break from each other for a while. I'll see if I can arrange something." Her first thought was to send her to the girls' favorite aunt. However, Mate was about to have another baby and was too busy.

During a visit to the Thompsons', Eliza quietly inquired whether they might be able to take Nellie into their home for several months along with Ruth, but they told her that one child was all they could manage at their age. So it ended up that her second oldest daughter went to live with Pierce's parents. Nellie was ten and old enough to help them with cooking and cleaning. It was farther for her to walk to school, though, and her strong personality did not mix well with the temperament of Pierce's mother Binnie.

By the time Nellie moved back home six months later, she had fallen behind in her schoolwork. She could not memorize multiplication tables. Eliza encouraged her, and Sadie tried to tutor her, but Nellie put her head in her hands and cried.

"I can't do anything right. No one understands me, no one cares how I feel, and everyone wants to get rid of me," she wailed. Eliza realized it was counterproductive to press the girl about her schoolwork.

Nellie did her chores dutifully, but she almost entirely stopped talking. She moped around with a sour expression and communicated mostly by nods and grunts. Eliza wasn't sure how to help her second oldest daughter. She bought her some new shoes, showed her how to knit and crochet, and allowed her to ride the bigger horses. Nothing cheered Nellie up for very long. She spent most of her time working in the vegetable garden.

"I'm sorry you're having a hard time, precious," said Eliza in a soft voice, squatting down beside her. "Sometimes I feel like not saying a word to anyone, either. But Nellie, whenever you feel like talking, I'm always willing to listen."

Irene offered to work together with her in the garden, but Nellie said she preferred to be alone. "Get a grip," Irene grumbled under her breath.

"For God's sake, I'll get her another damn dog," offered Pierce.

"Wait, let's not do that yet," replied Eliza. "Right now, she's preoccupied with Glenn, and they have a wonderful friendship. It's the only thing that brings her out of dark thoughts. She rescues Glenn when the big kids play too rough or tease, and she protects him from the geese."

Irene was in second grade, and very social. She wore two petticoats under her dresses and charmed everyone with her quick smile and enthusiasm. Although she had a good mind, she was more interested in Red Rover and Drop the Handkerchief than in arithmetic. She danced around with the relaxed, slightly furtive confidence of someone who knows she is pretty and wonders what one could do with this splendid gift. Eliza reminded her to be kind and to look at things also from the other person's point of view.

As to Irene's sweet and generous side, she made hand cream and glycerin soap for her mother and sisters in various herbal scents. She gave her mother a cake of lavender soap for her birthday, and Eliza kept it under her pillow.

Ralph and Sadie had started going to high school. Ralph had long legs, broad shoulders, and rugged facial features. He worked in the fields afternoons and weekends. Since he liked to build things, he fixed up a stall in the barn as a workshop.

"Good Lord, boy," said Pierce. "You're getting to be a beanpole."

Sometimes the older boys would carry one of the geese to the top of the windmill, to see it spread its wings and soar. The geese must have enjoyed it also, to put up with the rough jolts of being carried up a ladder.

Sadie, who had developed a womanly figure, read all the books she could get her hands on. When she was taking care of the little ones, she kept them amused by telling them stories. Sadie and Irene worked together to plan and take care of the flower beds. Nellie and Eliza did the vegetable garden.

Ross plugged away at school, but what he liked most was horses. John did fine in school, although the teacher said he daydreamed too much. When they walked to school, Reenie would chatter away to John while the older ones were silent, thinking their own thoughts. She talked a lot at home too.

"Yak, yak, yak," Pierce complained. "That kid never shuts up."

208

Nellie dropped out of school and experimented in the vegetable garden to see which varieties grew the best. She also spent a lot of time with the horses, particularly if one of them went lame or was getting ready to foal. She was fond of one little filly named Trixie, and Pierce showed her how to train her to ride. Enid and Glenn had a playhouse and made mud pies or played with the cats. One of the chickens, Henrietta, was tame enough that they could carry her around.

That summer, the heat was stifling. The sun-scorched earth was cracked and dry, the weeds brown-edged and drooping. The crops shriveled in the fields. The plowed furrows were bleached by the unremitting sun. Clouds of grasshoppers, arriving with a loud hum, gobbled weeds and brush in the ditches and then fed on what was left of the crops. Many of the songbirds disappeared. There were no orioles or meadowlarks to be seen, and only one pair of barn swallows had a nest in the eaves of the barn. Robins, sparrows, and red-winged blackbirds flew around sluggishly or sat silently in a bit of shade.

Determined to save what she could, Eliza let the chickens into the garden to keep the grasshoppers down. Only for an hour at a time, or else they would peck at the vegetables and scratch hollows under the plants to make a cool place to sit. When baby Glenn took his afternoon nap, Eliza herded the geese over next to the bean field. She didn't stay outside very long because grasshoppers would eat holes in people's clothes. When the men had to go out, they tied the bottom of their trousers tight around their boots so the insects would not bite their legs.

Eliza tried to look on the bright side of the disaster. "One good thing about this drought is that the chickens and geese are getting fat from eating so many insects," she said.

Pierce said, "As long as you keep water on the garden, we'll have vegetables. The field crops aren't worth a damn, but if we get rain soon, the buffalo grass in the pastures will recover quickly enough to save the cattle. At least I have most of my land in pasture now rather than in crops."

The family had a tomcat that persisted in killing kittens, which upset everyone. Pierce got so mad at it that once he tossed it through a window.

One day the boys caught a black snake. They wanted to keep it for a pet but Eliza said, "Not in the house!" So they tied the snake to the tomcat's tail and turned the cat loose. It scurried away but when it glanced back, the cat was horrified to see that the snake was still following. The cat walked faster, and the snake came faster as well. The cat walked even faster, but the snake, being tied on, of course kept bumping along behind it. The boys ran to see what happened, and Eliza watched from the kitchen window. The cat became frantic and started to run. Eventually, the string broke, and at last the cat was free of the snake. The whole family had a good laugh.

"Oh, those boys!" Eliza told Pierce later, smiling and frowning at the same time. He thought it was hilarious.

To a great extent, Eliza recovered her health. She went back to baking, entertaining, and gardening, although she gave up horseback riding.

She and Pierce liked to get together with neighbors for card games and dances. When they were the hosts, she would serve a meal, then everyone would roll up the rug, shove the furniture to the wall, and dance on the linoleum floor. Someone would play music on a squeezebox, mouth harp or fiddle, and the adults and children would dance in all combinations of partners.

Around this time, Pierce joined the Masons. "Lodges do a lot of charity work," he told Eliza, "and it's a good way to get know the bigwigs of this county. I'd like to run for County Commissioner sometime and if I join the Masons, I could probably count on their support in an election. Eastern Star is the related organization for women, and it might be good for you to join that."

Eliza did join Eastern Star, and she also became a member of the Rebekah lodge, which many of her women friends belonged to. It was a similar, quasi-religious community service organization. She also belonged to the Big Timber Club, a women's sewing club. Eliza had a talent for developing deep friendships with other women.

1907 (one year later)

On a hot day in June, Ralph and Ross were working in the fields. Pierce had gone to town, and the other children wanted to go swimming. Eliza and the older girls gathered up supplies for a picnic, and they walked down to the swimming hole.

Eliza threw rocks into the river to scare away snakes, and the children stripped down to their underwear. The older children waded into the murky water, feeling around in the muck and among the slime-covered roots to find crawdads. They chased tadpoles, salamanders, granddaddy longlegs and water striders. Farther out, where the water was cleaner, they could paddle their feet and actually swim.

Eliza found a shallow section in a bend of the river and settled down on a blanket under a big elm tree with Enid and Glenn, who began to dig in the soft river bank, saying they wanted to make a turtle house. The sun glinted through the leaves and birds twittered in the branches above them.

"No turtle is going to live in your old turtle house," scoffed Irene.

"We're going to make it anyway," said Enid. "*Baby* turtles could live in it." She and Glenn played in the mud for some time, then Eliza picked up Glenn and waded into the water. She washed most of the mud off him and wrapped him in a towel so he wouldn't get a chill. Enid washed her arms clean and ventured over to the deeper part of the river, about four feet deep, where the other children were noisily playing.

"Yoo-hoo, Sadie, Nellie, Enid's coming over," said Eliza.

"Okay!" replied Sadie.

"Can't catch me," called Irene, as she splashed over to the other bank.

"No fair," said Nellie. "You didn't give us a chance."

"Let's have a race," suggested Sadie. "I'll say one, two, three, go, and you can see who is the fastest."

"Okay," chorused John and Reenie. "The start can be here by this rock, okay?"

"One, two, three, go!" called Sadie, and the older children either dog-paddled or ran through the water, splashing and squealing. Their sleek heads bobbed up and down in the river. Then they had another race. Eventually, they drifted back to where Eliza was sitting and threw themselves on the ground.

"Mama, I'm hungry," said Reenie.

"Starving," agreed John.

"Where's Enid?" asked Eliza, her eyes searching.

Sadie looked around, alarmed. "I thought she was here with you. She didn't like all that splashing and went back."

Eliza leaped to her feet. "She's not here. We have to find her." Her mouth was set in a firm line.

Without discussion, Nellie took care of Glenn, and all the others ran to the swimming hole to search for Enid, who was nowhere to be seen. Eliza and Sadie called Enid's name, waded into the muddy water, and felt around the rocks and fallen branches.

Then Sadie said, "I think I see her!" A head of dark hair was half-submerged in the water. She rushed over and pulled Enid to the surface. The child hung limply in her arms. Eliza grabbed Enid, bent her over her knee, and pounded on her back. There was no response. She checked that her mouth was clear and then she shook her violently.

212

Enid made a small movement. Eliza tipped the child forward again and slapped her on the back. A rush of dirty water came from her mouth, and Enid let out a thin, high-pitched shriek.

"Cough it all out!" Eliza ordered. Enid coughed, cried, and vomited until at last her face reddened. Then she began to shiver.

"I have to get this poor child back to the house," said Eliza, almost in tears herself as she wrapped Enid in the blanket. Sadie and Nellie silently packed up the food and dirty towels. Eliza left them to it and, with some difficulty, she carried her youngest daughter back up the gradual incline to the house. In addition to carrying a whimpering, shaking six-year-old, her own dress was heavy with water and mud.

"You're going to be fine, Enid," Eliza kept saying, radiating a sense of calm. "You've had quite a scare, but you're going to be all right. We'll get you into some dry clothes, and you can have a nice nap."

When Pierce got home and was told what had happened, he was livid. "For chrissake, couldn't you watch her better than that? Three people old enough to be responsible, and you couldn't prevent this dreadful accident?" He slapped the table and pulled at his hair in despair.

During supper, Pierce held Enid on his lap. She didn't want anything to eat and, in truth, Eliza thought it was probably better that she didn't eat for the rest of the day. Enid clung to her father and pressed her face into his overalls. The other children were subdued.

"I'm so sorry," said Sadie.

"I'm sorry, too," said her mother. "We all are, and if we could do it over, we would pay more attention. Thank the Lord that this turned out as well as it did."

After a few days, life was more or less back to normal. However, Pierce continued to be irritable. He ridiculed Sadie about her pimples, teased Glenn about being a mama's boy, and was abrupt with Eliza.

"I don't blame you for Enid's accident," he said. "I know you're a darn good mother, and children can slip out of sight pretty fast. At least it wasn't worse."

Ralph was now a strapping boy of sixteen, and Pierce trusted him to harness the horses or mules and hook them to the plow, harrow, or cultivator by himself. When Ross did field work, Pierce checked up on him more often.

Pierce got frustrated because the boys never kept at the work long enough to suit him. He told the boys, "Keep your head down, your tail up, and keep headin' for the barn."

Irene liked to know everything that was going on and would tell Eliza or Pierce if any of the other children did something wrong. Despite Eliza's best efforts, the previous closeness that the children had had as a family seemed to be fading away.

1908 (one year later)

Back in eastern Kansas, Eliza's sister Jane married a widower who had a little girl, and they moved to another town fourteen miles from Lecompton, which left Eliza's parents with none of their children living with them. However, two years later Mate got a divorce and, along with her five children, she moved back in with Alexander and Elizabeth.

Chapter 19

1909 (one year later)

The two older boys were almost grown, and Pierce was eager for summer, for then Ralph would graduate from high school and be able to work on the farm full-time. Ross had dropped out of high school after one year, as school did not interest him. Currently, he and Pierce did most of the field work, albeit with frequent disagreements.

Nellie, on the other hand, decided to go back to school. "I'm not dumb, like some of you seem to think," she said with a sour expression. Over the next year, by working hard and skipping some grades, she caught up her lessons and entered high school with students of her own age.

Pierce and the older boys hunted deer, pheasants, and ducks, depending on the season. It took a lot of food to feed a bunch of teenagers, and the whole family loved Eliza's venison stew.

Ross got up in the wee hours of the morning to check his traps. He caught muskrats and skunks along the creek and, once in a while, a mink, which was quite valuable. He skinned the animals and sold the pelts for several dollars each to a dealer who came through the county once a month.

One day, Pierce came back from town with a black and white puppy. "I've been needing a cattle dog for some time, and this one comes from a litter that is supposed to be good herd dogs. You can play with him, but in a few weeks, I'll take him out with me and begin his training." The children named the dog Shep.

When spring arrived, Nellie planted a lot of vegetables, and Enid was eager to help her in the garden. They made a companionable team. Enid was quiet, and she liked to hoe and weed.

Nellie didn't wear shoes when she gardened. "Saves all that work cleaning them." She preferred to do anything outdoors rather than stay in the house and clean or cook. Nellie was quite proud of how much food she contributed to the family by her gardening.

At the end of May, Ralph and Sadie graduated from high school, and Pierce and Eliza were very proud of them. The whole family attended the graduation ceremony, and Ralph and Sadie had their photographs taken.

"Now don't get swelled heads and think you are smarter than the rest of us," said Pierce.

"You have a good education now," Eliza told them, "and your whole lives are in front of you. You can do anything you decide to do."

"Don't say that," said Pierce, scowling. "It's hogwash. Sets 'em up for disappointment."

Irene was busy going to parties and asking people to sign her autograph book. It was her job that year to get the family's flower garden back in shape after the winter, and she worked very hard at it. In summer, when the flowers bloomed, the pink ones spelled out Eliza's name.

"What a lovely gift, honey!" said Eliza. "So creative."

Eliza and Sadie canned so much that summer that they had to enlarge the cellar to hold all the jars. John, Irene, and Enid found grapevines along the creek and kept an eye on when the wild grapes would be ripe. Irene made herself a shirtwaist dress with pintucks in the bodice. The older girls too sewed clothes for themselves, including fitted brassieres.

Glenn mostly kept out of people's way. He didn't like conflict, and he especially didn't want to be bullied by Pierce. He played with Enid and with the cats. John taught him how to play poker. Glenn borrowed Ross's art supplies and made drawings of motorcycles and Model T's. Ralph carried Glenn on his shoulders when they went down to the creek or on long walks.

Pierce now had 80 acres in alfalfa, 20 acres in beans, and 300 acres in pasture. Smallpox had popped up again in the community, and for some weeks the family stayed home from community events for a while to avoid being exposed.

One night in bed, after Enid and Irene had fallen asleep, the older girls were whispering, their heads close together. Sadie confided to Nellie, "Pierce keeps touching me. I told him to stop it, but he just laughed."

Nellie replied, "He's bothered me too. He touched my breast once, 'accidentally.' He says I have a womanly figure. Tee-hee. What a miserable old geezer! We should probably tell Mama what he's doing."

Sadie shook her head. "No, don't tell her. She'd get really upset. Just avoid him."

"Well, I think it's disgusting how he tries to get in a sly touch now and then. We have to make sure to stay out of his reach."

One day near the end of June, when the family had just finished dinner, Eliza stopped and stared out the kitchen window. "I don't like the looks of that sky, Pierce," she said. He went out immediately to look at the clouds.

"Something's stirring for sure," he said. "The swallows are flying low, and there's an odd tang in the air." Over the next half an hour the sky filled with dark thunderheads. The sky took on a yellow cast, and a funnel cloud was visible on the horizon. Pierce and Eliza hastily gathered the children, called for Shep to come, grabbed blankets and a lantern, and they went down into the cellar. Just after Pierce, with some difficulty, pulled the heavy cellar door shut, a downpour began.

For about an hour the family sat on blankets on the floor of the cellar, listening to the increasing volume of the wind and rain. "Tornadoes cause a lot of damage," said Pierce, "but usually just in a narrow swath. Impossible to tell whether they'll destroy the farm or skate right by."

Hail hammered in waves on the cellar door, so loudly at times that it was impossible to talk. Then, all at once, they heard an ominous train-like rumble. Irene screamed, Enid whimpered, and Glenn started to cry.

"Now *that's* a tornado," said Pierce. "Sounds like it's pretty close. I hope to hell the suction doesn't pull off the cellar door. I should figure out a way to bar it shut from down here." He looked desperately around the room. There was nothing firmly attached that a person could hold onto. If the cellar door gave way, they would be in grave danger. They heard things being tossed and banged around in the yard.

"There goes the wagon shed," said Pierce.

After a few minutes, it was hailing again. The wind moaned.

"Wow!" said Irene. "Wait till I tell the other kids at school that a tornado went right over our heads. This is exciting!"

After another crunching sound, Pierce said, "There goes the toilet, I bet." The boys laughed. "The wagons will be reduced to kindling. . . to say nothing of what will happen to the livestock." His face was grave.

An hour later the wind let up abruptly, and the rain had almost stopped. Pierce lifted the cellar door cautiously, then opened it up wide, and the family climbed out. The barnyard smelled like a freshly-mown lawn.

There was an eerie calm—no animal noises, no bird song, no insects. The sky, slowly clearing of clouds, seemed wider, stretching from horizon to horizon. The house and barn were wet and glistening. The farmyard was littered with twigs and boards. Weeds had been pounded to stubble, bushes stripped of leaves, and crops pounded into the ground. Pierce rubbed both hands over his face and shook his head in disbelief.

Over the next several days the extent of the damage from the storm became apparent. Seven tornadoes had touched down in Norton County that afternoon. All the Rural Telephone lines were down, and many houses had been destroyed. Dozens of cattle had been picked up in the air and hurled to the ground or injured by hail.

At Pierce's farm, the house and barn were intact, though their roofs were damaged and their windows shattered. Three steers that had been almost ready to sell had been killed by flying debris, but otherwise the cattle, mules, and horses were all right. The horses and mules had been safe in the barn, and the cattle had huddled together.

"Come on, boys, we got to save what there is to save," said Pierce. Ralph, Ross, and John were tall and broad as men now and, together with their father, they dragged the carcasses of the dead steers to the farmyard and worked through the night, using debris from broken wagons and sheds to build a smokehouse. Usually, a butcher was hired to come out when they slaughtered beef, but with so many local people in the same predicament, the family was obliged to do the butchering themselves.

The next day, Pierce had a stitch in his back and, while waiting for supper, he lay on the couch and fell into a deep sleep. Enid saw him lying there, got out his straight-edge razor, and shaved off half of his mustache. Later, when he woke up and hobbled stiffly to the table, the others burst into laughter.

"What the heck? I was just taking forty winks."

"It was me! I did it." Enid chortled and danced around to the other side of the table. Pierce hurried to look at himself in a mirror.

"You little monster!" he said and pretended to chase her. If it had been any of the other kids, he would have been furious. Since it was Enid, he just shaved off the other half of his mustache, saying, "Maybe I look better clean-shaven anyway."

In November, Pierce was awarded the Shriner degree of the Masons. He got along well with his lodge brothers and began taking on leadership positions in the group.

Nellie was becoming increasingly heavy-set. She didn't eat an unusual amount at mealtime, but she often went to the kitchen for snacks. If Eliza inquired, Nellie would merely say, "I was hungry." *Perhaps her stomach is bothering her again.*

Sadie, on the other hand, seemed to have lost her appetite. "Nothing tastes good," she said. She looked pale and exhausted, and spent a lot of time sprawled on the bed, reading. The younger children could not persuade her to tell them stories.

One morning when Eliza was alone with Sadie in the kitchen, she asked, "Tell me, honey, is something wrong?"

"Mama, I'm scared I'm pregnant." Sadie began to sob.

Eliza inhaled sharply. She put an arm around her shoulders and bent down to look directly into her face. "Oh, sweetheart. Dear me. Well, it's not the end of the world. With so many children around the house, what's one more?" She stroked Sadie's arm.

"Who's the boyfriend, honey? I didn't know you were seeing someone."

Sadie cried so hard she got the hiccups.

Eliza folded her oldest daughter in a warm embrace. "Baby, baby. Don't cry. We'll get through this together."

Sadie fidgeted for a few minutes until she was able to speak. "Mama, it's not my fault! I tried to get away." Her face was flushed, and her voice rose to a hysterical pitch.

"What? Who?"

"Well, this is embarrassing to talk about, but I was in the pasture, bringing the cows in for milking, and Pierce came out and chased me. He grabbed me and was kissing me. I screamed and ran away, but he caught me and threw me on the ground and attacked me. It was horrible!" She began to cry again.

Eliza gazed out the window, her face contorted. She held her weeping daughter and caressed her hair. "Pierce, Pierce, how could you?" she whispered. Her chest felt constricted as if her breath were being pressed out of her. *Did I make a terrible mistake after all by marrying Pierce? Have I been so distracted by the daily tasks that I didn't make sure the girls were protected?*

Eliza was sick at heart. It was almost as if the love and affection that had bound her and Pierce together was dissolving. *What to do? There is no way I can go away with the girls and leave the boys behind. Besides, I have deep roots in this community now. This is my home, and where I belong.*

That evening, she went out in the yard to meet Pierce, Ralph, and Ross when they came in for supper. "Go on in, boys," she said. "I need to talk to your father."

As soon as they were alone, she said, "Pierce, you should be ashamed of yourself!"

"What the hell you jabbering about, woman?" He stepped back and took a wide-legged, aggressive stance.

Eliza wrung her hands and turned her face away as if it were painful to look at him. "Sadie is pregnant. She says you raped her."

Pierce shuffled his feet like a scolded schoolboy. "Well, blast! Got one in the oven, does she?"

Eliza looked aghast at him, and her mouth hardened. "Pierce! When we got married, you promised me solemnly that you would never bother my girls."

"I'm a red-blooded man. It's damn hard to ignore all these shapely young women running around the house. I didn't mean to do it. It just sort of happened. Sorry!"

"You gave me your word!" she shrieked. Dark blotches appeared on Eliza's cheeks. She wrapped her hands in the ends of her shawl and held them tight around her body.

He raised his palms. "Forgive me, Eliza. I'm sorry."

"For God's sake, how can I forgive something like this?"

"I know it was a dang fool thing to do."

"You raped my child!"

"Well, you forgave me before."

Pierce lifted his chin. "Well, I forgave *you* when you almost let Enid drown." He leaned forward belligerently.

Eliza recoiled. "This is completely different." She turned and rushed into the house.

She had always pictured herself to be like Martha in the Bible, staying in the background and quietly caring for her family, but now, disasters seemed to be happening one after the other, and she was beginning to feel like Job. What more could go wrong?

That night, getting ready for bed, Eliza spoke to her husband again, making an effort to control her rage.

"How can I ever trust you again, Pierce, after what you've done?"

"I *said* I was sorry. Maybe I'm over-sexed." He gave her a sheepish grin. "Anyway, she didn't resist that much."

"She's a vulnerable female child, and you are a liar! She said she tried and tried to run away. And even if she hadn't fought back, you wouldn't be off the hook. Where is your *conscience*? For some years now I have thought of you as a good man. Was I mistaken?"

"Look, Eliza, I used poor judgment, okay? I admit it. And she was getting too big for her britches. Seeing her flounce around the house every day like she owned the place, well. . . Besides, she's got a curvy, seductive figure. I couldn't help myself."

"Pierce, Pierce, Pierce!" Eliza slumped against the headboard and spoke in a monotone. "Can we not keep our children safe in their own home? The worst thing I could have imagined has come true." She closed her hands into fists so tightly that the fingernails dug into her skin. "What kind of man are you, to be so cruel?"

He abruptly came over and knelt beside her bed. "Please forgive me, Eliza. But let me explain something. The fact of the matter is, I am illegitimate. A bastard. Not my father's child. He treated Charlie like a real son, and just tolerated me, so I never felt like I got as much love as I deserved. That's the honest-to-God truth. Maybe that's why I did it." He pressed his face into the blankets, and his shoulders shook with sobs.

Eliza caressed his head and replied slowly. "I'm very sad that your father never accepted you. Children are a gift from God, however they are conceived. You got the short end of the stick, it's true, but you have nothing to be ashamed of. The sin was your mother's, not yours. And be that as it may, painful experiences in the past are no excuse for harming other people."

"I don't know what comes over me sometimes. Maybe I have a screw loose. Maybe someone put a curse on me."

"Well, I have heartaches too, but I strive to be a person of integrity, regardless. And anyway, sex is not the same thing as love."

"Let me buy you a nice necklace to show how sorry I am."

Eliza gasped and pushed him away from her bed. "No, no, a thousand times no! My girls are not for sale. Get out of my sight! I have to concentrate on helping Sadie." Her eyes were blazing. "And stop bothering the girls! Don't touch any of them, ever, ever again."

"I won't, I swear," he said in a small voice, alarmed at the hardness in her eyes.

She turned her face away from him and spoke quietly. "I may still love you but I am completely out of patience with your antics. If you ever do anything else of the kind, you will face your sins publicly."

He turned pale but did not reply. He got to his feet, turned out the lantern, and climbed into his own bed. The two of them lay awake in the dark for a long time, without speaking.

Eliza and Pierce did not discuss the situation with their other children, but Nellie knew what was going on, and Irene soon found out as well. The youngest children simply were aware of a sudden chill that had come over the family, and they kept their heads down.

All the girls worked in the garden, but Nellie stayed there for hours, reproaching herself for keeping Sadie's confidences and not telling their mother. Perhaps this tragedy could have been prevented if their mother had known what was going on.

Eliza was sick at heart. *What should I do? I can't support eight children by myself. Is this God's punishment because I didn't leave Pierce in the beginning?*

Ralph tried to lighten the atmosphere by making Enid a jump rope out of twine and teaching Irene and John how to saddle and ride the horses. Ross showed Glenn how to make traps for prairie dogs and squirrels. Although Glenn didn't catch many animals, he enjoyed it, and it kept him occupied for hours.

When Eliza and Sadie were canning tomatoes, Sadie confronted her mother. "How is it that you pick such bad men for husbands? Of all the men in the world, you seem to choose ones with something wrong with them. Surely, most men aren't mean."

"Yes, darling, lots of men are good. The men in my family were perfect gentlemen.

"What happened to you was inexcusable. But I can't just close the door and leave. How can I abandon children who call me Mama?"

"Well, this horrible thing happened to me because of Pierce. Did you have any idea he would do something like this?"

"Well, as a matter of fact, the reason I married him originally was that he forced himself on me and I got pregnant."

"And you married him after that? That's ridiculous! If you're mistreated, you should leave. After all, you left our father."

Eliza took off her apron and sat down. Tears rolled down her face. "I'm so sorry, precious, and I don't blame you for being angry. I thought I had protected you. When I married Pierce, he promised me solemnly that he would never touch you girls."

"And you fell for that?"

"The choice I made at the time seemed to make sense, but maybe you're right, and I shouldn't have stayed." Her heart was pounding in her chest. "When you make a decision about something complicated, you never know for sure how it will turn out. And it's impossible to live in the world without trusting the people around you.

"Men are a different kind of creature. They are hunters and protectors, and some of them never find the right balance between being a hunter and being a protector. It depends on their character.

"You have probably noticed that it's women who hold a family together. They bring forth life, and day after day they keep watch over everyone, trying to make sure the others have what they need. Women are like gardeners, they plant seeds and keep them watered, and hoe the weeds as best they can."

"I don't care!" Sadie exploded. "You ought to stab him in his sleep!"

"Oh, sweetheart, that would make things even worse. There's little I can do at this point. God will judge him."

She continued in a softer tone of voice. "You cannot always outrun evil. Bad things can happen anywhere. Each person has crises that test their character, and you have to do the best you can with what happens."

Sadie exhaled loudly. "It's not fair," she said, subsiding. "He just takes what he wants, like some ancient warlord in the storybooks." She turned abruptly and left the room.

Standing at the stove, Eliza stared vacantly into the distance. *What have I done? My number one goal in life was to make sure the children were protected, and I have failed.*

Later Pierce told Eliza, "This situation with Sadie is an absolute, stinkin' mess. I want to run for County Commissioner next year, and I can't afford a scandal."

"Pierce Griffith! Is that the main thing you're concerned about?" Eliza's voice faltered, then rose to a shriek. She took a deep breath. "It's inconvenient for you, sure, but imagine what poor Sadie is going through." She glared at him with red, swollen eyes.

"Well, something has to be done about it!"

Eliza stepped back and folded her arms. "There's nothing to be done. Sadie will stay right here and have her baby. If having a baby out of wedlock makes it hard for her to get a husband, then she will live with us as long as she likes. None of this was her fault. And as for you, may the Lord have mercy on your soul."

Chapter 20

It was early spring. The snow was melting, and the river overflowed its banks. One morning, Pierce and Eliza were roused from sleep by the persistent bawling of cattle.

"Something's wrong," said Pierce. "Maybe a calf was born early, or a coyote is scaring the herd."

Eliza put on old clothes and accompanied him down to the pasture by the light of the moon. Pierce searched out the best path with his large overshoes, and she placed her smaller overshoes in his footsteps. They waded through slushy snow and cold, muddy ankle-deep water. Most of the cows stood on higher ground, bellowing and swishing their tails. Seeing the people approach, most of the cows stopped making noise and watched them.

One cow continued to bawl hoarsely, and Pierce and Eliza turned in her direction. Next to that cow, in a few inches of water, was a trembling newborn calf, its eyes dull, its tan coat dark with moisture.

"Blast!" said Pierce. "That calf looks half dead." He crept closer. The cow eyed him warily, then put her head down and jerked away.

"What a beautiful baby," he crooned. Eliza distracted the cow with lumps of molasses meal while Pierce approached from the other side and picked up the 60-pound calf. "Let's get you and your baby somewhere warm." He started walking toward the farmyard, carrying the calf.

The cow walked close behind them, breathing heavily. Trying to lick her calf, she kept nudging Pierce, almost tripping him.

Eliza offered the cow more molasses. She refused the food, but at least she quit jostling Pierce. After a tiring walk, their footsteps at last crunched on gravel, and the barn loomed ahead. The cow mooed impatiently.

"So boss, so boss," Pierce called. He wanted the cow to wait, to let him go into the barn first. Otherwise, she might turn around in the doorway and trample him, trying to get to her calf. "So boss."

"You've got a dandy little calf. Once she is warm, she'll nurse."

Pierce shifted the weight of his burden and climbed the steep step into the barn. The cow clambered in slowly behind him, and Eliza followed. They put mother and baby in a stall and rubbed the calf dry. Then they fixed them up with hay and straw and a bucket of water. The little calf was saved.

The next week, when Pierce returned from a trip to town, Sadie was working in the garden by herself. "Here, I have something for you to drink," he said. "It'll help you feel better."

"I don't want it, whatever it is," Sadie replied, shrinking away from him. But Pierce was adamant. He grabbed her and forced the liquid down her throat.

"What *is* that stuff? It smells like licorice. Why did you make me drink it? It tastes disgusting!" She clutched her stomach and tried to cough it up.

"I'm only trying to help you, doggone it. It's a mixture of herbs I got from a woman who knows about that sort of thing." Sadie ran into the house.

That night, she developed a fever and writhed with painful cramps. The next day, she began to bleed. The herbs had induced a miscarriage, and Pierce was pleased. However, Sadie's face took on an unnatural pallor, and she spent a lot of time in bed. Eliza fed her liver paste sandwiches and molasses cookies and hot beef broth.

A week later, Sadie's bleeding had not stopped. Eliza insisted they get the doctor. Pierce saddled his horse and set off at a brisk canter.

The doctor arrived in a couple of hours and examined Sadie privately in her bedroom. His face was grim. "Okay, what did you take?"

"I don't know. Pierce made me drink something. It tasted terrible."

The doctor closed the buckle on his leather medical bag and came out to the kitchen to speak with Pierce and Eliza.

"What the devil was in that drink you gave her, Pierce?"

"I don't know. The person I got it from didn't explain."

"This is a bad business. Who did you get it from?"

"I can't tell you who it was." Pierce paused. "You know I cannot say."

The doctor snorted. "Well, it worked. Sadie's had a miscarriage all right, and she'll recover from that. Unfortunately, it was too strong a dose and damaged her heart. From now on she must avoid any extra exertion. If she lives a calm life and rests every afternoon, she should be able to resume regular activities after a month or two."

Later, Eliza had a special talk in the kitchen with Sadie, Nellie, and Irene. "I'm sorry to say this, girls, but you need to be careful around Pierce, in case he might try to interfere with you in a sexual way. Especially you, Nellie, as you're fifteen and developing a buxom figure. As you probably know, Sadie has had a terrible experience, and Pierce has promised to leave you girls strictly alone in the future, but no point giving him an opportunity. That sort of thing must never happen again."

Nellie began to cry. "He's been bothering all of us girls lately. We didn't want to tell you, Mama. We thought you'd get upset. Maybe if I had told you earlier, this wouldn't 've happened to Sadie."

Eliza's head was reeling. *Here I had been proud of myself for raising my daughters in an intact family, with a mother and father and enough money to support them. And now this.*

"Honey, this is not your fault. I do wish you had told me. I had no idea he was up to such mischief. In a few years all of you girls will be married and gone but, in the meantime, stay together with one of your sisters whenever you go outside. Or ask me to go with you."

She looked at them intently and sighed. "At the moment, I cannot think of what else to do—unless you want to live somewhere else." She put on an apron and picked up the skillet.

Turning back, she asked, "Would any of you girls like to live in Lecompton? You could stay with Grandma and Grandpa Glenn and Aunt Mate. I know they wouldn't mind. Or you could help Aunt Alpha at that hotel where she is the manager."

"Only if you came, too, Mama," said Nellie. "I want to be with you."

"I couldn't leave all my friends," said Irene.

Sadie said, "I want to stay with you, Mama. Besides, I don't think I have enough energy right now to do housework."

Eliza placed her hands on the table as if trying to draw strength from it. "My place is here. I have chosen this life. Besides, leaving Pierce would not put things right." She shook her head in despair.

"I just wish everything would get back to normal," said Irene, frowning.

Eliza gazed sadly at her three older daughters. "I will protect you girls the best I can. We will get through this."

For the next several years Eliza was a bundle of nerves, watching over the girls and keeping an eye out for where they were at all times. The girls did everything in twos and threes. They acted carefree and chatty as usual, but with an undercurrent of tension. Pierce was aware of the change in their behavior and stayed out of their way. The older boys retreated and began to do things just with each other, spending a lot of time training horses.

One day Pierce brought home three jewelry boxes, and as the family was beginning to eat supper, he handed them out to the older girls. "Here, these are for you." Everyone looked at him in surprise.

Sadie, Nellie, and Irene opened the velvet-lined boxes. Inside were identical bracelets of heavy gold etched with a flowered design.

"Ooo, lovely," said Irene. She put hers on immediately and stretched out her arm to admire it.

"Thank you," said Sadie. She held the bracelet in both hands, considering it with a resigned expression.

"Must be expensive," said Nellie, trying hers on. "Blood money, eh?"

"Don't look a gift horse in the mouth," remarked Irene, pursing her lips.

"Where's a bracelet for me?" asked Enid, hopping up and down.

"Maybe in a few years, sugar," said her father. "These are just for the older girls."

Eliza was shocked. "Where did you find bracelets like these?"

"Special order from New York City!" He leaned back in his chair, smiling, and folded his hands over his stomach. "They arrived yesterday by train. Cost a pretty penny." He snorted. "Surprising for an old tightwad like me, eh?"

Late that night, in their bedroom, Pierce said, "I'm truly sorry about Sadie's heart trouble. How was I to know those herbs would do that? Gol durn it, I was trying to help her."

"This whole thing should never 've happened," said Eliza. Her expression was more sad than angry. "You're a grown man and should be past such immature behavior. Besides, I wish you'd talked it over with me before giving Sadie the herbs." Eliza lay motionless on the bed and stared at the ceiling. She felt as if her limbs were slowly turning to stone.

"I do believe she liked the bracelet," Pierce said finally, staring at his fingernails, bruised and ragged from handling horses and machinery.

Eliza spoke in a quiet voice. "Yes, but it hardly makes up for the tragedy you have caused. How much did the bracelets cost, by the way?"

Pierce said, "About $200."

"Good heavens!"

"Yah, I had to sell a goddamn bull to pay for them."

"Oh dear." She winced and shook her head. "Next year we might not have the usual number of calves."

"You see? It was a real sacrifice."

"Sacrifice!" Eliza screeched, clenching her fists. "What do you know of sacrifice?"

1910 (one year later)

Although Sadie gradually recovered, her health was never the same. Her face looked thin and drawn, and she got short of breath whenever she walked any distance. Her hair became lifeless and dry, full of split ends. She rested often during the day and spent a lot of time sitting near Eliza and doing embroidery while her mother worked.

The kitchen was filled with a delicious aroma as Eliza baked bread. She always made six loaves, putting them into the oven three at a time. In a pan on top of the stove, a dozen eggs bumped and tapped against each other in the boiling water. They were going to make deviled eggs.

Eliza and Sadie listened to the rumbling of the boiling water and the click-click of the eggs. The kitchen window steamed up with moisture.

"What am I supposed to do, Mama?" Sadie wailed. "I wanted to teach school, at least until I got married. Now I probably will probably never get married. When I walk around, my body feels heavy, as if I was dragging around a wooden leg. My whole life is ruined because of Pierce!"

Eliza shook her head and sighed. "I am so very sorry that things turned out this way, sweetheart. What I thought would preserve us as a family has turned out to put you girls in danger. You have a hard row to hoe, Sadie, but it won't help to sit and brood. Why not go ahead with your plan to teach? I'm sure you could do it, and they'll need teachers at one of the country schools next year. You have a natural bent for teaching, precious, and you could sit down much of the time. Just tell them you'd like the job."

That summer, there were again a few cases of smallpox in the county, so when Enid got sick in the night, Eliza and Pierce sent for the doctor at once.

The ten-year-old had a fever and severe spasms in her face and neck. The doctor explained that Enid had a case of lockjaw (tetanus). He gave her an injection of antitoxin, which he said would probably keep the disease from being fatal.

"This is very serious," he told them. "Keep a close eye on this child, day and night. Feed her liquids and soft foods. Don't let her get dehydrated. The disease will have to run its course. If you take excellent care of her, it's possible she will pull through."

"Mama, my throat hurts terrible," said Enid. "I can hardly swallow." She was sweaty and restless. Eliza made a bed for her on the couch in the front room and gave her something to eat or drink every hour. She massaged her youngest daughter's limbs and back when she had muscle spasms. She read books to her. She put warm compresses on her jaw and neck. Sometimes Enid would arch her back and cry out with pain. The light bothered her, so they darkened the room most of the day. Pierce, Sadie, Nellie, Ralph, and Eliza took shifts to care for her around the clock.

One day Eliza was feeding Enid some pudding, and as the girl slightly opened her mouth for the spoon, her teeth clamped tight and she could neither open nor close her jaw. This was actually a stroke of luck, for if her jaw had 'locked' when her mouth was completely closed, she would only have been able to eat liquids dribbled through her clenched teeth. This way, she could eat soft foods as well, for instance soup, buttermilk, applesauce, and ice cream. Her jaw was frozen in place for a number of days, and then it gradually improved. After a few weeks, she was fully recovered.

In the summer the family went to community events held on the banks of the Solomon: tent meetings, rodeos, traveling shows, and speeches by politicians. Eliza and other members of the Willing Workers Club provided refreshments.

That September Sadie began teaching in a nearby one-room country schoolhouse. Pierce drove her to and from the school with a horse and buggy, because the walk would have made her overtired. Sadie had twenty students, ranging from first grade to eighth grade. Enid and Glenn attended a different country school nearer to their farm.

"You drive that girl to school and pick her up," Eliza had told Pierce, "It's the only thing you can do to make partial amends. It's essential for Sadie to succeed at this job. And don't lay a finger on that girl!"

"Don't worry. I won't. If I did, she might have a heart attack and die on the spot."

"I like being a teacher," Sadie told her mother after a few weeks, "and it feels good to be doing something useful. Helping children enjoy books and learn things is really fun, and also it's easier than I thought it would be."

On December 24, 1910, there was a huge ice skating party at the old mill dam. Young men piled dry wood and logs high near the river bank and set them on fire. Up the stream a hundred yards they built a second fire. The whole community came. The young people skated arm in arm and the oldsters hand in hand. Others sat by the fire and sipped coffee. Just before the evening ended, Santa came dashing down the bank by horse and sleigh, tossing small sacks of candy and nuts.

1911 (one year later)

On Saturday, December 2, 1911, 4:30 a.m. Ralph knocked firmly on the parents' bedroom door. "Mama! Wake up! Something's happened to Sadie!" Eliza and Pierce hastily jumped out of bed, and Ralph pointed them toward the front room.

Sadie was lying on the couch, her face covered with a blanket.

"She's dead," said Ralph, in a cracked voice.

"No! No!" cried Eliza, touching her daughter's cold cheek. "Tell me it's not true!" Her face crumpled. She threw herself on the floor next to Sadie's body, sobbing, her braid askew and coming undone.

John patted Eliza's arm. Tears were running down his face.

"Where was she?" asked Pierce in a quiet voice.

Ross explained. "We boys just came in from hunting, and as soon as Ralph lit a lantern, we saw her lying in a heap on the kitchen floor. We ran to help her, but she was already dead."

As morning came, Eliza roused herself enough to dress and make breakfast, but she kept moaning and whimpering. The atmosphere in the house was restless and brittle. Pierce and the boys had somber faces. Nellie and Irene sniffled. The younger children, eating at the table, did not make a sound. Their eyes flitted from one person to another.

After breakfast, Pierce hitched the horses to the wagon and left for town. In a few hours, the farmhouse began to fill up with people—the doctor, the pastor, friends. A neighbor woman took over the kitchen and kept a pot of hot coffee and something to eat on the table.

The coroner came in the afternoon. "There's no injury on the body, and she was fully dressed. What happened?"

Pierce explained, "Well, the older girls all went to the box-cake dance last night. I don't know who won the bid for Sadie's cake, but anyhow around eleven Eliza and I had just gone to bed when we heard the girls come home. They were in high spirits, talking and laughing. For all we knew, they had gone right to sleep."

After interviewing each person in the family, the coroner decided that Sadie must have come back out to the kitchen for a drink of water and had a sudden heart attack.

People remarked later that Sadie had looked especially pretty that last night. Maybe the dancing had been too much for her weak heart.

The Thompsons and some of the Griffith relatives came the next day to pay their respects. Gram kept patting Ruth's arm, and when they left, they took Enid and Glenn home with them to stay for a couple of days. The Griffith grandparents sat quietly with their eyes on the floor and did not stay long.

For Eliza, the time passed by in a blur. She hardly registered what people said to her. When Pierce tried to embrace her, she pushed him away. *How to survive the hours until I can sleep and not be aware that she is gone. . .* It was as if a weight on her ankles was pulling her into oblivion, into the earth where she could be with Sadie.

One of Eliza's friends cut locks of Sadie's hair as keepsakes for Nellie, Irene, and Enid. Pierce sent a telegram to Alexander and Elizabeth Glenn.

As for the younger children, all they knew was that when they went to sleep, Sadie was alive, and when they woke up, she was dead. Enid thought maybe her father had strangled Sadie to keep her from having a baby. Glenn believed that Sadie had killed herself. No one ever explained to them what had happened, and they were too scared to ask.

At the funeral, the sanctuary was so full that some people had to stand. After the burial, there was a funeral dinner in the church basement. Relatives, friends, neighbors, and the families of Sadie's pupils shook Eliza's hand and said what a wonderful person Sadie was, and what a pity that she had died at only twenty years old.

Back home again, Eliza sat for several days hunched in a chair in rumpled clothing, staring into space. She had no appetite and hardly ate a bite. The younger children ran noisily in and out of the kitchen, and she paid no attention. Nellie and Irene cooked a lot of beans and sausage. Pierce slouched around and kept to himself.

Nellie and Irene were concerned about their mother. They had never seen her fall apart like this. "Don't worry," she told them distractedly, with a wave of her hand. "I can eat later. I'll just get a cup of coffee."

Eliza sent her white shawl to be dyed black, and she gave Sadie's gold bracelet to Enid. She turned picture frames to face the wall and soaped the mirrors. Pierce ordered a large gravestone engraved with a flower design.

For Eliza, Sadie had been almost like a second self. Most everyone that Eliza had known, Sadie had also known. They had talked each day, worked together, and organized the household together all these years. Eliza listened to the wind and stared at the mending in her lap. Her chest felt heavy and torn. One day dissolved into the next.

She was carrying the coffee to the table one morning when suddenly her mind registered the sad, upturned faces of the children. Eliza, known in the family for her great memory for birthdays, realized with a start that the next day Glenn would be seven years old. And Ross's birthday was the week after.

She trudged into the kitchen and began making an applesauce cake with white fudge frosting. *Life is for the living*, she told herself. She could not spend her days pining for Sadie. The other children would be neglected.

Glenn came to the kitchen table and put his arms around Eliza's waist. "Don't worry, Mama. I don't have to have a birthday this year."

"Bless your heart!" she replied, giving him a hug. "Of course you'll have a birthday this year! Seven is a very important birthday."

Later she asked Nellie and Irene, "Can you girls figure out a present for Glenn? I can't think that far right now."

The next day they had a birthday meal, and the Thompson grandparents came over. Eliza stayed at the edge of the celebration, keeping her thoughts and feelings to herself. They sang "Happy Birthday" to Glenn and gave him a few books and toys. Ruth brought him a scarf; she had just learned to knit.

Ralph took Sadie's place as the teacher at the country school, finishing out the rest of the year. A few weeks later Eliza received a postcard from one of Sadie's students, a little boy in third grade. The penciled message read, "We like Ralph all right for a teacher. But it is not any thing like it was when Sadie was here. From a friend, Clarence."

Eliza's parents were not well enough to travel and come to the funeral. Mate was caring for them now, and their daughter Jane helped also, as often as she could.

Although Alexander Glenn rarely put pen to paper, he wrote Eliza a letter in his characteristic meticulous script. He talked about the need for patience and courage in the face of adversity and told of the deep sadness he felt whenever a child or grandchild of his was laid to rest. Reading his letter, Eliza felt his loving presence surround her.

Chapter 21

1912 (one year later)

The Thompson grandparents were now in their seventies, and in early spring Ruth moved in with Eliza and Pierce. The Griffith farmhouse was filled with teenagers bustling around, going on dates, and applying for jobs. Pierce was taciturn and kept mostly to himself.

Eliza was filled with foreboding. She was not so much worried about the boys, but the girls. . . She felt responsible for their safety, and for their futures.

"Everything seems different since Sadie died, Mama," said Nellie.

"We miss her, don't we, precious?" said Eliza. "She was a blessing to us all."

Daily routines kept their hands busy and their minds occupied. Eliza took time to talk especially with each one. Enid was learning to cook, Irene sewed new bedroom curtains, Pierce and the older boys dealt with the livestock, and Eliza, Nellie, and Glenn took care of the garden. They planted a bed of petunias by the milk house where, for some reason, Shep liked to dig holes.

"If you get into my flower bed again," Eliza told the dog, "I will cut off your tail right behind your ears!" Glenn giggled at that, knowing his mother would never do such a thing.

Eleven-year-old Enid was increasingly subdued. Eliza could tell that her youngest daughter was troubled with many questions that she didn't know how to express. One afternoon after Enid came home from school, Eliza put an arm around her and gently pulled her onto her lap.

"My dear girl, let's have a serious talk. I'm very unhappy with what your father did. I couldn't keep it from happening. Sometimes a person does their best, and things still turn out badly.

"But there's no need to hate him. He's your father, and he has good in him. Even if I left, it wouldn't solve anything. What's important is for you and me and all of us to do the best we can to help each other and be good persons ourselves." Enid's face took on a strange expression.

One Saturday morning when most of the family had gone to town, Nellie handed her mother a notebook. "Look, Mama, I found this under our mattress." Eliza paused, then took it. She opened the cardboard cover and scanned through a couple of pages.

"It seems to be a diary, Sadie's diary. It's her handwriting."

"That's what I thought, too. It would be like Sadie to keep a diary." She looked at her mother fiercely. "I didn't read it."

"Of course not, honey. You did the right thing by bringing it to me." Eliza closed the notebook and stared at the cover. She was very much tempted to read it. *Would Sadie want to share her thoughts with me, or not?*

"Well, since Sadie wanted to keep those thoughts private, that's what we should do, don't you think, Nellie?"

Eliza hugged the notebook to her chest for a long minute, then handed it to Nellie, who went to the cook stove and pushed the notebook in among the burning embers in the firebox. Eliza sighed.

Nellie put her arm around her mother. "I know I'm not Sadie, Mama, but I'll help you like Sadie used to. You can count on me."

Eliza hugged Nellie hard around the waist and her eyes filled with tears. "My beautiful Nellie! Thank you."

One day a few weeks later the family had just finished eating split pea soup with biscuits and cheese. Pierce and the older boys left for the barn to do something with the horses.

"Aunt Eliza, I have a question. Why did Sadie die?" asked Ruth. "I always wondered what really happened."

"It was her heart, darling. She had a weak heart."

Ruth frowned. "She wasn't very old."

"Well, she was going to have a baby, and the herbs she drank damaged her heart."

"I don't understand."

Eliza sighed. "You and I probably need to have a private talk, and now might be a good time. You could sit in too, Enid. Glenn, sweetheart, would you please go out in the barn with your father? I need to speak to the girls by themselves." Glenn slipped out the door.

"You see, Ruth," she went on, "Sadie got pregnant, and Pierce gave her some herbs to make the baby go away. The herbs worked, and she was no longer pregnant, but they also damaged her heart."

"Why didn't she just marry the boy?" asked Ruth. "If she liked him, I mean."

"I'm sorry to have to say this," said Eliza, "but what happened was that Pierce had forced himself on her. There's no need to spread that about, but that's the ugly truth." The girls listened solemnly, wide-eyed.

"But *why?*" persisted Ruth. "Fathers don't do bad things like that."

"You're right, dear, but unfortunately, Pierce seems to have a character flaw in regard to womenfolk. What he did was wrong, and I'm terribly sorry that he is that way sometimes. So we females have to stick together. Never let yourself be alone with Pierce. Just stay with your sisters or with me. That sort of thing must never, ever happen again." All the girls nodded.

"And there's no need to talk about this with your brothers. I wouldn't want to take away their love for their father. It's best we handle this among ourselves. Hopefully, the harm won't go any farther. And it's worth it to protect the family's good name so we can hold up our heads in this community.

"Such things happen in other families too, of course. Outsiders never know. But in a few years you will be grown up and married and out of danger." She took a deep breath and smiled. "I love each of you so much. We'll get through these years together." Eliza's face was serene and resolute.

1924 (12 years later)

It was Christmas Day. The light was thin and bright, the air crisp and cold. As usual, the Griffith family had gathered at Eliza and Pierce's. All eight children were married now, with families of their own. On holidays everyone came out to the farm, wearing their good clothes and bringing pies and casseroles. There was Ralph, Ross, John, Nellie, Irene, Enid, Glenn, and Ruth, their spouses, and twelve grandchildren, including two babies.

Everyone loved those big family dinners. The grownups got to have a good visit, and the cousins enjoyed playing with each other. In summer, everyone brought freezers of ice cream. One of Eliza's daughters-in-law said that everything she knew about keeping house and taking care of children, she had learned from her.

Eliza was a little bit stout now, with gray streaks in her hair and well-defined laughter lines at the corner of her mouth. Under her full-size apron she wore a plain gray-blue dress with an open collar. "It's wonderful to have a big houseful again," she said. "Reminds me of old times. I've missed you all." *No turning back the clock, is there?* Pierce was getting a little thin on top, and irascible as ever, but still robust and energetic.

The little house overflowed with aunts, uncles, and cousins. The younger women had bobbed hair in the current fashion. Nellie greeted the grandkids by saying, "You better behave, or I'll take you down and sit on you!" They laughed, but they knew she wasn't just kidding.

In the morning, everyone opened their presents, then the women got the food ready. Three extra leaves were put into the table, and the wall sconces were lighted. Pierce shouted at the grandchildren, who were chasing each other around the house and yelling. Eliza handed each of the kids a pancake with a piece of bacon rolled in it and told them to go run around outside. Ralph and Ross went out to keep an eye on them.

"Taste this gravy, would you?" Eliza asked the girls, "Tell me if you think it's about done."

At last, dinner was ready. Enid called out the door, "Come and get it, or we'll throw it to the hogs!" Everyone laughed and came to the kitchen and sat down. Eliza carried a big platter of roast goose to the table. There were also mashed potatoes and gravy, baked beans, coleslaw, sweet cucumber pickles, bread-and-butter pickles, and canned peas.

Looking around at all of her family, Eliza had tears in her eyes. Her heart was bursting with love and pride. She remembered her first years on this farm, and how she had worked so hard to raise these children who had now grown to be fine people, with families of their own.

Irene had been the first of the children to get married. Eliza well remembered the day Irene had told her, "Mama, I'm pregnant! Ray and I are going to get married!"

"Congratulations!" she had replied, and gave Irene a big hug. "I'm very happy for you. But honey, you're only sixteen! Have you thought this through?"

"Don't worry, Mama. I'm plenty old enough to know my own mind. Ray makes lots of money playing cards at the pool hall. Oh, Mama, I knew you would understand."

Then Ross got married, and then Nellie. When the war came, Ralph and John enlisted. As it turned out, none of the boys ended up staying on the farm. The three older sons went into business, and Glenn wanted to go to college and become an electrical engineer.

"Wash that notion out of your head, boy!" Pierce had told him. "That's a jacket job. Stick with me, and I'll show you what real work is."

Eliza had urged Pierce to give Glenn money for college, but her husband wouldn't relent. "If Glenn wants it that bad, he can do it on his own dime, like Ralph did." Glenn didn't argue but, as a teenager, he spent a lot of time with the beer drinkers who hung around the Edmond garage where Ross was a mechanic.

After the kids left, the farm was quiet and peaceful but, for Eliza and Pierce, it was wonderful seeing them all crowded around the big table once again.

Everyone declared the food delicious, and many conversations were going on at the same time. After dinner, Nellie and Irene told their mother to go sit down and relax, that they would put away the food and wash the dishes. They thought they were being kind to her, but the truth of the matter was that Eliza wasn't happy unless she was working in the kitchen with the others.

After the dishes were finished, the women took off their aprons and sat in the front room to talk. Eliza mostly listened. The older kids peddled out music on the player piano, and the men had a pitch game going at the kitchen table. They teased Ray about his flashy plaid jacket.

Later, the men took over the front room. Pierce was in his favorite spot, in the corner of the chaise longue next to a side table that held his big radio and a sprawling asparagus fern.

"How are things going with you, Art?" he asked Enid's husband.

"Pretty good, although I wish I was rich instead of so good-looking!" replied Art. That got him a big laugh.

Ralph had a new Studebaker, and the others wanted to hear how he liked the car. He told the others that he planned to buy the Densmore garage, and John was going to work for him. Ross worked at a garage in nearby Edmond, and Glenn farmed a rental place.

"Ever get the hang of your Model T, Dad?" asked Ross.

Pierce scratched his armpits and grimaced. "That doggone car is nothing but a miserable hunk of garbage! It never does what the hell I want it to."

"Like I keep telling you," said Ralph, "when you back up, let the clutch out a bit faster once it begins to engage. And don't keep revving it. Go easy on the gas."

"I'm afraid I'll kill the engine, boy, don't you see? Aw, hell, one of these days I'll buy a different one.

"The other day a car salesmen came out to the farm, some city slicker, and he tried to sell me a new car. We went out for a ride, and I told him to try that real steep hill over here. You know it's one heck of a hill. No car can make it up that incline. So the crazy coot starts the car up the hill. The engine pulls like hell but can't make the grade. I told him, 'Why don't I get out and help push?'" They all laughed.

Glenn didn't mind the others doing most of the talking; he was a naturally quiet person. He and his wife Lucille were newlyweds. They had met the previous year during a big blizzard. Lucille and her dad had gotten their car stuck in a snow bank. Pierce and Glenn happened to drive by in their car and stopped to help. They fetched the mules and pulled the car out. From that moment on, the two young people had been inseparable.

"Anyone want to ride Ol' Babe?" asked Eliza. Shooing the chickens away from the front door, she walked out to the barn, followed by the grandchildren. She and Nellie and Enid put as many little kids on Ol'

Babe's back as would fit, and then Nellie led the horse around and around the farmyard. Its ears twitching, Ol' Babe paced evenly along, no matter how the children shouted and squirmed. Enid walked beside them to make sure none of them fell off. The older grandchildren took turns riding Trixie and Star.

Eliza also let them pet the three Jersey calves, and she kept an eye out that the gander didn't chase the children. He patrolled the area and if anyone got too close—and he decided what was too close—the gander would put his head down, stretch out his neck, and come charging.

Later, the grandchildren came back inside to get warm, and Eliza brought out a round oatmeal box filled with pennies. The grandchildren rolled the coins back and forth to each other on the linoleum floor. When a quarrel sprang up, Eliza came over and put her hand on their shoulders and the quarrel evaporated.

In the afternoon, Eliza served coffee with pumpkin pie made her special way, with maple flavoring. "You shore know how to cook," said Irene's husband Ray. Then the men sat in the front room and listened to a prize fight on the radio, which had a big horn-type speaker.

John's shy wife Elsie said to Nellie, "These kids tear around like crazy. How do you keep up with them?"

"Oh, I'm used to it." Nellie grabbed her six-year-old son as he ran by, gave him a rough hug, and let him go. "This one's my surprise baby," she said. "I was out on a horse one day, helping Floyd with the cattle, and I had such awful pains I had to go back to the house and lay down. Sent for the doctor, we all thought there was something terrible wrong. Turned out, it was Gilbert! Didn't even know I was pregnant. That's the gospel truth."

"Wow." Elsie was in awe of the women in the Griffith clan. Each of them was so distinctive: Irene with her bubbly personality, beautiful earrings, and perfume, Nellie with her baggy clothing, bare feet and raucous laugh, quiet Enid with her graceful movements and mysterious smile, Glenn's wife Lucille keeping the whole family in stitches with funny stories, and Eliza, the calm, quiet person in the center of activities.

The only problem that day was that whenever Elsie walked by Pierce, he would gently stroke her bottom. Elsie hated it but was reluctant to start trouble with him. He was, after all, her father-in-law. She simply didn't know how to deal with the situation.

"I'm so sorry," said Eliza, when she heard about it. "No matter what I say, he keeps on being ornery like that. I guess a leopard can't change his spots."

"He's a real stinker!" said Lucille. "But watch this! I'll show him a thing or two!"

She walked over and stood near where Pierce was sitting. Unsurprisingly, he cupped his hand around Lucille's bottom. She shrieked, "Pierce! For heaven's sake! Stop that! What are you doing? You're embarrassing me!" She went on and on. Hearing her loud and resonant voice, everyone in the house stopped and came to see what was going on. Pierce's face got red under all that scrutiny. Eliza smiled faintly and shook her head. The men began to tease Pierce, and he moderated his behavior for the rest of the day.

Later, in the kitchen, the women had a good laugh, saying, "Boy, that took the starch out of him!"

Eliza stood back and looked with eyes of love at everyone gathered there in their little house. *All in all, I am a lucky woman—I had a wonderful childhood, escaped from a violent first husband, experienced many joys with my second husband, and earned an honorable place in the community. I have my health, am married to a good provider, and we raised a houseful of smart and healthy children. We have had challenges and heartaches, but then, who hadn't? In good times and bad, we're a family, and we love one another as best we can. That's what a family is.*

Afterward

This story is based on the life of my great-grandmother Eliza Griffith, who died two years before I was born. Her daughter Enid was my paternal grandmother. Eliza's other children were my great-aunts and great-uncles, and I knew most of them personally. Family stories portrayed Eliza as a serene, unfailingly kind person, beloved by all who knew her. I wanted to honor her memory, and also to try to understand how she was able to come to terms with Pierce's shortcomings without losing her inner equilibrium.

The materials for the book came from family stories that were handed down, old letters, historical documents, and detailed memories told to me by relatives, in particular my father Doyle Foss and his cousin Harpo Griffith, grandsons of Eliza and Pierce.

What Parts Are True

I did not change any known facts for the sake of the story. The people in the family are called by their actual names, and I kept their appearance, personalities, and typical habits of expression as close as I could get to true life. Eliza had a dark complexion, and was known for her strikingly beautiful eyes.

Eliza did escape from the island by herself with her girls although, other than the 1897 article in the Topeka newspaper, I don't know the details. The time frame in which things happened is accurate. I don't know the cause of Harry Benjamin's death. It is true that Joe falsified his name and later moved away and remarried.

Pierce and Eliza's house and farm are described to the best recollection of several people who knew it well, and from photos. The details of life in the early 1900s are as accurate as I could find from family stories and from other historical information in books and online.

I don't know the exact money arrangements Pierce made with Eliza about her housekeeping job, but we do know that he was a penny-pincher. Pierce's letter offering her a job is dated March 14, 1900, and he asked her to come out before April 1 if possible. They were married May 8. Family stories say that she married him because she got pregnant after he raped her, and that before agreeing to marry him, she made him promise never to bother her girls in a sexual way.

When she was growing up, Ruth lived primarily with her Thompson grandparents. Eliza raised geese for many years. I have assumed that Sadie and Nellie lived with Mate the summer of 1900 because the census that year does not list those two girls as living with Pierce and Eliza, and in later years the girls always felt close to their Aunt Mate.

Enid had beautiful eyes, and as a child she was Pierce's favorite. There were several outbreaks of smallpox in the county around this time. Their hired man Edwin got married and moved away in 1903. Pierce was reluctant to let the boys be educated beyond what he thought was necessary.

Many of the Griffith children's toys and pastimes are ones I have heard them talk about. I know nothing about Eliza's pregnancies. Irene had trouble in later years with her hip, and people said it was because as a child she had carried Glenn around on her hip when he was too heavy for her.

There was some kind of difficulty with Nellie not getting along with others in the family, and she lived for six months or so with the Griffith grandparents, although that proved to be unsatisfactory for all concerned. She returned home and quit school. Later, however, she got a high school diploma. The year of the bad grasshoppers is true, as is the story of the boys tying the snake to the cat's tail.

I invented the story of Enid's near-drowning, but Enid was always deathly afraid of drowning, so some incident must have happened to scare her that much. Their dog was named Shep, and the horses' names are accurate. Nellie and Enid particularly enjoyed gardening. The incident of Enid shaving off half of Pierce's mustache is true. The big storm with seven tornadoes is true.

252

Pierce's rape of Sadie, and many of the details regarding it, are a vivid and well-known element of stories handed down the Griffith family. Pierce surprised Sadie when she was alone in the pasture and forced her to drink the herbal mixture. It caused an abortion, and after that she had a weak heart. Pierce bought three gold bracelets for the older girls, and some of the bracelets are still in the family. I invented the idea of Sadie writing in a journal, but of course she might have.

It is true that Enid had lockjaw when she was ten years old, and her jaw froze with the spoon between her teeth when her mother was feeding her pudding. Pierce driving Sadie to and from her teaching job is true. The details around Sadie's death are accurate, including the postcard from the little boy. The information about the circumstances of Sadie's death came from John. Ralph finished out Sadie's term as schoolteacher and then taught one more year.

Eliza was known for putting on many big family dinners and usually serving roast goose. The story of Nellie not knowing she was pregnant until the day Gilbert was born is true, as well the story of Lucille embarrassing Pierce at the family dinner.

After Eliza married Pierce, she went by the name Anna for the rest of her life. However, the change of her name proved confusing to readers of this book, so I called her Eliza throughout.

Everyone who knew Eliza said she was sweet, kind, patient, and generous. Lucille said that her mother-in-law had taught her everything she knew about how to raise kids and keep house. Eliza was a very quiet person with an air of serenity. She was especially known for listening at great length to children and being interested in what they had to say.

The author wishes to acknowledge the generous comments, support, and encouragement received from a number of people, some of whom contributed numerous detailed suggestions for this book:

*Margaret Laliberte
*Laura-Lee Bennett
*Harpo Griffith
Jan Schwarz
Bob Kimberly
*Warren Dent
Nick Pasch
Donna Hadlock
*Arlene Foss
Barbara Altwegg
Janice Foss
*Eva Peoples
Kathleen Galvin
*Michelle Ainslie
*Brunella Costagliola
Ken Osborne
Sandy Heidergott
Samantha Smith
*Julie Brown
Rosemarie Peterson
*Marie-Anne Johnson

Appendix

Eliza/Anna's autograph book, entries from 1884-1886, just before her first marriage.

Joe and Eliza, wedding picture

TRAGEDY OF THE ISLE.

Fortunately Mrs. Vaughan Escaped From the Island in Time.

There was trouble between the monarch who reigned over Vaughan's island and his spouse and late yesterday afternoon Judge Hazen divorced the couple.

Vaughan's island lies in the Kansas river just north of Tecumseh. It has been in the Vaughan family for some time and is used for a truck farm, but little is raised upon it except watermelons. Joel Vaughan raised watermelons all summer and his wife testified that at odd times he quarreled with her and occasionally came home intoxicated.

"We were on the island," said she in her testimony before Judge Hazen, "and he thought I could not get away, so he treated me worse than he ever had. Before we moved to the island we used to have a little trouble occasionally, but it never amounted to much. The last time he swore at me and said all manner of things to me. He also took down the razor and ran his finger over the edge, and said he would kill me and the children and then kill himself. After that I left and went to my father's home with the children."

Mrs. Vaughan, who held a 3-months-old babe in her arms, cried while she was telling her story. Mr. Vaughan was in the court room when the case was called, but when his wife took the stand he left the court room. He agreed to a division of the property and Mrs. Vaughan was given the custody of the three children.

Alexander and Elizabeth Glenn, Eliza's parents

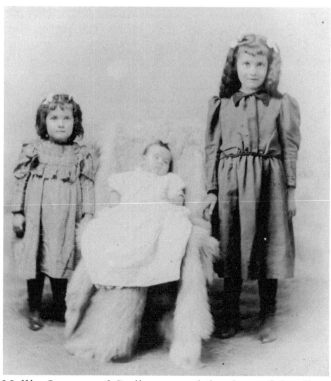
Nellie, Irene, and Sadie, around the time of the divorce

Pierce and his children, taken after Nanny died
(one year before Eliza came to live with them)

Pierce and Eliza's wedding picture, 1900

Griffith farm, around 1904

Nellie

Irene

Enid

Sadie

Irene, Sadie, John, Pierce, Enid, Eliza, Edwin, Ralph, Ross, and another hired man eating watermelon at the barn.

Glenn and Enid

Enid with the mules, and Ralph keeping watch

Nellie, Enid, and Irene, with Eliza

Eliza, Enid, Pierce, Ruth, John, Irene, Ross, Glenn, Nellie, and Ralph, around 1912

Eliza

A family dinner at Eliza and Pierce's house with all the kids and grandkids, 1923